The Devil is Loose

Canton fell sideways, spraying blood in the doorway. Richard stared, unwilling to believe what had happened. "God's legs!" he muttered. "I came to find my brother . . ."

The alarm had alerted the household, and men were approaching on both sides. Richard braced himself in the doorway, his mind in turmoil.

"Stop short!" he bellowed. "Are you possessed?"

There was a heavy thud above their heads, and the knights turned towards a sagging, wooden staircase. Marking their positions in his mind, Richard followed their gaze. He heard footsteps on the floor above, saw high-heeled boots, the hem of a linen shift, bejewelled fingers and bare arms, and then the jaw and face and head of John Lackland.

"You?" John mouthed. "You!"

Available in Fontana by the same author

The Knights of Dark Renown
The Villains of the Piece

GRAHAM SHELBY

The Devil is Loose

Collins
FONTANA BOOKS

First published by William Collins 1973
First issued in Fontana Books 1975

© Graham Shelby 1973

Made and printed in Great Britain by
William Collins Sons & Co Ltd Glasgow

For Sallie, of course
and for
N.J.B. I.R.H. A.C.W.

CONTENTS

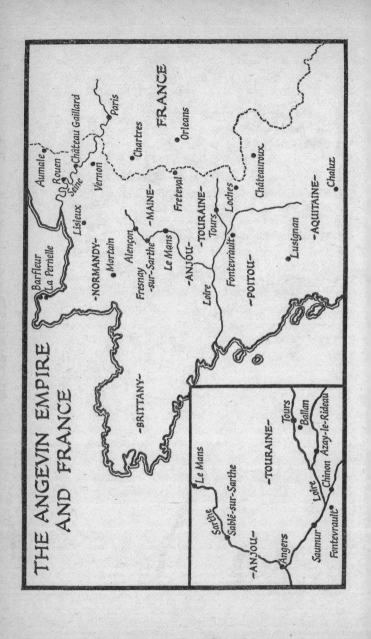

THE ANGEVIN EMPIRE
AND FRANCE

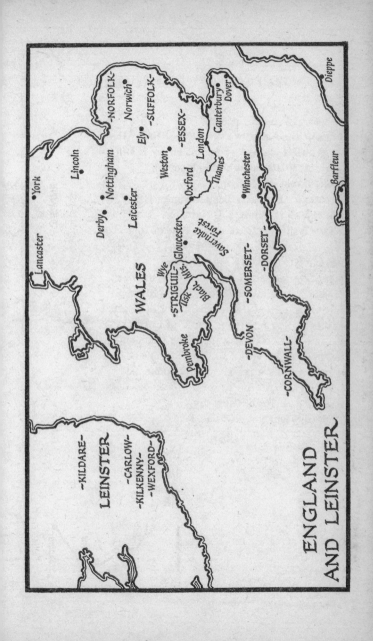

ENGLAND AND LEINSTER

PRINCIPAL CHARACTERS

HENRY II King of England
ELEANOR OF AQUITAINE Wife of Henry II
RICHARD LIONHEART Son of Henry II and
  Eleanor; later King of England
JOHN Brother of Richard
GEOFFREY FITZROY Bastard son of Henry II
BERENGARIA Princess of Navarre
HADWISA OF GLOUCESTER Wife of John

PHILIP AUGUSTUS King of France
WILLIAM MARSHAL later Earl of Pembroke
ISABEL DE CLARE Wife of William Marshal
WILLIAM LONGCHAMP Chancellor of England
RICHARD FITZ RENIER Sheriff of London
ROGER MALCHAT Steward of the Kingdom
RANULF GLANVILLE Justiciar of England
WILLIAM DES ROCHES Knight Commander

HENRY Emperor of Germany
LEOPOLD Duke of Austria

Chapter One

RUN TO EARTH

June, July 1189

At midday men were sent out with flaming torches to fire the suburbs. They were accompanied by archers who touched pitch-tipped arrows to the fire-brands, then loosed the shafts at the outlying buildings. Before long the houses to the south were burning briskly, and the smoke had drawn a curtain between father and son.

Inside the walled city of Le Mans, King Henry II of England prepared to make his stand. This was merely a figure of speech, for he could neither stand nor sit in comfort. He suffered from an anal ulcer, and the poison in his blood had all but robbed him of the use of his legs.

A mile to the south, beyond the billowing curtain, stood Henry's son and enemy, Richard Plantagenet, Duke of Aquitaine. He was an impatient man, but he knew that by their very nature fires burned down. He would not have long to wait.

The adversaries held their positions for two hours, and then the erratic wind shifted and the flames wafted back against the city and drenched it with sparks. Thatched roofs caught alight and collapsed, bringing down the supporting beams. Walls fell inward, or subsided into the streets. Trapped animals bellowed, and the city gates sagged on their hinges. The king's supporters read the signs and lifted him gently on to his horse and escorted him northward, out of the city.

Henry's father had been buried in Le Mans, and he himself had been born there, so he had a special affection for it. Now, however, as the flames spread, forcing him out, he found the strength to jab a gloved finger at the sky and croak an old man's curse. 'God . . . You listen to me . . . You choose to drive me from the city I love most on this earth . . . The city where I was born and raised . . . Where my father is buried . . . You do it to increase my shame and for no other reason . . . So I shall pay You back, coin for coin . . . Mark my words . . . You turn away from me in my distress . . . Very well . . . Then I shall take from You that which You love most in men . . . I deny You my soul . . . Do what You will, for

You have already lost me . . .'

And so he went on, until fatigue overcame him and his escort edged closer, to hold him in the saddle.

An hour later, when the south gate of the city had become so much charred wood, Richard Plantagenet mounted his horse and led a group of riders through the blackened archway. He was so eager to continue the pursuit that he went in without sword or shield. Such an omission by the man who would one day be known as the Lionheart, the Champion of Chivalry and the greatest warrior in the West, was proof enough of his feelings for King Henry. If he could not kill him with a sword, he would batter him down with a mailed fist, then trample him beneath the hooves of his destrier. No more than his father deserved . . .

There were those on both sides who acknowledged that it should never have come to this. The race to tragedy might have been halted, though the path had been laid twenty years before.

In those days, the Kingdom of France had been ruled by the ingenuous Louis VII. In an attempt to end the historic enmity between France and England, Louis had encouraged the betrothal of his daughter Alais to Henry's twelve-year-old son, Richard Plantagenet. The betrothal guaranteed English dominion of the Vexin, a vast tract of land on the north-east border of Normandy, together with the extensive fief and fortress of Gisors. Alais was sent to England and placed in the care of King Henry, on the understanding that she would marry Richard on his fourteenth birthday.

Ten years later she was still waiting, and there was a widespread rumour that Henry had taken a fancy to the girl, and had seduced her . . .

True or false, the news enraged the French nation and reawakened traditional animosities. If it was true, it made a monster of the English king, for what manner of man would swear to safeguard his son's bride-to-be, and then keep her for himself? And if it was not true, why had there been no marriage?

Alais had been twelve years in the English court when King Louis died, and the crown passed to his son, the chilly and far-sighted Philip Augustus. As Alais's brother, Philip had every reason to avenge the hapless girl. As King of France, he was equally determined to drive the English monarch – and seducer – back across the Channel. Throughout the next nine years he had schemed and plotted, devoting himself to the eventual downfall of the Angevin empire. During that time he had discovered that his most powerful allies were Henry's own sweet sons.

In short, Philip had managed to convince Richard Plantagenet that his father intended to disinherit him in favour of Richard's younger brother, John. It was hard work, for Richard was no fool. But neither was he a politician, and, seven months ago, in the village of Bonmoulins near Mortain, Philip had brought father and son face to face, and he had fed Richard his lines.

Would Henry arrange an immediate marriage between Richard and Alais, and make over to Richard the Vexin and Gisors?

No, he would not. In time, certainly, but not yet.

Would Henry instruct his barons to swear fealty to Richard as heir to the throne of England, and so ensure John's exclusion?

No, not until Richard curbed his warlike ways, and showed himself fit to govern.

Would Henry at least allow his eldest son to take control of Maine, Touraine and Anjou, three of the most important English possessions abroad?

Again, no.

Concealing his satisfaction, Philip extended his hands, palm uppermost, and Richard knelt before him and laid his own hands palm downward, so that the two men touched in the gesture of homage. Then, in his deep, raucous voice, raised for his father's benefit, Richard swore to defend Philip in the English dominions of Normandy, Anjou, Poitou, Touraine, Maine and Berry, and all the fiefs on that side of the Channel. For his part, Philip gave his new-found vassal a variety of castles, and then the two men rode away, leaving Henry to his own devices.

Since then there had been open war. It had gone badly for Henry, but never so badly as now, driven out of his birthplace by God and wind and fire, hunted by the implacable Frenchman and his own son. The King of England was fifty-six years of age, and his bleeding ulcer made him wince with every lift of the saddle.

The hurried retreat from Le Mans was directed by Henry's favourite knight, William Marshal, and by one of Marshal's closest companions, William des Roches. The former knight was remarkable for many things, not least that he resembled an Arab. He had brown hair, brown eyes, a thin cut-butter nose and skin that had been scarred and darkened by a life-time in the open air. He was forty-three years old, and looked it, as any man will look his age if his life is given over to tournaments and warfare and hard riding. His name presaged his title, though he did not yet know that. It was enough for his vanity that the world addressed him as Marshal, and that he was King Henry's right arm – and in these sad days, his legs.

Marshal's companion was rather more substantial, at least around the belly. But a heavily-built knight owes nothing to a thin one; there are simply more links in his hauberk.

Now, with their cloaks and faces speckled with soot, Marshal and des Roches guided the ailing king along the east bank of the River Sarthe. Henry moaned on, blaming God for his situation, but his protectors paid no heed to his mouthing. Each kept a hand on his shoulder, holding him in the saddle.

Behind them came the seven hundred knights who comprised the remnants of Henry's force. There were no foot-soldiers, for they had been unable to keep pace with the fleeing horse-men. But no matter, the infantry were expendable. The im-portant thing was to save the palfreys and destriers as vehicles for the knights.

Two bridges spanned the river north of Le Mans. The first was a trestle structure, built to take sturdy, ox-drawn wagons. The other, a few hundred yards upstream, was a stone, hump-backed affair, its walls so close set that riders could only cross in single file. Marshal peered at it for a moment, then led the king across the wooden bridge and on to the west bank. The knights followed, four and five abreast.

When the last of the English riders were across, Marshal and des Roches gave Henry into the care of his steward and factotum, the reliable Roger Malchat, and told him to conduct the king to Fresnay-sur-Sarthe.

'Follow the river road,' Marshal said. 'Fresnay is twenty miles to the north. We'll catch up with you.' Then he clapped des Roches on the arm and the two men rode back on to the still trembling bridge. Each knew what the other was thinking and as yet there was no need for discussion.

Below them, the Sarthe was running low, the result of a week's dry weather. Nevertheless, the banks were steep, and the only ford was several miles south of Le Mans. If the wooden bridge could be destroyed, and the stone one defended –

Marshal turned in the saddle, raised a hand above his head to identify himself and roared, 'My lord John! To me, if you will!' He waited for the king's youngest son to emerge from the mass of knights. When John did not appear, he asked des Roches, 'Did you see him go across?'

'No, nor since early this morning,' des Roches growled. 'And small loss in my opinion.' Then, warned by Marshal's scowl, he added, 'He's probably mixed in with his friends. Give a shout for Belcourt, or Peter Canton. They never leave his side.'

Marshal did so, though without results. Cursing under his breath, he glanced southward for signs of pursuit. The curtain of smoke obscured the city, though there was no doubt that Richard and his men were back there somewhere. And Philip Augustus and *his* men. And those barons and knights who had reason to hate King Henry. And mercenaries, in it for the money. And the usual rabble of camp-followers, prostitutes, looters and turncoats who swelled the ranks of any army.

But where was John?

Marshal shouted again, this time for the twenty nearest knights. They clattered on to the bridge, then shook their heads in answer to his question. Like des Roches, some of them said they had seen John in the city, yes, with Belcourt and Canton, but that had been shortly after dawn. Had not the prince ridden on to Fresnay, perhaps, with his father?

'It's possible,' Marshal admitted, 'but why did no one see him go by?' He shrugged irritably, then pointed at the bridge. 'Time's against us; we can't wait. I want this brought down. Chop it, or fire it. Both, if you can, I'm not choosy. So long as it's made impassable.'

Des Roches leaned over one of the side rails. Using his big belly to push himself upright, he said, 'There's a mass of rushes on this side. Use them to kindle the wood.' He signalled to the knights to start work, then strode over to Marshal. 'We should not let the king get too far ahead,' he murmured, 'not without a proper escort. For all we know, the French may already have taken Fresnay.'

Marshal grunted agreement. 'Send the army on then. But hold back a few of them. There's still the other bridge to care for.'

They regained the west bank and dispatched all but a dozen of the riders. The twenty-strong work-force were busy below the ox bridge, piling bundles of reeds against the trestles, or hacking at the upright posts with swords and axes. Marshal dismounted and slithered down to where one of the knights was blowing sparks into flame. 'When you've finished here,' he said, 'go on to Fresnay, and find the king. If he has recovered his senses, tell him I'll be with him by nightfall. And tell Roger Malchat.'

The knight waited until the flames had taken hold, then asked, 'How severe *is* his illness, Marshal? Every day we hear he's dead, or recovered. No one seems to know.'

'Make no mistake,' Marshal told him, 'he'll outlive the lot of us.' Then he turned away, in case the doubt showed in his face.

With care and the right medicines, there was no reason why Henry of England should not recover. His ulcer was deep and malignant, but by no means incurable. The physicians of the West had learned much from their Eastern counterparts, particularly in the treatment of sores and abscesses, to which the Crusaders were most vulnerable. But no physician, whether Christian or Moslem, could cure a man on the run. Above all else, Henry needed rest, and time out of the saddle. Until then, the fistula would continue to poison his system as surely as if he had been stabbed with a rusty blade.

The knight scratched flints under a second pile of rushes. 'You'll be with him by nightfall,' he echoed. 'And until then?'

'Up there, on the stone span. If you can get this bridge down, and we can hold the other – Well, it may be enough. We have reinforcements at Alençon, and Richard and Philip will think twice before invading Normandy.' He watched the man use the blazing rushes to ignite other bundles, and said, 'Give me one of those. I'll get some more started.' A moment later there was a shout of alarm – 'Get back! It's through!' – and the knights scrambled clear of the bridge. It did not come down, but sank to one side, springing the planks and splitting a number of supports. The men waited until the bridge had settled, then went back to work while the rush fires spread to the wood.

Des Roches had elected himself watchguard, and now, standing at the top of the bank, he pointed in the direction of Le Mans. 'Men coming out,' he growled. 'We'd better get upriver, Marshal, if we're to block them.'

At that instant another post was chopped through, and the bridge twisted, contributing to its own destruction. A side rail snapped, and another sprung plank fell into the river. A courageous horseman might still cross, but his mount would have to step with care, and be unafraid of fire.

Marshal climbed the bank, then called down to the knight with whom he had been working. 'We're going on. Put one of your men up here to keep watch. They may have archers with them.' He opened his hand in a brief farewell and hurried over to his horse. Des Roches had meanwhile assembled the twelve knights who would help them hold the narrow stone bridge. As soon as Marshal had mounted, the riders spurred northward along the river road. Ahead of them hung a dark pall of dust, marking the passage of the English army. Marshal pulled his horse to one side and looked back, first at the tower of smoke above Le Mans, then at the twisted bridge. He heard a sudden creak and splinter of wood and saw the western end of the structure collapse into the flames. The work-force gave a ragged cheer and appeared, one by one, at the top of the bank. There was no more to be done. For several hours the Sarthe would be impassable at this point. The knights ran to their horses and followed as a third group on the road.

As he spurred on to rejoin des Roches, Marshal allowed himself a humourless smile. The English, it seemed, were adept at burning things, whether by accident or design.

Leaving the dozen members of the rearguard at the western end of the stone bridge, the commanders took up their positions on the eastern bank. They heard the work-force pass behind them, and then the hoofbeats died away and there was only the drone of insects and the snort of horses and the soft babble of the river.

The two men were dressed and armed alike. Each wore a knee-length, link-mail hauberk and a simple, acorn-shaped helmet. Des Roches' headpiece had a nasal, but Marshal had yet to find one that did not skin his bony beak. Each carried a lance and a long shield, rounded at the top and narrowing down to a point. Their cloaks were tied back over their shoulders, leaving their sword hilts exposed.

They wore the commonplace battle-dress of the day. Not for them the new-fangled plate armour, or a spiked ball on a chain, or a double-bladed axe, inherited from the Vikings. they were content with what they had, proven armour and lethal weapons.

They sat quiet, des Roches deep in thought, Marshal letting his gaze roam the countryside. To the north was the large dust-cloud, dispersing in the wake of King Henry and his army and the bridge wreckers. To the south were the two plumes of smoke, the larger sculpted by currents in the upper air. Marshal sighed extravagantly, as though by expelling his breath he could disperse the marks of retreat.

The sound brought des Roches from his reverie, and he nodded in the direction of the new dust-cloud, rolling north-ward from the city. 'Here they come. I'll wager Richard is among them.'

'Too safe a bet,' Marshal dismissed. 'I'd be wasting money.' He muttered a short prayer, heard his companion do the same, then glanced around to see if the rearguard were in position. They were, and one of the twelve was already on the bridge, poised to come forward and replace whichever of the commanders was first to fall. It was small comfort to know there was an avenging angel at one's back.

He faced front again and watched the enemy gallop into view. There were forty or so in the group, spreading out as they neared the bridgehead. Had they swept forward *en masse*, Marshal and des Roches would have been quickly over-whelmed. But they were blinded by the dust, and were still fifty yards away when someone roared at them to move aside. They did so, allowing two of their number to ride onward, out of the cloud.

Richard of Aquitaine, and someone with a feather in his helmet.

King Henry's eldest son was a gigantic, broad-shouldered man, a full head above average height. At thirty-one, he was not yet at his prime, though at any gathering he was the focus of attention. His hair was a mixture of ginger and cinnamon, capped today by a plain, pot-shaped *casque*. His face, like theirs, was speckled with soot, but he had made no attempt to wipe away the flecks. As he emerged from the group, his wide-stretched grin faltered and shrank, and he dragged desperately at the reins.

No explanation was conclusive, but it seemed that Richard had thought the bridge deserted, and had decided to charge across it, ignoring the fact that he would crack his knees on the narrow walls. It was a display of bravado he would remember and regret.

Marshal measured the distance, then dug in with his single-point spurs. As his horse plunged forward he shouted at des Roches, 'Take the feather!' He heard an answering growl and saw the bulky knight couch his lance and ride at Richard's companion. Weight and accuracy were with des Roches, and he caught the rider full in the chest. His lance splintered along the shaft, and the Frenchman – if he was a Frenchman – was lifted from the saddle. Marshal saw the start of his fall, but after that he was too busy to watch.

Richard had continued forward, unable to slow his destrier. He saw his adversary's lean, Arabic face, saw light glint on the lance-tip and on the metal that edged his shield, and he realized that the charge could not be halted.

It was over quickly, but it was an incident that scratched a mark in history. There were few occasions in Duke Richard's life when he had shown fear, or chosen precaution. But this was one of them.

Still fighting to control the destrier, he used his favourite oath and yelled, 'God's legs! Don't kill me! I'm unarmed, can't you – *I'm unarmed*!'

Marshal had little time to react. Collision was inevitable, as it should have been, for no one knew this type of work better than the champion of Europe's tournaments. But there was time enough to open his fingers, relax his hold on the lance and see the point dip from the chest of the man to the chest of the mount. Then the lance struck and was wrenched from Marshal's grasp. He felt his body buckle with the impact and used his left hand to drag his destrier to the side. As he did so he saw Richard's horse stumble, throwing its rider. Dust rose from the hooves of Marshal's mount, and from Richard's stricken destrier, and from the sprawling body of the Duke of Aquitaine.

The victor reined-in, less than twenty feet from the enemy knights. But he had nothing to fear, for they were glued to their saddles, their mouths hired out as fly-traps. Not for several moments more would they accept what they had seen.

Walking his horse in a circle, he glared down at his fallen adversary. He could not remember when last he had felt so angry. To be challenged by none other than Richard of Aquitaine, second only to Philip Augustus as a sworn enemy . . . Then to be told by Richard that he had forgotten to bring his weapons . . . To hear him shout pax . . .

Christ in heaven, did he think this was a *game*!

His face fattened with anger, Marshal snarled, 'Don't fret, sire. I shall not kill you. That's the devil's work, and it can be safely left to him.' His horse was still pawing the ground, and the dust hid Richard's expression. It doesn't matter, Marshal thought, I don't need to see him. He knows he's had a fall.

With a final glance at the enemy knights, he rode back to the bridge to rejoin des Roches. As after any such skirmish, they were wide-eyed and trembling. A man does not risk a lance in the throat and come away whistling a tune. Indeed, it was no hardship for des Roches to stay silent and allow his friend time to cool. He knew how close Marshal had come to slaying Duke Richard, and he sensed what it had cost him not to do so. Had he been less honourable . . . Had his reflexes been less quick . . . Had his mind been fuddled by drink, or poisoned by revenge . . . Had he sought to win King Henry's praise . . . Christ and His angels, but wasn't Richard the lucky one?

They sat quiet again, waiting for the enemy to charge, or the arrows to fly. They were both exhausted, but des Roches made an effort and gestured to his rearguard to furnish them with lances. The rider on the bridge brought them across, and volunteered his admiration. Then he saw Marshal's expression and hurriedly retired.

A few moments later another dust-cloud followed Philip Augustus from Le Mans. The thin-faced king halted and stood up in his stirrups, then asked what had happened. By now the fly-trap knights had found their tongues, and Richard could be seen waving his bruised arms and making threatening gestures, as though he wished to go through it all over again. Eventually, Philip managed to calm him, and the enemy stood off at a distance. Well now, Marshal wondered, has French practicality prevailed, or English commonsense?

King and army and work-force and rearguard were reunited at Fresnay. Marshal and des Roches and their twelve knights had remained at the bridge until sunset, but the enemy had not attempted to force a crossing. When last seen, in the fading light, they were still on the east bank, half a mile from the bridge.

At Fresnay, the king had sunk into an exhausted sleep and had been carried into the small castle and laid on a couch in the ground-floor chamber. The castle could only accommodate a handful of visitors, so the seven hundred knights had billeted themselves in the surrounding villages. The tents and pavilions had been abandoned at Le Mans, along with the foot soldiers and most of the personal baggage. Henry's supporters were now not only tired and hungry and in retreat, but reduced to the clothes they wore and whatever money they had on them.

Sensing the futility of their position, a number of them rode out under cover of dark, some returning to their own lands, others to Le Mans to offer their services to the enemy. Philip Augustus stayed awake all night to welcome the deserters, while, for his own information, Richard recorded their names on a sheet of parchment.

Next morning, the middle day of June, King Henry awoke within his senses and summoned his senior barons. When they heard what he had to say, they wished he had slept on.

Rejecting their arguments out of hand, the pain-racked king insisted on going south, into his long-held county of Anjou. Marshal and the others reminded him that his strength lay to the north, in Normandy, where there were fortresses to shelter him and fresh troops to be recruited.

'King, we have more men at Alençon than we have here. If we send for them, and for the others around, we can drive the enemy clear back to Touraine. We have an extensive armoury at Alençon. There are even siege machines in store; mangonels and trebuchets, towers and mining equipment, everything we need.'

But Henry would not be swayed. Stubborn and irrational, he told two of the senior knights to lead his army-in-retreat to Alençon, leaving him an escort of seventy men. These would see him safe to Anjou. With long pauses between his words, he whispered, 'The smaller the royal party, the less chance of discovery . . . Marshal, you stay with me . . . And you, des Roches . . . There are not so many I can trust, these days . . .'

He may have been thinking of the barons who had deserted during the night. Or of his son and enemy, Richard Plantagenet. Or of his favourite, the vanished John. Whoever it was – and Henry had the world from which to choose – Marshal exchanged a glance with des Roches and said, 'You know we are with you, lord king.'

Henry blinked acknowledgement and croaked, 'Get started, messires . . . Normandy is my last sure possession, this side of the water . . . I could not bear it if it was lost . . .' As the warlords filed from the chamber, he crooked a finger at Marshal and murmured, 'Do something for me . . . Fetch my physicians . . . I'm bleeding again . . .'

From then on they were fugitives in their own lands. With the bulk of the army restrained at Alençon, the royal party dared not travel by the known routes, or in the open, or in clear weather. Instead they zig-zagged southward, at night and along forest tracks, covering two hundred miles in a week. They were not intercepted, but Henry's condition continued to deteriorate.

They reached the rock-girt castle of Chinon, on the north bank of the Vienne, and Marshal immediately conferred with des Roches and Roger Malchat. The tough bald-headed steward assumed responsibility for the food and fuel, while des Roches set about restocking the armoury with arrows, crossbow bolts, jars of vinegar, barrels of pitch and river sand. When needed, the pitch would be warmed in a cauldron, poured into leather sacks, and a length of pitch-soaked tow inserted in the neck. The tow could then be set alight, and the sack hurled down from the ramparts. More times than not, it would split on impact and the blazing mass would stick to whatever it touched. The vinegar and sand would be used to extinguish enemy fire bombs.

A head count revealed that there were less than eighty able-bodied men within the walls of Chinon, and that these included priests and clerks, gardeners and household servants. King Henry's escort doubled the number, but even so the castle was dangerously under-manned. The watchtowers held

three men in place of six, and the wall-guards were so widely
spaced that they were almost patrolling the walls like common
men-at-arms, while the commanders took their turn at stacking
barrels and lowering foodstuffs into the storepit below the
keep.

Three days after their arrival at Chinon, they were paid a
surprise visit by emissaries from Philip and Richard. King
Henry was too ill to receive the messengers, so they were
taken before Marshal. He was disturbed that the enemy had
so quickly discovered Henry's whereabouts, for it made
further flight impossible. Philip would not have dispatched
his emissaries unless he had already encircled Chinon, so the
reason for their visit was clear enough. They had come for
Henry's surrender.

Reading aloud, the senior emissary informed Marshal that
King Henry of England was invited to attend a conference at
Azay-le-Rideau, a few miles north-east of Chinon, on Friday,
30th June. It was hoped that a peace treaty could be signed,
and the family feud forgotten. However, if Henry rejected
the invitation, Philip and Richard would immediately lay
siege to the citadel of Tours, capital of Touraine. The King
of France and Duke of Aquitaine expected Henry of England
to act with his customary wisdom, and they awaited his reply.

The man stopped reading, and Marshal gazed quizzically
at him. 'No terms? Are we not to know what's to be discussed?'

'When King Henry attends, then he will be furnished with
the terms.'

'I see. In which case, when the king has finished with his
other, more pressing affairs of state, you will be furnished
with his reply.' He nodded at the emissaries, the guards escorted them to their horses.

There was, of course, no question of Henry attending the
conference. The flight from Fresnay had aggravated his condition, and he was now losing more blood than his system
could create. He had a high fever, and his skin had begun to
purple. Marshal had concealed the truth from the emissaries,
and the physicians were the last to admit it, for their reputation
was at stake, but they agreed amongst themselves that the
king was dying.

The commanders at Chinon waited until the afternoon of
the 29th, then they, too, accepted that they could no longer

dissemble the king's condition. Word was sent to Philip, asking that the conference be postponed until Henry had regained his strength.

Philip's reply was counter-signed by Richard.

'It is our understanding that Henry, by the grace of God, King of England and Duke of Normandy and Count of Anjou, seeks to decry our attempts at reconciliation, and continues to do all in his power to prolong this unhappy war. We do not accept that Henry, who, not long ago, made the arduous journey from Fresnay, is now too unwell to meet those with a claim against him. It is our belief that Henry of England has not yet lost the taste for battle. We shall therefore press forward with our attack and, under God, triumph over our enemies.'

In a desperate effort to halt hostilities, Marshal told one of the king's physicians to find Duke Richard and convince him of the gravity of his father's condition. 'I don't care if it heartens the French, so long as Richard comes to terms with reality. Let him know the truth, that Henry is a dying man. Invite him to see for himself, if he wishes. Even if he does come, it will be a death-bed reunion.'

The physician delivered the message, and Richard called him a trained liar and a charlatan. 'God's legs!' he roared, 'I *know* my father! He never yet sat when he could stand, or walked when he could run. He's feigning, and if you cannot see that, it shows how little you know your trade. Your patient is King Henry of England, strap-bone, not a snared squirrel!'

Richard loved to shout. It put air in his chest and brought the colour to his face. 'Listen,' he went on, 'if I offered him a virgin to deflower, a girl like the luckless Alais, or agreed to let my pasty-faced brother inherit the throne, Henry would come running. You go back and tell him I have such a girl. Tell him I'll keep her warm at Azay; all he has to do is come and collect her. We'll listen for his foot-fall!'

Attendant knights howled with laughter and dredged their minds for jokes about virgins and women given as gifts. They did not yet know that, beneath the banter, Richard Lionheart was not one for the women.

A few days later, the occupants of the Chinon learned that

Tours had fallen to the French. This, together with Le Mans and all the English territories to the east, put Philip and Richard in an unassailable position. They again invited Henry to confer with them. If he rejected them a second time, they threatened to lay siege to Chinon itself and mount a full-scale invasion of Normandy, Anjou and Touraine. The girl is still waiting, they added, and itchy with desire.

Marshal, des Roches and the bald-pated Malchat discussed the situation with their peers. It was eventually agreed that, for the sake of the English dominions abroad, Henry should be led or carried to the meeting-place. The decision was not arrived at easily, for the commanders knew that any further movement might kill the invalid. But, if they stayed at Chinon, and allowed the vast Angevin territories to be overrun . . .

No, not even the life of a king was worth the loss of so mighty a kingdom.

The conference had been set for 4th July, in the village of Ballan, between Azay and Tours. The weather was sullen and overcast, and thunder echoed along the river valley. Rain soon dappled the riders, and Henry was transferred from his horse to a canopied litter. He looked small and insignificant, more of a mascot than a monarch. Marshal and Malchat rode beside him, and they masked their distress as his querulous voice rose through the rain.

'Oh, God, messires, this pain is intolerable . . . It creeps all through me . . . I feel it in my feet and my legs . . . And now it is everywhere, clawing at my heart . . . I tell you, I have neither body, nor mind, nor . . . Are we there yet . . . I would like to be set down awhile . . . Where is he, John, have you seen him . . . John . . . Is he with us today . . . Aah, Christ, it's strangling me . . . *Inside* . . .'

Malchat told the four soldiers who bore the litter along the riverside path to show their pace. Why hurry the king to his end? Meanwhile, Marshal leaned down to reassure him. 'Your son John is well, sire. He has been to see you several times these past days, but he was asked not to disturb your rest. He's behind us somewhere, but not far away.' He caught Malchat's sidelong glance and reined-in, allowing Henry to be carried ahead.

In answer to the steward's unspoken question, he said, 'Yes, it's a lie, and I shall continue with it. What else am I to tell him, for God's sake? That John deserted us at Le Mans and has not been seen since? Come on, Malchat! If you can find a better story – '

'Calm yourself, Marshal. It's not your doing, that's understood. I'm as anxious to find him as you are. And when he does appear, I shall need an explanation for his absence, when his father needed him most.' He looked at the rain-soaked litter, then at Marshal again. 'Have you any idea – '

'None. He was at Le Mans when we started the fires, and gone when we left. He may have fled eastward, or been burned alive in some whore's bed-chamber, I don't know. But somehow I think it's unlikely he was trapped. The others, Belcourt and Peter Canton, perhaps, but not Prince John. He's too slippery for death to catch him, just yet. But,' he measured, 'so far as the king is concerned, John is here and well. It's surely enough for a man to have one son sniffing his blood. Don't you think so?'

Malchat nodded quickly, reminding himself to curb his inquisitive glances.

Nevertheless, the lie seemed to satisfy the tortured king, and the sad company continued on to Ballan, where scouts reported that Philip and Richard were already on the field, waiting near an isolated oak tree. There were four or five hundred troops at their back, while several hundred more were drawn up beneath the walls of Tours.

Leading the English party on to the field, the bulky des Roches shook his head in disgust. What did Philip think? What did Richard imagine? Why assemble an army to face a dying king and a handful of riders? *Jesu, Jesu,* the ground was knee-deep in mistrust.

Henry came briefly to his senses and insisted on being lifted on to his horse. 'I may be ill, but I am not incapable . . . This is your doing, Marshal . . . Get me mounted, sir! You think I would stay in bed to meet them?'

They lifted him from the litter, and he bit the wrist of his gauntlet as the movement stirred his poisoned blood. Near to fainting, he was at last settled in the cushioned saddle and led forward across the field. He wore his battle-crown – a simple, silver coronet welded to his helmet – and a purple cloak edged with marten fur. His red hair, the mark of the Plantagenets, curled around the rim of his helmet. Rainwater escaped through holes in the coronet and dripped into the fur collar.

When the king was ready, Roger Malchat nodded at Marshal and des Roches, and they escorted Henry toward the isolated oak. The English riders remained near the edge of the field, as though unwilling to risk the derision of the French army.

The thin-faced Philip Augustus approached, and his perpetual frown deepened as he noticed Henry's discoloured appearance. He was clearly upset at the condition of his enemy, and he unclasped his own cloak, folded it and offered it as a pillow for the Angevin. 'Climb down and be comfortable,' he said. 'On my word, brother king, I did not know it had come to this.'

Marshal said, 'You were told it had,' but Philip turned away to snarl quietly at Richard. 'So he is feigning, is he? He'll come running at a woman's beck, eh? You know your father, isn't that what you said?'

Richard shrugged inside his massive, silver-mail hauberk, but before he could reply they heard Henry growl, 'Keep your pillow! England does not sit at the feet of France, never! *I* am the senior monarch, and I'll *not* be put down!'

His steward touched him on the arm to calm him, but Henry pulled away, grimacing with pain. 'Well?' he mouthed. 'You've invited me here. And what for? To hear your terms. Then read them, messires, read them.' He was puffed with pride and shrunken by illness, and his left foot had begun to kick involuntarily. It was a heart-breaking sight, but when Marshal looked at Richard to see if he was at all affected by it, he met only the angry gaze of the man he had unhorsed. Even in the rain, the Lionheart's expression was clear and legible. We've a score to settle, you and I, when this is over.

Marshal was tempted to return the exaggerated shrug, but decided against it. There was already enough enmity to go around.

The King of France had tried to make things better for his enemy, but now he looked away and beckoned his chancellor. The man hurried forward from the sparse shelter of the tree. He slid to a halt on the wet ground, watched for Philip's nod, then read aloud from the carefully prepared document. It was lengthy, framed by formality, and couched in precise, well-polished language. But the gist of it was plain enough, and the opening words captured the bitter flavour of the piece.

Holding the document so that only a few lines at a time

were exposed to the rain, the chancellor intoned:

'Henry, King of England and Duke of Normandy and Count of Anjou abides by the will and counsel of Philip, King of France and accepts that whatsoever Philip commands or ordains, that will Henry do to the utmost of his ability and without contradiction.'

He twisted the paper, rolling it toward the top. Des Roches looked at his king, but the old man sat impassive, blinking water from his eyes, his left foot twitching. The chancellor found his place and continued.

'In order that peace may be restored between Henry of England, Philip of France and Richard, Duke of Aquitaine, the following provisions must be met.'

The chancellor rolled the parchment again, settled himself flat-footed on the grass, and read the terms. In the moments that followed, the invalid king learned his fate.

He was henceforth to recognize his son Richard as his sole heir, and was to command his barons to swear fealty to him . . .

He was to place Philip's sister Alais in ward to Richard's nominees until such time as Richard and Alais were wed . . .

He was to accompany the King of France on Crusade to the Holy Land and was, in addition, to contribute 20,000 silver marks towards Philip's Crusading expenses . . .

He was to surrender the territory of Auvergne and various scattered baronies, and make over the already captured citadels of Le Mans and Tours, plus two others . . .

And, finally, he was to kneel before King Philip and renew his homage to him, and thus end the conflict abroad . . .

The chancellor licked rain from the air, rolled and tied the parchment, then retired under the tree. He thought he had read the thing rather well, in the circumstances.

Marshal and des Roches moved in as Henry swayed in the saddle. His body seethed with pain, and his mind was numbed by the immensity of the demands. In the name of God, what did they *not* want from him? This was not a treaty! It was a humiliation, the long-sought vengeance of a minor king and a treacherous son. And where was John in all this? What place was left for him? Poor John, known as Lackland, because in any queue he came second to Richard. What provision for poor young John?

Unable to control himself, Henry jerked forward, slamming himself against the pommel of the saddle. His battle-crown slipped from his head, hit the back of his hand and fell to the ground. He pressed a stiffening hand to his face and the opposing forces heard him weep. It was an ugly sound, for he, less than anyone, was practised in sorrow. In all his life he had not apologized a dozen times. Until this past year he had possessed more fingers than failures, and had regarded defeat as some obscure and foreign disease to which he was, anyway, immune. He had ruled England and the great Angevin dominions for thirty-four years, the supreme monarch and administrator, the man against whom other kings measured their worth.

And now it had come to this, to treason and vengeance and disgrace. A victorious reign, a lifetime, come to nothing.

He let his hand fall away from his face. He took the helmet that someone had reclaimed for him and jammed it on as though it was a woodman's cap. Then, in a dull, flat voice he said, 'I accept the terms,' and turned his horse. He had no more interest in the proceedings. One does not stay at the dice table when all one's money has gone.

But he was not yet allowed to leave. Richard leaned over and spoke quietly to Philip, then rode forward to embrace his father and exchange the kiss of reconciliation. Marshal and des Roches moved away, leaving father and son to make their private peace. But the knights were not too far removed to hear Henry mutter in his son's ear, 'I pray God I live long enough to see you utterly destroyed, as I have been, my sweet boy. You will burn forever, and be torn apart, and each morsel of your flesh – '

Richard reared upright, roaring a laugh. Then, shaking his head with pleasure, he rode back to his lines. He would never again see his father alive, not that he cared a spit.

Henry was taken back to Chinon. Papers were placed before him and, with someone to guide his hand, he affixed his seal. On 5th July, the day after the conference, he asked for a list of those who had conspired against him, or deserted him, or financed the enemy. There was nothing he could do to them, he knew that, but the names would make interesting death-bed reading.

He took a sudden dislike to Malchat and des Roches, but he nodded when Marshal told him John had been by twice, only to find his father asleep. 'Whatever I have lost,' Henry croaked, 'John will regain . . . No one sees as deep into him as I do . . . You protect him, Marshal, and he will establish you in the realm . . .'

Next day a French messenger delivered the list to one of Henry's servants. Henry told the man to read each name aloud, slowly, so that he would have time to recollect. But the unfortunate servant did not get beyond the first name, for it was that of Henry's twenty-one-year-old son, poor John, known as Lackland.

The shriek of anguish brought Marshal and others running to the chamber. Two of the knights caught hold of the servant and flung him against the wall. They wanted to know, quickly and brutally, if his plan had been to kill the king with a knife, or stifle him with a cushion.

'Neither!' the man screamed. 'I was reading the list! This! Here! *This*!' It was snatched from him and passed to Marshal, crouched by the bed. He looked at it, saw the first name and let his breath stir the parchment. If the signature was real, and not some cruel forgery, it explained John's unseen departure from Le Mans.

Beside him, Henry murmured, 'Things may go where they will . . . I no longer . . . I want no more of them . . . I am finished with them now . . .' Then he rolled heavily on to his side, his face to the damp stone wall.

By nightfall he was dead. His physicians sought out Malchat and des Roches and Marshal, and announced that Henry had succumbed to fever, aggravated by blood-poisoning. The diagnosis was accepted, for neither the knights, nor the physicians, were trained to recognize a broken heart.

Chapter Two

RECKONINGS

July 1189

The thieves waited until Henry's knights were at prayer in the draughty chapel at Chinon. Then they crept upstairs, attacked and murdered the men-at-arms who guarded the king's chamber, and broke into the room. They plundered the treasure chest, carted away the clothes boxes, tore the weapons rack from the wall. Not content with that, they stripped the corpse, dragged the coverlet from the bed and left Henry's naked body sprawled on the floor. It was the most profitable work they had ever undertaken, and they escaped unnoticed.

The alarm was raised at the next guard-change and, while Marshal led the garrison in a foot-by-foot search of the castle, des Roches took a second group into town, where they kicked their way into every house and byre. They returned empty-handed, to learn that a tunnel had been discovered, leading southward from the cellars of the keep.

The shamefaced members of the garrison denied all knowledge of the subterranean passage. None of them were among the original occupants of the castle, nor had they ever seen plans of the layout. On their oath they had not known of the tunnel's existence. It was what it purported to be, a well-kept secret. That was how it had been designed, and –

'Enough!' Marshal snapped. 'Don't go on with it. I accept your ignorance.' Armed with sword and torch, he made his way along the tunnel, closing his mouth against the rat-fouled air. He noticed that webs hung in tatters and the dust had been stirred and flattened underfoot. The ground was scored by the corners of the clothes boxes, and the low roof had been chipped, presumably by spear-tips. He counted his paces and, at one hundred and nine, emerged among thorn bushes on the rocky hillside. Here he found the boxes, emptied of all but an old belt and a boot with a broken heel. He pushed his way quietly clear of the bushes and stood, listening for the sound of muffled hoofbeats, or the chink of metal. But he was too late; the thieves were far and away, and with them the wealth of a king.

He shouted up at the guards on the south wall, and workmen were sent out to block the hillside entrance. The same would be done in the cellar, in case the secret was known by the French. The empty boxes were carried back into the castle, as though that somehow minimized the theft.

In a touching attempt to reinvest the king with at least a semblance of dignity, his sickened knights searched among their own meagre possessions. Someone produced a clean linen shift. Another gave a woollen cloak. A third offered a pair of unworn shoes. From elsewhere came a cherished ring, a carved wooden replica of the stolen sceptre and, most pathetic of all, a strip of yellow embroidery to serve as a crown.

Inexplicably, Henry's war sword had been discarded by the thieves, although they had taken the decorated scabbard and the belt with its elaborate silver buckle. So the bare blade was laid beside him.

'He'll use it,' one of the knights said, 'to extend the boundaries of heaven.' His companions were not sure if the remark was prompted by admiration, or sarcasm.

By the time the sad work was complete, the sky was lightening. Marshal arranged for the murdered guards to be buried in the castle graveyard, then sent a servant to find Roger Malchat. While he waited for the steward to join him, he crossed the inner courtyard, hauled a rope-bound bucket from the well and doused his head with cold water. He needed sleep, not a drenching, but there would be no sleep today – unless it was eternal, induced by Richard's sword.

Malchat emerged from the keep, crossed the narrow entrance bridge, then stumbled as he descended the steps to the bailey. If the outer defences of Chinon fell to an attacker, the members of the garrison would retire to the keep. Then the wooden bridge would be chopped through, leaving the steps as an isolated pyramid, twenty feet from the wall. The heavy door would then resemble a shuttered window, fifteen feet above ground level. But until that happened, anyone wishing to enter or leave the keep had to traverse the unrailed bridge and scale the steep stone steps.

As the steward approached, Marshal shook his head, spraying water. He tapped the bucket and said, 'You, too? If we can't sleep, we may as well be more awake.'

Malchat hesitated. He had been with Marshal at prayer in

the chapel, and had joined in the hunt for the thieves, but he had not attended the burial of the murdered guards. Instead, he had snatched an hour's sleep in his chamber, from whence he had been roused by the servant. But one glance at Marshal's dark, drawn face told him that Henry's champion had not slept at all, and would not appreciate Malchat's stolen hour. So, more in spirit of contrition than refreshment, he scooped water over his bald head and managed, 'Yes, that's right. Anything to help us keep going.'

Marshal brushed his hands over his ears, squeezing the water from his hair. Then he nodded towards the gate that led to the outer bailey. 'Come on. Let's see the day in. It will be one to remember.'

Given the choice, Marshal preferred to walk and talk. If necessary, he would argue across a table in a conference hall, or discuss from a high-backed chair. But he felt more at ease on the move. He believed that the motion of the body drove the blood, like the current of a millstream, and that blood turned the mill-wheels of the mind. None of his less agile friends had been able to convince him that monks and clerks did their thinking at a desk, and were often accounted brilliant. 'One thought a day,' he dismissed, 'and a week to write it out.'

Now, with Malchat hurrying to keep pace, he strode through the outer yard, signalled to the gate-guards and went on to the path.

Looking westward from the castle approach, it was possible to see the junction of the Loire and the Vienne, and the flat, fertile land between. Low cliffs hemmed the south bank of the Vienne, and there were hills to the north, beyond the Loire. It was a beautiful part of the country, at its most beautiful on this summer morning.

Marshal walked to the edge of the path and gazed down at the town and the meandering rivers. There were still patches of mist on the water, but even as he watched they dissolved in the sun. The village and meeting-ground of Ballan were too far away to be seen, though his memory of them served well enough.

Turning to Malchat, he said, 'There's something I want you to do; something we cannot entrust to a messenger.'

'Yes, I can guess at it. To tell Duke Richard his father is dead.'

Marshal nodded. 'God knows if he'll listen to you, or respond, but he must be told today. The king's body is – well, there's no delicate way to put it – it's ready for the ground. So, if Richard wishes to pay his respects, he'd be advised to hurry. He will not take the word of any common messenger, and I, myself, would go, but – '

'No, you will not,' Malchat said firmly. 'You saw the look he gave you at Ballan. He will either strike out at you before you are off your horse, or hold you for ransom.' With a faint smile he added, 'And for us the second course would be the worst. We'd have to put a value on you.'

'That's how I see it,' Marshal said. 'Duke Richard is anxious to make a reckoning with me, but he has nothing special against you. He'll probably be free with his insults, but if you can close your ears to them – '

'You forget,' Malchat told him, 'I was King Henry's steward. If every insult heaped on me was a grain of sand, I'd be buried in a beach! There is nothing Duke Richard can say that his father has not already told me. Don't worry, my friend. I'll get there and back.'

I hope so, Marshal thought. You're worth too much to us to be savaged by the Lionheart.

As they turned back towards the castle, Malchat asked, 'When he comes here – *If* he comes, I should say – what will you do?'

'That will depend on him.'

'He'll want an apology from you, that's assured. From what I've heard, you made a prize fool of him at the bridge.'

'I dropped him on his arse,' Marshal said, 'let's be clear about it.'

'Well then, when he demands his apology – '

'When he does that, I shall tell him he's damn lucky to be alive.' He grinned at the astonished steward who had never until now regarded Marshal as a braggart. 'Don't look so miserable, Roger. He'll adore me for it. You'll see.'

'Will he?' Malchat retorted. 'Well, I don't. I'm already sweating like a kept cheese.'

During the morning the king's body was taken from the upper chamber and laid in the chapel. It was where it belonged, and the chapel possessed the added advantage of being one of the coldest rooms in the castle. Henry may have craved warmth during his final hours, but it was not good for his corpse. As it was, the honour-guard was changed every hour – the limit of their endurance.

While Roger Malchat made his way towards the French camp at Tours, Marshal sent other men in the direction of Le Mans and Alençon. They went unarmed, and dressed as common wayfarers, in the hopes that the French patrols would let them pass. Their task, other than avoiding arrest, was to learn the whereabouts of poor John. The commanders acknowledged that the invisible prince might still be with Philip and Richard; he must, after all, have put in an appearance in the French camp, in order to add his signature to the list of deserters. But with John Lackland, nothing was certain. For all they knew, he could be on his way to England, or, having suffered another change of heart, be assembling his father's troops in Normandy. Or drunk in Orléans. Or at prayer in the cathedral at Chartres. Or in a haystack with a whore.

In the event, the unarmed scouts failed to find John, though they did make contact with another of Henry's offspring.

Of the king's five legitimate sons, only Richard Lionheart and John Lackland were still alive – if indeed John *was* alive. But Henry had also sired numerous bastards, and it was the most important of these, the thirty-seven-year-old Geoffrey FitzRoy, whom the scouts met on their way north.

There were many who regarded Geoffrey as a more likely Angevin than either Richard or John. True, he shared Richard's energy and physical courage and, to a lesser extent, John's natural cunning. But he was more persistent than either of them. It was said that Richard could be halted by flattery, and John by a brandished feather. But Geoffrey had inherited his father's stubbornness and tenacity, and he was not so easily put off. He was six years older than the Lionheart, sixteen years older than Lackland. And, as with most high-sired bastards, he was required to work harder and look further and move faster, in order to earn his keep.

Apart from this, two things separated him from his brothers. His hair was prematurely grey and, if the list of deserters was reliable, he was the only one to have remained loyal to the king.

He was on his way to Chinon when the scouts brought him the bad news. He had just completed a tour of Normandy, where he had gained the support of the powerful Norman barons. Instill some sense in your father, they'd told him, and we will supply him with an army. But he *must* make his way north; we will not fight across three rivers to be surrounded by the French.

However, Henry Plantagenet would only travel to a grave-yard now, and his only support would come from his pall-bearers...

Geoffrey took the news calmly. He had half-expected it and, if there was any weeping to be done, it would be in private. He asked if William Marshal was in command at Chinon, and was cheered by the answer. In return, the scouts inquired as to the whereabouts of John Lackland.

'I have no idea,' he told them. 'I've neither seen nor heard of him since Le Mans. Has he not been with the king?'

The scouts shook their heads. They knew John's name had topped the French list, but they were soldiers, not sacrificial lambs. Let someone else tell the volatile Geoffrey about the death-dealing signature.

They took him back the way they had come, avoiding the French patrols, then left Marshal to show him the parchment that had broken Henry's heart.

'How well do you know John's writing?' Marshal asked. 'Is this his hand?'

'Hell!' Geoffrey erupted. 'What does it matter? If that vermin had been truly loyal to our father, as you and I have been, they would not have attempted such a trick. If it had read "William Marshal" where it reads "Prince John", King Henry would have howled with scorn. You're over precise, sir. It's the effect that proves it, not the cause.'

Give him time to cool, Marshal told himself. This is as bad a blow as a man can take. And perhaps he's right. 'Perhaps John's absence is proof enough.' He realized with a start that he had spoken the last few words aloud.

'Present or absent,' Geoffrey snapped, 'I tell you, it doesn't matter. It satisfies me that my brother's actions do not *disprove* the signature. It's the nature of the beast that counts. If he did not personally put pen to paper, he gave the forger his blessing. He's with Philip and Richard now, rely on it. Oh, not in their camp, necessarily, but with them, none the less.' He glanced at the list again, then tossed it aside, as though it had been used to wrap some diseased carcase. 'It is at times like this,' he said, 'that I favour bastardy.'

Malchat returned from the French camp to report that Duke
Richard was on his way. He greeted Geoffrey FitzRoy in the
main hall of the keep, then told the weary commanders, 'He
says – and these are his words – "I'll come 'as soon as I've
eaten." I saw the food being served as I left.'

'It's a terrible thing,' Marshal commented dryly, 'to witness
a sorrowing prince. Between mouthfuls, did he say how many
mourners would keep him company?'

'He did. Among other things. His actual message was that
you and des Roches are to stop trembling. He will not bring
an army, for fear of suffocating you with the dust. He'll arrive
with only twenty men, and knock politely at the gate. Two
light taps, so you'll know it's him and not be terrified.' He
looked directly at Marshal. 'You did say he would be free
with his insults.'

'Was John there?'

'Not that I saw. Nor Belcourt or Canton, or any of his
coterie. King Philip was present, though he contributed
nothing. He seemed saddened by the news, but he sent no
message. And as for John, he could be anywhere, the French
are in Tours and along both banks of the river.'

Des Roches could take no more of it. He stamped forward
and slammed a mailed fist on the edge of a long, trestle table.
Forgetting that he was in the presence of Richard's brother,
he cursed the Lionheart for a traitor and a coward. 'We'll
see who trembles, and who shows fear! Christ seal his mouth,
or leave it to me! I swear, that man will be held to account
before long. I'm to stop trembling, eh? Yes, and then he'll
start trembling!'

Geoffrey made no attempt to still the outburst, but Marshal
said, 'Let it lie, *confrère*. There's no profit in being goaded by
his childish taunts. Twenty men, did he say? Well, let's be
cautious, and stand to arms. I'd hate to be overrun by such a
well-fed prince.'

Geoffrey nodded agreement, and in a while the towers of
Chinon were bristling with arrows and crossbow bolts, a
barbed welcome for England's heir.

He rode through the gate and into the outer courtyard,
followed by his armed companions. True to his word, he had

limited the escort to twenty.

The riders had noticed the archers in the towers, and had reined-in at the foot of the approach path. Then Richard had said something to them and spurred forward, his barked laugh carrying up the hillside to the castle. Heartened by his words, the knights had grinned at each other and continued upward. But by the time they had reached the barbican gate they had erased all traces of humour.

He advanced to the centre of the bailey, nodded left and right at certain members of the group, then swung himself to the ground. Six of the knights dismounted, gave their horses to the remaining riders and followed their master towards the inner gate. He had been to Chinon before, and his knowledge of the palace allowed him to make his way without directions. It also enabled him to ignore his bastard brother and the men who had baulked him at the bridge. Sparing them no more than a glance, he went on into the inner courtyard and up the steps to the keep.

His knights were not so willing to slight Geoffrey FitzRoy, but, when none of Henry's commanders moved to intercept them, they clattered after Richard. A few of them noticed that Malchat had positioned himself in front of des Roches, and that when des Roches edged to the left, the steward went with him. They noticed, too, that the thick-set knight kept his hand on his sword.

Relying on memory, Richard crossed the gloomy hall, waited scowling for his escort to appear, then ducked through an archway at the rear of the chamber. The six knights followed, though they did not stoop so low. Beyond the arch he turned left, corrected himself and went the other way along a short, unlit corridor. Then, sniffing the air, he turned into the chapel and made curt obeisance before the altar.

Henry's body lay at the foot of the cloth-covered table, the dreadful corpse guarded by four whey-faced knights. They had served their hour and were waiting to be relieved. Richard dismissed them with a jerk of his head, and they deserted their posts without a second bidding.

His own contingent hung back, appalled by the smell, trying hard to convince themselves that he wished for privacy. They masked their faces with their cloaks, and coughed into the linen. Their eyes watered, not entirely from sorrow, and two of them removed their helmets, which seemed suddenly tight against their skulls. Geoffrey had already paid his last respects to his father, but Marshal and Malchat arrived in the doorway, anxious to see how Richard would commune with the king.

The chapel was illuminated by a dozen sputtering candles, and a thin cross of light admitted through a window above the altar. As the knights peered into the room they saw, or imagined they saw, a trickle of blood leak from Henry's left nostril. It did not begin until Richard gazed down at the body, and it ceased the instant he turned away. But to those who believed their eyes, the meaning was clear – the victim had named his murderer.

Richard knelt again, down and up, and stood over his father for as long as it would take to gabble a prayer. Then he turned on his heel, brushed past his escort and strode from the chapel. As he shouldered his way between Marshal and the steward, he said, 'You. William Marshal. Follow me out.'

Malchat opened his mouth to remonstrate – keep that tone for your dogs – but Marshal nudged him silent. This was not the place to trade insults; nor to draw breath.

Preceded by the Lionheart, and followed by the six armed mourners, they went back along the corridor and into the hall. Geoffrey and des Roches were there, and it was clear that Richard had once again ignored his brother.

The young giant made his way across the creaking bridge, and Marshal said, 'I'm going out with him. Keep these six at a distance. If it comes to blows, it is to remain between Duke Richard and me.' Turning to the escort, he asked them if they understood. They did not like it, but they nodded, and continued coughing foul air from their chests.

With an unsuccessful smile for his companions, Marshal crossed the weather-warped planks and went down to the yard. He realized that he was at a grave disadvantage. He had no desire to kill Richard of Aquitaine, but the duke seemed less reluctant.

Richard stood with his back to the keep, twenty feet or so in front of the steps. The archers and men-at-arms had come down from the towers and were now spaced along the walls, looking down into the yard. Richard's fourteen riders were still in their saddles, though they had been allowed to come through the second gateway into the inner bailey. They, too, were spaced out under the cross-wall, and Richard faced them as he heard Marshal descend the steps.

Turning slowly, so that his words carried around the yard, he boomed, 'In your own time, sir. When you are ready. I'll hear your defence.' That brought him face to face with Marshal, who said, 'You will not, Duke Richard. But all Chinon can hear you. If I was intimidated by noise, I'd keep clear of battles and country fairs.' He moved forward, clear of the steps. If it *did* come to blows, it would not help to snap his sword on the pyramid. 'Now, what am I supposed to say, that I regret unhorsing you?'

'Why not? It will do for a start. You realize we came close to killing each other. Had your lance taken me and not my horse – Had I not deflected the weapon with my arm –'

'One moment!' Marshal snapped, his voice as loud and intense as Richard's. 'You should have learned more about me, prince. I have participated in more than two hundred jousts, around here, and in Normandy, and in your own duchy of Aquitaine. I have made my living at it for years, and you may be assured that I strike where I aim. You did not turn my lance. I lowered the point through sheer good sense. And you are unhurt because of it.'

Richard had already realized his mistake, and sought another line of attack. What Marshal claimed was true. He was without doubt one of the foremost chevaliers in Europe, and for ten years or more he had travelled from tourney to tourney, competing for the prize-money. To say he could not align a lance was to tell a Viking he was lost at sea. Richard almost wished he had not started the shouting match.

'Say what you will, it's fortunate for you that I survived.'

'For both of us,' Marshal corrected, 'though I had no intention of killing you. I told you so at the time. I did not wish to add to your foolishness; merely to stop you.'

Until now, Richard's anger had been largely a test of memory, an attempt to recapture his feelings at the bridge. But this last accusation refreshed his fury.

'Foolishness, was it? You guard what you say, William Marshal, before I cut you out!'

'I'll take care. But you might also be advised, and wear a sword and shield before you next run mad.'

At the head of the steps, Geoffrey FitzRoy braced himself,

sure that the blows would now be struck. Malchat and des Roches watched from the doorway of the keep, the steward praying that the adversaries would hold themselves in check, des Roches willing Marshal to strike first. Throughout the castle, soldiers and servants heard the exchange and waited for the onset. One did not call Richard of Aquitaine a fool and a madman. Nor did one tell Marshal how to couch a lance.

Drawn to his full height, Richard was a terrifying sight. He was one of the tallest men of the day, and one of the broadest in the shoulder, and anger ran through him like strong, coarse wine. In the years to come he would dominate armies and strengthen the resolve of nations, and would be seen storming up from a Syrian beach, or striding inland to subdue the islands of Sicily and Cyprus. Equipped with a personality that blossomed in indignation, he would show why he was called Lionheart, and why, throughout the West, mothers warned their children to behave, lest *Coeur-de-Lion* came to swallow them alive.

But the magic was not yet perfect, and the spell was not working at Chinon. Richard held Marshal's gaze until his vision blurred, then heard himself laugh and say, 'All right, it's good advice. I should have dressed for the occasion. Mind you, I was not to know you had interrupted your retreat.'

'No,' Marshal agreed. 'You were not.'

The young prince let his shoulders sag, and his hands came away from his sword. An audible sigh drifted above the yard, for although every man there had seen insults turn to blood, they would not have enjoyed anything more than the vicious skill of the duel. Whoever had triumphed – and with a sword it would most likely have been Duke Richard – Christendom would have lost a champion. These two were not white-faced courtiers, soured on wine or jealousy, but serious men, loyal to their cause. Until now they had been enemies, the one supporting his king, the other fighting to gain his inheritance. But the death of either would have meant an irreplaceable loss, as much for the victor as for England.

Richard laughed again, and this time there was some warmth in the sound. He was about to show that other part of his nature that endeared him to those he could not crush – his extraordinary magnanimity.

'You insist you could have killed me, had you wished?'

Marshal shrugged, leaving an affirmative impression.

'And you are quite unrepentant of what you did?'

Don't crow, Marshal warned himself. This is a new side to the man. Don't force him to conceal it.

Nevertheless, he said, 'I cannot repent for having halted an adversary. And I only cost you a horse, not your life.'

'A damn fine horse,' Richard exclaimed, '*and* a blackened arse! I think of you every time I'm seated.' Then, never less than dramatic, he extended his arms and clasped Marshal in an embrace. With complete sincerity, and able to forget the bloody year that had passed, he said, 'If my father had had a thousand more of William Marshal, he would not have come to such a – such a paltry end.'

He leaned forward, his head bowed over Marshal's shoulder, and as he mourned the circumstances of his father's death, the occupants of Chinon were treated to the sight of England's heir weeping on the neck of his erstwhile foe. Geoffrey clicked his tongue and went into the keep to find some wine. He did not believe that Richard possessed one stalk of genuine emotion, but saw him as a consummate actor, the kind that travelled the country, slaying demons at midday, and expiring at dusk. Tomorrow he would kill the same, straw-filled monster, and the villagers would roar approval; tomorrow he would die again in the service of some badly-rehearsed story, and the audience would weep. It was enough to turn a man to the jar.

For his part, Malchat accepted the reconciliation, and thanked God for it. Now, perhaps, England could be raised from her knees, and the lost territories regained. Richard Lionheart with William Marshal; yes, that was something to be applauded.

Beside him in the doorway, des Roches thought his friend well placed to draw a dagger and stab Richard in the side. While they are clung together like that. Go on, he's at your mercy . . .

But he was to be disappointed, for when Richard had controlled his tears, he and Marshal walked arm-in-arm around the yard. The riders withdrew to the outer bailey, while the wall-guards returned to their stations. Des Roches and Malchat joined Geoffrey at the trestle table and invited Richard's escort to share the wine. Before long, dice appeared, and sword-belts were thrown haphazardly against the wall.

Richard removed his helmet and brushed at his red-and-yellow
hair. 'Tell me,' he said. 'It seems remarkable that you have
been so long without lands. What are you, forty? Forty – '

' – three.'

'Forty-three, and still without a fief. It's unjust. Did my
father never promise you anything? He was in the devil's
grip at the end, but if he did make some assurance – '

'Yes,' Marshal said, 'he did.'

'Then tell me what it was, and I shall see it's honoured.'
He glanced across, in part to see if his new friend was
inventing a claim, but more because he suspected that Marshal
would not yet confide in him. But that was stupid. They were
comrades now. He admired the knight!

Marshal sensed the look and said nothing. Only a fool
would put his trust in reconciliatory promises. They were
made with too much passion and, like passion, they tended
to grow cold. If Richard was serious, he would ask again.

'Did you hear me? If my father made an assurance to you,
I shall see it's honoured.'

With fine timing, Marshal said, 'You might think I'd
invented it. You have only my word for it; there's nothing
written.'

'God's legs, I swear you're out to affront me again! I said
I would honour it, and so I will. Tell me what he – '

'The hand of Isabel de Clare.'

' – promised you and – Isabel de Clare? The Earl of Pembroke's daughter?' Marshal nodded equably. 'Do you know
of her, prince?'

'Yes, I – But do *you* know the extent of her holdings!'

'The king said it would make me a man of some importance
in England. I believe the lady will bring me the Lordship of
Striguil; that's a hundred square miles or so between the Wye
and the Usk. And the manor of Weston in Hertfordshire.
And Chesterford in Essex. And Badgeworth in Gloucestershire.
And the county of Pembroke in Wales; all the land between
Carmarthen and St Bride's. And the Lordship of Leinster in
Ireland; with that I shall get the counties of Kildare and
Kilkenny, Carlow and Wexford, Queens and a portion of – '

'That'll do,' Richard told him, unable to hide his confusion.

'You've obviously been with the clerks.' He moved away to think things over, turned back, then dismissed his own unspoken comment. And *he* had felt sorry for Marshal. Still without a fief. Landless at, what was it, forty-three? And now to be told this.

'Is it too much,' Marshal asked, 'for yesterday's enemy?'

'What? No, no, of course not. My father was right to – You did say it was never written out, his promise?'

Be careful, Marshal thought. It can still be lost. He did not think Henry would make so much of me, and it worries him. With justification, for if I was to rise against him as Earl of Pembroke, I could recruit an army from my own lands.

'No, prince, it was not put down on paper. But it was announced before we retreated to Le Mans. In the presence of the entire court. So I can furnish proof.' *And you will be bound to honour it.*

But Richard had already come to terms with the situation. Marriage to Isabel de Clare would indeed make William Marshal a man of importance. Yet he was no self-seeker, and throughout his life he had been loyal to the king. God willing, he would be as loyal to King Richard.

'I have proof enough,' he said. 'You're as good as ennobled.' Then with a strangely diffident expression, he asked, 'Have you seen this woman, Isabel de Clare?'

'I have heard she is a beauty, and only nineteen or so, but no, I have not yet set eyes on her.'

'Hmm. You are one for the women, are you, Marshal?'

'Aren't we all eager – ' Marshal started, then stopped abruptly. 'Yes,' he amended. 'I look forward to marriage.'

'And why not?' Richard murmured. 'It suits some people.'

Marshal watched him, and kept his thoughts to himself. Like his brothers, Richard of Aquitaine had a ribald sense of humour, and possessed a wealth of bawdy stories. But, unlike John and Geoffrey, he did not sweet-talk the ladies,, or seek the more intimate services of the maidservants. It was rumoured that he found his bedmates among the knights and squires of his court, and that he was unnaturally attracted to the disdainful Philip Augustus. But no one dared publicly accuse him of homosexuality and as yet it did not much matter. It would only cause concern if, as King of England, he refused to marry, or married and sired no children. Until then, his hours were his own.

On 8th July, King Henry II of England was buried in the
Angevin church at Fontevrault. The service was attended by
Richard and Geoffrey, though there was still no sign of
brother John. Marshal had inquired among Richard's entourage and been assured that it was indeed Lackland's
signature that topped the list of deserters.

'Then why is he not here? It took eight men to set that lid
on Henry's tomb; he won't rise up. Is John now afraid of the
dead, along with everything else?'

'Not the dead,' they told him, 'but maybe of Richard.'

Within hours of the burial service, he understood what they
meant.

Richard produced the list he had made in the French camp
at Le Mans – the record of those English knights who had
ridden down from Fresnay – and matched it with the more
comprehensive list that Henry had demanded on his death-
bed. He then told Roger Malchat to draw up another, com-
prising all those who had remained faithful to the old king.

When it was ready, Richard checked the one against the
other, to make sure there were no discrepancies, then worked
his way down the list of deserters, disinheriting every man
who had come over to him.

Where the turncloaks had looked for reward, they found
rejection. Where they had anticipated honours, they earned
hatred. Yes, they had sided with the victor, but no, they
would not be thanked for it. The Lionheart loathed cowards
and indoor men, but above all else he detested changelings.
How could he rely on a man who had already abandoned
his father? What sense was there in setting a proven thief to
guard the silver?

Name by name, the deserters were stripped of their lands
and titles, then fined, or banished, or imprisoned. In the space
of a day, the nobility of England was given a new face. Those
who had hewed unswervingly to the father – or the son – were
treated as equals, and the confiscated properties were shared
between them. They stood in line to swear fealty to their
future king, then hurried away to inspect their new holdings.
Richard saw them off with a smile, aware that his reputation
for generosity travelled with them. He had made enemies of
those he had disinherited, but what harm could they do,

stripped naked? His new men, on the other hand, would do whatever he asked them. And, when the time came, pay for their privileges.

When the give and take of property was concluded, he sent for the dark-skinned commander, and they discussed the one woman in Richard's life – his mother, Eleanor of Aquitaine. She was sixty-seven years old now, but still elegant and witty; or with as much wit as one can muster after sixteen years in prison . . .

In 1173 this extraordinary woman, who had been married to King Louis of France, divorced by him, then married to King Henry of England, was arrested and accused of fomenting rebellion. Her inquisitors claimed that it was she who had turned Henry's sons against him, while Eleanor maintained that the king merely sought an excuse to have her put away in favour of his current mistress, Rosamund Clifford. The Fair Rosamund, Henry's supporters called her. *Rosa Immunda,* the Rose Deflowered, was one writer's cruel pun.

Since then, Eleanor had been confined in various English castles, and manor-houses. Her sons had continued to wage war against their father and, even as a prisoner, the strong-willed queen had exerted considerable influence over the Angevin brood.

When Rosamund Clifford died suddenly, it was rumoured that Eleanor had administered poison. The queen derived sour comfort from the story, and told one of her handmaids, 'They must think I fly in and out of the window like a bat. If Henry is ever killed in the field, someone is bound to say they saw me strike the blow. I wonder why they bother to lock me in, if I'm to be credited with these far-flung crimes.'

Nevertheless, her influence did not get her released during Henry's lifetime. It was only now, when the king lay in his sealed stone coffin, that Eleanor's favourite son told Marshal, 'I want you to go and free her. I shall be detained on this side of the Channel for some weeks yet, but she's to be set at liberty without delay. She knows and trusts you, Marshal, even though you fought for the king. And you have a special place in your heart for her, so I've been told.'

'You have been told right,' Marshal nodded.

The two men were seated in a narrow, low-beamed hall, part of the Bishop of Fontevrault's palace. Richard had commandeered the building, and had already carved his name in one of the chair arms and cut a cross in an inlaid writing-table. He was at work again now, defacing, or as he thought, improving, the chiselled border of a bench. He glanced up from his labours, tapped the blade of his dagger against a bare knuckle and said, 'Tell me about it. I love stories that speak well of my mother. She is the finest lady that was ever born; under God, she is. There'll never be one to equal her. Anyway, not that I shall meet.' He gave a sigh and shrugged, and the simple gesture illustrated his attitude to women. Why struggle against his predilections, when the only woman he liked was his mother?

He whittled at the bench again and said, 'Go on. What did she do for you?'

'She set me on the road,' Marshal told him. 'I was, what, twenty-one? So you were ten, my lord.' He smiled at the thought of the giant as a downy-haired stripling, then stood up and paced the chamber.

'I had just returned from England with my uncle, Earl Patrick. He'd been summoned by King Henry to suppress a revolt in Poitou. It was the middle of winter, I remember that, and bitterly cold. We used to wrap hot stones in our clothes, and hold burning branches to warm our metal gloves. The Poitevins said it was the coldest winter in living memory, and we were not inclined to argue.'

'About my mother.'

Marshal stopped pacing. 'This is my story,' he said evenly. 'Allow me to tell it as it comes.'

Once again the air between them was charged with antagonism. Richard interrupted his woodwork, and the two men gazed at each other.

'You like to hold the floor, don't you, Marshal?'

'I like to tell the story I was asked to tell.' He waited a little while, then asked, 'Well, my lord, do I go on?'

'Of course go on! Nobody said stop.' He dug the knife into the bench, and ran his tongue noisily over his teeth. God's legs, Marshal was as touchy as a Provençal troubadour.

'So,' Marshal continued, 'the middle of winter, and we had just taken the castle of Lusignan. King Henry had gone on elsewhere with the army, leaving Queen Eleanor and Earl Patrick and myself in the castle. We were under constant attack from the Lusignan family, and in one month we must have repulsed a dozen assaults. Your mother was magnificent. Nothing was too menial for her, and I swear she spent as many hours on the walls as any of the guards.'

All encouragement now, Richard asked, 'Did she dress the part?'

'In armour? Yes, my lord, certainly. We would scarcely have let her go up there unprotected.'

'I tell you,' the young duke blurted, 'she is as good as *any* man! I'd be as willing to have *her* beside me in battle – ' He stabbed the bench, wrenched the knife free, then stabbed down again, pitting the buttock-smoothed wood. There was something vehement in his enthusiasm, and Marshal pressed on with his story.

'Eventually the attacks lessened, and one day we took the opportunity to ride outside the walls. We went heavily-armed at first, but when nothing happened we grew careless, and that's how they surprised us, the Lusignans, trotting along without a hauberk or helmet between us.' He saw Richard point accusingly from the bench and said, 'I know what's on your tongue. How dare I lecture you about the business at the bridge, when I myself have committed the same sin? Well, for that very reason. It courts disaster.'

Richard curled his finger and went back to defacing the bench.

'While Earl Patrick sent Queen Eleanor into the castle, we tried to keep the Lusignans from the gate. Unhappily though, one of them rode behind my uncle and drove a spear into his back. Without his hauberk he was as vulnerable as a child. I went for them as best I could, but they cut my horse from under me and stuck a sword in my leg. After that, I was in no shape to fight.'

'And Earl Patrick?'

'They killed him. The queen was safe inside by then, but it was a bad day for us.'

The story contained all the elements that appealed to Richard; courage and cowardice, the excitement of battle and, as a rare advantage, the presence of his mother. He was somewhat disappointed that she had been sent from the field, but he could see the sense in it.

'Then what?' he asked. 'You were lucky you weren't skewered where you lay.'

'By rights I should have been, for I was worth nothing in

ransom. But the Lusignans were not to know that.'

'Aah, false modesty,' Richard chided. 'You had a reputation, even then. King Henry would have paid for you.'

'Perhaps he would. But it was the queen who purchased my release, out of her own coffers. When the ransom was settled and I was returned to the castle, I found that she'd sent all the way to Rouen for a reliable physician.'

'Is that what you mean by being set on the road?'

'In part, though my indebtedness to your mother does not end there. As I said, I possessed nothing of material value, but when my leg had healed Queen Eleanor summoned me to her chamber and said, "These chests are cluttering the place, Marshal. This is not a storehouse, you know." '

'What chests?'

'Two great iron-bound boxes. I explained that I owned no chests, but she waved aside my denials and told me to check through them. So I opened them up and found a lifetime supply of *pelissons*, leather *gambesoms*, gloves, belts, several cloaks, boots and shoes, even a painted clasp. Oh, yes, and behind the chests armour and lances. She had omitted nothing, save a fresh horse and its trappings.'

'Which was waiting for you in the yard.'

'Wrong,' Marshal said. '*They* were waiting. A palfrey, a pack-horse – which, by God, I needed – and a tub-chested Norman destrier. *That's* what I mean when I say Queen Eleanor set me on the road.'

Richard mutilated another section of the bench, then with complete sincerity remarked, 'I'm glad I did not kill you at the bridge, Marshal. It would have caused my mother great sadness, I can see that now.'

Next morning, Marshal and Roger Malchat set out for England, with orders to release the widow queen from her prison chambers in the palace at Winchester. That done, the steward would go on to London and prepare for Richard's arrival. For his part, Marshal would be free to claim the hand of his unseen bride, Isabel de Clare.

Richard would follow later, when he had settled affairs in Normandy and Anjou. And ferreted out brother John.

Chapter Three

BROTHER JOHN

July, August 1189

It was said that he slept in his boots, for fear of being caught short. True or not, the only men who saw him barefoot were his bath attendants, and the only women, those he bedded. It was painful enough to be known as Lackland, without giving the world the opportunity to cry Dwarf, or Curtcount.

He compensated for nature's parsimony by having his boots and shoes made with three-inch heels, and by taking his position on any available step or dais. His companions had grown used to his ways, and the diplomats among them wore slippers in his presence and stood stoop-shouldered. Needless to say there were few tall men around John Lackland.

Although he measured less than five-and-a-half feet in height, he was well-proportioned, at least at this time of his life. He was proud of his thick reddish hair and his elegant fingers, and he had developed a mannerism that showed them both to advantage. Presented with a problem, or regaled with a joke, he pressed a hand to his head and held it there, fingers outstretched. Over the years the mannerism had become instinctive; during the last few days it had become incessant.

John had last seen Duke Richard at Tours, the day before their father had died. On that occasion he had added his name to the list of those who had deserted Henry, and had then left the citadel as invisibly as he had left Le Mans. It was with mixed feelings that he had signed the scroll, for he sensed it would destroy the ailing king. But in the past few months Richard and Philip had established complete superiority over the English forces, and it had become increasingly clear that Henry was a doomed man. For too many years John had listened to his father's promises, and lived in the expectation of lands and largesse. He *was* Lord of Ireland, but his only visit to the place had ended in disaster, and Henry had hurriedly appointed a justiciar to clean up the mess. At the time, John had been accused of irresponsibility, embezzlement and gross discourtesy to the Irish nobility. But they were charges he refuted. In his opinion, the Irish were uncouth peasants. They wore beards to their waists, and spoke a language that was quite incomprehensible to any but themselves. To hear *them* tell the story, John had gone over with a group of indolent courtiers, insulted the native priests and princes, raped the women and all but drowned in drink and debauchery. It was a wild exaggeration, of course, but what else could one expect from a nation of hirsute barbarians? A few beards *had* been tugged in play, and a few appointments overlooked, and a few women impregnated, and the money *had* run out before the soldiers could be paid. But was that so terrible? It happened all the time, and if one's name was Lionheart instead of Lackland, nobody complained.

Nevertheless, he was Lord of Ireland in name only now, and otherwise as landless as a pilgrim.

So, with Henry unable to turn his promises into reality, John had changed sides and signed the list. Then, accompanied by Belcourt and Canton and a few other trustworthy friends, he had left Tours and returned to his hideout, a small village on the Sarthe. His original plan had been to let Henry and Richard and Philip come to terms, then rejoin the family in the hopes that somebody would give him something. But events had taken a different path. Henry had surrendered unconditionally, and died without making any provisions for his youngest son. And now the latest reports spoke of Richard avenging himself on all who had signed the list. It wasn't fair, and it wasn't what he'd been promised.

John Lackland was twenty-one years old, petulant and embittered, and in fear of his life.

Marshal and Malchat reached Dieppe, where they took ship for England. On their way through Maine they had passed within a few miles of John's hideout, but they were no longer interested in the turncloak. They had ladies on their minds; Eleanor of Aquitaine, and Isabel de Clare.

Marshal ungallantly suggested that the heiress of Pembroke and Striguil would probably resemble a gargoyle, and that if she cut her hand, she would leak water. 'I've heard she's a beauty, but how can she be, if she's worth so much, yet still unmarried?'

The serious-minded steward saw no humour in the comment. 'Because Henry kept her for you,' he said, 'that's how. I'd say he had her in mind as your wife long before he told you. She has been put by, so think yourself lucky.' They rode on, and then Malchat relented enough to say, 'I know why you're so harsh. You imagine her as satanic in order to avoid disappointment. But what if she *is* as ugly as a griffon, what then? Will you still marry her for her property?'

'Hell, yes,' Marshal laughed. 'She can always be sent to one of her holdings, when I'm not there. If I was to marry a woman for her looks, I'd be hooked by now. Hooked but not landed, so to speak.'

'Have you never been in love?'

'Yes, my inquistive friend, I've been in love. And brokenhearted. But such emotions are easily come by. A slice of England is not.'

'Are you so suddenly hungry for power? You never were before.'

'Well, let's say I've worked up an appetite.' There was a note of finality in his voice, and Malchat decided to let it go. Even so, he hoped Isabel de Clare was reasonably presentable. For her sake.

When it came to it, John Lackland was not hard to find. On 14th July, exactly one week after Henry's burial, Richard's scouts reported that his brother, along with Belcourt and Canton and ten others, had made their home in a derelict water-mill, near the village of Sablé-sur-Sarthe. Richard immediately took his leave of King Philip, having agreed to rejoin him at Rouen within the month, and set out for Sablé. He was accompanied by a strong bodyguard of knights, but when the riders reached the outskirts of the village he told them to wait, and went on alone.

They settled themselves in a riverside meadow and sent two of their number in search of wine. It was already too dark for archery, or stone-throwing contests, so they contented themselves with six-dice, and impromptu recitations. One of their favourite poets was Guillaume of Aquitaine. He had been dead these past sixty years, but had left a wealth of poetry, ranging from the courtly to the obscene. Knights revered his work, for, although they were often the butt of his mordant humour, they were also extolled as the real champions of liberty. He dismissed clerks and priests as unworthy of a lady's attentions, and advised the heroine to find herself a bold young knight. In his less spiritual moments, he had composed works of unparalleled obscenity, and these could

always be relied upon to enliven the evening. Many of the
young knights recited the poems by rote, aware that their
memory far outstripped their experience. Was *that* really
possible between a man and a woman? Would even the lowest
whore submit to *this*? Well, apparently so, as Guillaume
described it.

On his way through the village Richard accosted a late-
returning farmer, who said yes, he did know of the water-mill;
it was beyond the last house, just north of a poplar grove.

'Do you know how many are in there at present?'

'I have never visited the place, master, not since they –'

'What? Since they what?'

Terrified, the man edged against the street wall. 'We were
warned off when they first came. I think there are twelve,
but –'

'Do they get their food from you?'

Again the man hesitated. He had never before set eyes on
the red-haired monster, and he did not know if he was there
to join the occupants. It was best to be cautious. And to
improve his mode of address. 'Yes, my lord, they take their
food from us.'

'Take it? And pay for it?'

The farmer said nothing, then suddenly shook his head. If
the rider became angry, or called him a liar, he would say
he'd had a fly on his face. It was a feeble excuse, but it was
all he could manage.

Richard urged his horse closer to the wall. 'How much do
they owe you, those at the mill?'

'How much?'

'Yes!' he snapped. 'How much money?'

'It's not easy to say, my lord.' He wanted to push the horse
away, but he knew better than to touch it. 'I would have to
ask the others.' He glanced along the street and saw two more
strangers, loaded down with wine-skins. Now where were
they going? The mill was the other way.

Richard said, 'I'm not here for a conference. Would five
Angevin marks balance the scales?'

'Balance the scales? I don't – Oh, you mean – Yes, my lord,
yes, more than enough for the bread and meat and things
we gave them, that they took. Yes.'

Richard sighed at the man's stupidity, and dug a handful
of coins from his purse. He intended to give five marks, but

when the coins were in his hand he could not bring himself to pick them out, one-and-two-and-three. That was clerk's work. But neither would he pass them directly to the farmer, as though he acknowledged the debt. This was to be an act of largesse, not settlement of a bill.

He glanced at the money, guessed that there were ten or eleven Angevin marks, plus an assortment of smaller coins, then tossed them at the man. They hit his legs and bounced off the wall, rolling back beneath the horse.

'More than twice your price,' Richard told him. 'So you will never forget me.'

The man nodded blindly and found sense to blurt, 'No, never, I swear it.' Had he known the identity of his benefactor, he would have been even more astonished, for to get money from the Lionheart was to get wine from a stone.

Bathed in the light of his own generosity, Richard left the man with a tale he would tell and embroider the rest of his life. '. . . Appeared without warning, out of the dark . . . Just unstrapped his purse and handed it to me . . . The Duke of Aquitaine, there's only one that looks like him . . . Coming through the village, and I stopped him and said we could not afford to keep those . . . Yes, he was surprised when I stepped in his path . . . Vowed he would never forget me . . .'

Richard saw the trees silhouetted against the evening sky and heard the rush of the river, and led his horse up to the silent mill. The windows were shuttered, but candlelight leaked through the weather-warped boards.

He tethered the palfrey and rapped on the door.

It was opened by Peter Canton, who immediately sprang back, shouting the alarm. Richard frowned, annoyed that Canton had failed to recognize him.

'I'm no demon,' he snapped. 'Don't you know your suzerain by now?' He stepped forward, so the idiot could see him better, and panicked Canton into drawing his sword.

'What is this?' Richard roared, his anger mounting. 'You'd show a blade to *me*?'

But his warning was lost on Canton, who made a desperate lunge at him. It was a fatal mistake, for in one well-practised movement, Richard unsheathed his own sword, parried the blow, then slashed his assailant across the neck. Canton fell sideways, spraying blood in the doorway. The young duke stared, unwilling to believe what had happened. Employing his favourite oath, he muttered, 'God's legs! I came to find my brother . . .'

The alarm had alerted the household, and men were approaching around both sides of the disused grinding-stones. Richard braced himself in the doorway, his mind in turmoil. Canton was mad, no doubt of that. He had shouted, 'John, take guard, he is here!' But surely, that meant he *had* recognized the caller. So why strike out?

And the others, those who were coming past the stones, were they also afflicted? The mill was a mad-house! Somehow, they had been bewitched, and –

'Stop short!' he bellowed. 'You, Belcourt, we are known to each other. Are you possessed?'

There was a heavy thud above their heads, and the knights turned towards a sagging wooden staircase. Marking their positions in his mind, Richard followed their gaze. He heard footsteps on the floor above, saw high-heeled boots, the hem of a linen shift, bejewelled fingers and bare arms, and then the jaw and face and head of John Lackland.

'You?' John mouthed. 'You.' Then he clutched the stair-rail and gaped at the blood-spattered doorway.

Richard, in turn, stared past his brother's head at a woman's naked legs. They seemed appropriate to the mad-house.

The young prince had drunk a lot that day, brought a willing girl from the village, then fallen asleep across her. When she realized he could not be aroused, she had squirmed free and crouched disconsolately on the bed, wondering if she would get paid. She had been to the mill before, so perhaps one of the prince's companions would make use of her. That would at least ensure her some reward for her labours. Then she could return to him before he had slept off the effects of his wine and, if he was sufficiently refreshed when he woke, she might double her earnings.

But she was still weighing the risks when Canton shouted from below.

The girl had not understood what he said, but he had called John by name, so she had swung round on the bed, pummelling at him. He had come blearily to his senses and allowed her to pull him upright. Richard's challenge to Belcourt had been lost on him, yet there was something familiar about the roar. His head throbbing, and uncertain how long he had slept, he had started stiff-legged down the stairs. To discover Canton dead in the doorway, and his brother with blood on his boots.

He put a hand to his head, fingers splayed, and scraped his tongue against the roof of his mouth. 'What have you done?' he croaked. 'Why have you killed him?'

The girl descended another step, and Richard turned his attention to the knights. 'Clothe your blades,' he commanded, 'or bear the penalty. Now!'

They looked to John for guidance, but he lifted his hand from the rail in a gesture of surrender. Night after night he had dreamed of this confrontation, but it had been he, and not Canton, who met Richard at the door. Sometimes he disarmed the duke with words, and in other dreams knocked his sword to the ground. Richard did not always come alone, but it made no difference, for John was more than a match for the callers, and they were glad to retreat.

Those were the dreams, but each morning he awoke to reality and the knowledge that he would never thwart the Lionheart.

His hand raised above the stair-rail, he said, 'Do as he tells you. He has an instinct for killing.' He watched his companions sheath their swords, then peered down at Richard. 'Well, brother, you've won. We are at your mercy, what there is of it, so you'd better tell us what we're to do.' He was not interested in the reply. If Richard wished to punish him, as he had already punished those who had deserted Henry, let him get on with it. All that mattered to John was that his head ached abominably, and that he had failed to take the whore. He stood on the stairs, sweating and shivering, too preoccupied with his own sickly condition to care what form his brother's vengeance would take.

Richard's frown deepened as he returned John's question. 'What you're to do? Why, you must do whatever you please, boy. The war is over now, haven't you heard? It's over, and we've won, and I'm here to collect you.' He nodded at the corpse in the doorway. 'I don't know what madness afflicted Canton, but he died for nothing.'

It took a long while for his words to penetrate John's pain-racked mind. Swaying on the stairs, he blinked with disbelief and clutched again at the rail. 'Then you are – You are not here to persecute us?'

'In God's name, what for?'

'But we heard – We heard the king was dead, and that you were taking revenge on all those who signed the list. That's why Canton barred your entry. He was protecting me from *you*!'

'But why?' Richard exclaimed. 'Is that what you believed, that I would hound my own brother?'

'You hounded our father long enough. And my signature –'

'That! It's the scribble of an infant. You're a foolish and stupid child, John. You bend with the wind, and dote on rumour. You always have. But a traitor? God, no; you do not possess the *conviction* for treason!'

'Then you were never against me?'

'No!' he roared, 'I was never against you. Would I have come here alone if I'd intended to seize you? They're a motley bunch, your friends, but not even I would go single-handed against a dozen cornered rats.' He swung round in exasperation. 'Christ have mercy on us, boy, for you are as guilty of Canton's death as I. You say he was protecting you, but who fed him the lie? Who persuaded him that I was your enemy? And who was first persuaded by some half-heard tale?' He rammed his sword into its scabbard, then told John to come down from his perch.

Watching from the stairs, the young prince realized fully for the first time that *Coeur-de-Lion* absolved him from normal judgement. Richard had always seen him as, yes, a stupid and vacillating child, but he had never before overlooked such a decisive act. John had signed the list voluntarily and spitefully, in order to bring King Henry to his knees, and had then retreated to await the outcome. He had not expected the sound of his name to kill the king, but later, when he had learned what had happened, he had thought himself the prime target for Richard's revenge.

And even in that he had been wrong.

'Come down,' Richard repeated. 'You've nothing to fear from me, boy.' He turned from the sight of the naked whore and so he did not see the expression that cooled like wax on Lackland's face. It was compounded of pain and fear and suspicion, but the ingredient that gave it its flavour was a slowly widening smile. Never again would John question the value of brotherly love; it had a greater purchasing power than gold.

He took his hand from his head and caressed the girl's inner thigh. Then he stumbled down the stairs and knelt at Richard's feet. 'Please,' he murmured. 'Please.'

Richard leaned down and laid his hand on John's fine red hair. 'Don't fret,' he growled. 'I'll take care of you. I'll guide you along.'

'Yes,' John said, 'I know you will.'

They reached England, Marshal and Malchat, and exchanged a grimace of agony. Throughout the crossing the ship had dipped and rolled, bruising the tethered horses and hurling the men about the open deck. Marshal had been the first to drape himself over the bulwarks, though the steward's complacency had been short-lived. With Dieppe still in sight, Malchat had found his own place at the rail and hung over it, as though awaiting the executioner's axe.

Six hours later they were still at sea, drenched and exhausted. It did not comfort them to know that both King Philip of France and Richard Lionheart were prone to seasickness, nor that the sailors aboard were astonished at the bad weather. Mid-July, when the Channel was normally calm beneath a cloudless sky. Extraordinary. Had you waited until tomorrow, messires, or crossed over yesterday . . . Like a duck-pond it was, yesterday . . .

More than nine hours after leaving Dieppe, the blunt-prowed *buss* had entered port at Dover, and the passengers had been helped ashore. The ship's captain directed them to a waterfront tavern and, while they huddled morosely in front of the fire, the tavern-keeper arranged for the care of their horses. Neither man could summon the strength to eat, though they managed to keep down a bowl of warm goat's milk spiced with herbal wine. They fell asleep in their chairs, aware that their weak stomachs had sentenced Eleanor of Aquitaine to another night in her prison suite at Winchester.

With a protective eye on his brother, Richard rode north toward Rouen. He had already told his escort that they were never again to use the term Lackland. Why should they, he asked them, when he intended to give John control of the English counties of Somerset and Cornwall, Devon and Nottingham, Derby and Lancaster? Why should they, when the youngster was to obtain the honours of Eye and Wallingford, Tickhill and Marlborough, Gloucester and Ludgershall?

Why would they, when his contrite brother was to secure the homage of the Welsh princes and be firmly established as Lord of Ireland and Count of Mortain?

In the face of that, Richard's entourage masked their expressions and drove the term from their minds. Amongst themselves, they marvelled that the Lionheart could be so easily hoodwinked, but they never again referred to John as a man without property. As Richard had said, why would they, when his brother had come into possession of half England and the better part of Ireland? John Lackland? Oh, no. He was now John Lavishland.

Six days later, Queen Eleanor's rescuers reached the palace at Winchester to discover that she was already at liberty. News of King Henry's death had encouraged her sympathetic gaoler to unbolt the doors of her suite, though she had shown no immediate desire to leave.

'I've grown used to this place,' she told him. 'I know it so well, I could mend clothes in the dark, or walk about without touching the furniture. Besides, Master Blet, sudden freedom is as upsetting as abrupt imprisonment. You mustn't evict me without fair warning.'

This was not what Blet had expected, and he began to regret his decision. No one had authorized him to free the queen. He had done so of his own volition, and in the hopes that her gratitude would keep the hangman's rope from his neck. But if she intended to remain in prison, he might as well re-bolt the doors.

'How long will you – I mean, should you not go straight to London, and –'

'Don't be piqued,' she smiled. 'You'll be rid of me soon enough. Just allow me to stay on as your guest for a while. If I have any friends left in England, they will look for me here.'

He managed to combine an obedient nod with a shrug of resignation and withdrew to the door. From habit he started to close it, then remembered and pushed it wide open. Eleanor watched him, amused by his manner, but aware that he had put his life at risk. 'One moment,' she called. 'You've been gentle with me, Master Blet. As you know, I have savoured a dozen prisons in this country, but I was never treated so well as here. It's courageous of you to slip the bolts, and it would be easier for you if I was to pack my bags and leave. You could say I had been released by men-at-arms, and I'd back your story. But I must see who comes, now that my husband is dead. Time is pressing, and I have no wish to make my friends trail after me. Now, if you please, you may lock me in again.'

He squeezed his knuckles while he thought about it. His own quarters were nearby, but he could drag his bed into the passageway, so he'd be better placed to hear any knock. For that's all she'd have to do, just knock. Day or night, whenever she chose. And then he'd unlock the doors and let her out. Any time at all. That way, his neck would stop itching in anticipation of the rope. But . . .

'They've all sunk on their hinges,' he said. 'I'll bring some wedges, to keep them open.'

Eleanor nodded, as though Blet had never been in doubt.

She spent the next few days writing letters and re-discovering the palace grounds. She spared hardly a thought for her dead husband, though Richard and John were ever in her mind. And the scheming Philip of France, the real architect of Henry's downfall. And Henry's bastard, Geoffrey FitzRoy, a shadowy figure for whom a place must be found in the new regime. Three brothers and the young French king, and each with a young man's appetite. It would take some pretty cooking to satisfy them.

She was in her rooms, with the doors wedged open, when Blet hurried to tell her that a certain Sir William Marshal and Roger Malchat, King Henry's steward, were waiting in the antechamber. Marshal's name brought a hum of joy to her lips. 'Bring them in, bring them – No, wait. They must have travelled from Anjou or Normandy. The least I can do is shorten their journey by a few paces. Have you offered them wine?'

'I have, my lady, *and* hard-boiled eggs and some white bread I had put by for your meal, but I'll send for some more, I know where I can get it fresh.'

'You're as excited as I am, Master Blet. Why's that?'

'I know that Sir William Marshal holds you special, my lady.' Worried that he should be in possession of such knowledge, he added, 'The world knows he worships you.'

'Does he, indeed? Well, go and attend him then. We must hold on to such a public friend.' She waved him off, shook the folds of her gown and turned slowly before an oblong, hammered-metal mirror. Exchanging a wry expression with her image, she thought, sixty-seven and grey in the hair, but not yet entirely destroyed. Your eyes are still clear, and you've kept your spine straight. You seem free of sores and blemishes, and best of all your mind is not addled. William Marshal, eh . . . Come to see his benefactress . . .

With a final, self-mocking glance at her reflection, she made her way through the palace and into the sunlit antechamber.

He was shocked by her appearance. During her sixteen years' imprisonment he had met with her twice – on those rare occasions when King Henry or his council had required her presence – but he had not seen her for more than five years. The shock was of his own making, he realized that later, for he could not repaint the picture he carried in his mind. It remained untouched by time, the vivid portrait of a tall, slender woman, whose expression changed at the flicker of an eyelid from amused detachment to narrowing condemnation. Surrounded by men who boomed their laughter, shuddered when they wept and turned purple and swollen in anger, Eleanor conveyed her feelings with the needle scratch of a frown, or the featherweight curve of her mouth. Unless she chose to disguise her feelings, one would know by looking. But afterward, it was impossible to say just how she had shown her displeasure, or registered her delight. The dish of the world would have to splinter, to make Queen Eleanor chew her lip.

And so with her voice. She could not have screamed since the midwives punched her, nor giggled uncontrollably beyond the simple jokes of childhood. Yet there was a greater reward in her quiet laughter than in the spluttering and shoulder-pounding of a hysterical court.

Neither old age nor imprisonment had robbed her of her magnetism, but she no longer matched the portrait in Marshal's mind. Where he wished her to be slender, she was thin, her long jaw-bone prominent, her nose as pinched as his, her eyes made large by the tightness of her skin. And her hair was grey, when he wanted it to be black.

The truth was, she had been old five years ago, but he had gone away entranced, and made her young again. Each time he saw her he was shocked, but even as he turned away in farewell, she was rejuvenated in his mind. It was the supreme accolade, and it was why mention of his name made her hum.

They were both on their knees, Marshal and Malchat, for they had heard her approach. She stepped on to the blue and grey tiles of the antechamber, looked from one to the other, then gauged the number of steps it would take to reach them. Marshal would not be pleased to see her stumble, her sight blurred by tears. And who was it, Malchat, Roger Malchat? Well, he'd expect something more regal from his master's widow.

She went forward and said, 'That's a hard floor, William Marshal, and you were never good at staying still. Get up and embrace me. I've been let out, did Master Blet tell you? He took it upon himself, so I want him protected. My husband introduced me to every important prison in the land, but it was not until this one that – Oh, God, Marshal, I am pleased to see you . . . I pray this is the end of it . . .'

Her voice and carriage had already lessened the shock. The perfect portrait was put by for later, and his carefully rehearsed speeches went for nothing. Coming to his feet, he said, 'You won't be imprisoned again, I promise you. Not while I live.'

Malchat pushed himself upright and studied the arrangement of the room. He affected not to see their gentle embrace, or hear their murmured reunion. He carried no portrait of Eleanor, though he had always regarded Henry's treatment of her as harsh and unworthy. True, she had rebelled against him; hardly the act of a wife and queen. But his scandalous flaunting of his mistress, Rosamund Clifford, and his obsessive desire to thwart Richard and advance John Lackland had already turned half the country against him. On the other hand, Malchat wondered, what would Eleanor have done if her rebellion had succeeded? Certainly no less than Henry had done to her.

He felt Marshal grip his arm, and acknowledged Eleanor's welcome. 'Even in prison,' she said, 'I hear the news. You are reputed to have been the king's most trusted adviser. It puts you across the fence from me, Roger Malchat, but it makes you one of the few who stayed loyal to either side.'

'I am not your enemy,' Malchat replied, 'no more than is Marshal. But Henry was the king, and had to be supported against his enemies in France – and in his family. You have been badly treated, as I see it, but you have not been hounded to death by your sons. King Henry was, and still nothing is resolved.'

'He was a tyrant-turned-monster,' Eleanor levelled. 'He despoiled King Philip's sister, and turned France against him. He imprisoned me on a charge of treason, then celebrated in Mistress Clifford's bed. He refused to recognize Richard as his heir, or to surrender the wretched Alais of France, or even to release John from a diet of promises. Don't make a martyr of him, Roger Malchat. A satyr, yes, and a vindictive old man, if you like. But all our troubles trace back to him, as they would to a man who lit a fire in a hayrick.' She paused, then allowed him a faint, disarming smile. 'I cannot argue with you dry. Give me a glass of wine. Blet has been a kind gaoler, but none too free with his drink. Ideal for men, he says, but destructive for women. I don't know which he feared more, my death from wine, or the loss of his most important prisoner. If Henry had had the sense, he'd have allowed me a barrel a day. They'd have found me drowned in bed, and no one to blame.'

There was no coyness as Marshal held the glass and Malchat filled it, for they were already under her spell. No wonder she had been married to two kings and survived them, then emerged from her long imprisonment as though from a wasting, but none too serious illness. Marshal offered her the glass, and she raised it in salute. 'God will that England is served by an honourable king, and that the king is served by honourable men. Men like you, Marshal, and you, Malchat.' She drank half the wine and nodded. 'Blet must approve of you; he's found a good flask.'

Three weeks ago they had been fighting for the man who had imprisoned her. Now they joined her in the salute.

In any country there are men who would make a better king than the king, and women more aptly fitted to be queen than the queen. But rarely is the best person offered the crown, and there are few who would dare accept it in such old age. But Eleanor of Aquitaine had twice been queen, and even now, at sixty-seven, she had lost none of her skills. This time she would not be married to the monarch – who, God willing, would be Richard *Coeur-de-Lion* – but she would mother him and guide him, and pass on her extensive knowledge of government. With Eleanor at his shoulder, Richard should not fail. And, when he was busy, she would find time to make John more charming, and Geoffrey less so.

She accepted Henry's bastard for what he was, an intelligent interloper and, although Richard was her favourite, and would remain so – she would see Geoffrey well-established in the regime.

If she had to make an assessment, it was this; Richard's present must be bestowed upon him in a crowd, so that he could bellow his speech and bathe in the applause. John's must be delivered in the evening, carried by a beautiful woman from whom all morality had been drained; then he would enjoy both the donation and the donor in darkness and seclusion. And for Geoffrey FitzRoy, some simple gift, beyond criticism. A bishopric would be perfect, combining the sacred and the secular. He would have a palace and property, a court-cum-congregation. If he wished to preach, he could do so, but he could also conserve his income and put the fear of God into the neighbouring barons. Yes, for Geoffrey, a bishopric.

And in detail, what for Lackland, the cynical, back-biting, youngest son? Something from Richard; the innocent income of a few counties, and a handful of manors. And sycophants who laughed at his jokes. And women who sprawled on his bed. John was no problem, so long as he was kept amused; so long as he had one hand on a woman's thigh and beads of wine on his lips.

And for Richard Lionheart, *Coeur-de-Lion,* Duke of Aquitaine and by now Duke of Normandy, what for him? The crown, of course, and as Eleanor's favourite, her constant attention. Richard would scorn a bishopric, and he would not be at all amused by John's bare-legged orgies.

But which of them should be offered the greatest protection, the Lionheart, or Lackland, or the Bastard? It was a difficult choice to make, for she had long ago decided that the most deserving would gain William Marshal as his guardian. If, as Blet had assured her, Marshal held her special, he would extend his protection to her chosen son.

The obvious choice was Richard, for he would soon be king. But what if he was killed on some pointless expedition, or in one of the noisy jousts of which he was so fond? Would

Marshal be prepared to change again, from Henry, to Richard, to – ?

To John, as the logical successor. But who, with a balanced mind, could see that feather-and-leathered creature sauntering down from his crowded bed-chamber to command the court? *King* John? No, it did not sit well on the tongue.

The last of them, Geoffrey, had no chance of becoming king. He was the most intelligent of the trio, but he was Henry's bastard, the son of a practised whore, and England would never accept him.

So, clearly, it was to be Richard who would feel the guiding pressure of Marshal's hand. If his grip was strong enough.

They stayed with her for three days. Marshal delivered a sheaf of letters Richard had entrusted to him, and Eleanor learned that she had been given complete authority in England during her son's absence. 'Show yourself to the people,' he suggested. 'No matter what it costs, outfit your household and travel the country in state. Let them see that their queen is returned to them. They need comfort, my lady, and you are as much England's mother as you are mine. Buy whatever takes your fancy; indulge in every comfort. Put on a show for them, and they will be reassured.'

Eleanor showed the letter to Marshal. 'He cares for me,' she remarked wryly, 'though, as usual, his brimming heart makes him forgetful. Unless your saddle-bags are stuffed with gold?' Marshal shook his head, and she mirrored the movement. 'No, I did not think they would be.'

Nevertheless, as supreme authority, the queen was able to call upon the resources of the treasury, and Richard's letter served as a key to the coffers.

On a lighter note, Marshal told her about Isabel de Clare, and asked if she had ever set eyes on the young heiress.

'No, though I have heard about her, and if I were you I'd waste no time in securing the claim. As a woman, I should dislike everything I've heard.'

'Why? Is she so unwholesome?'

'I could love her for that,' Eleanor said. 'It would still my envy.'

'Then she is – '

'Beautiful, so they say. Courteous, that's another term

used. Nineteen, according to the calendar. Sweet heaven, Marshal, go and find out for yourself. I'm not a paid jongleur, employed to sing her praises!' Her smile belied her impatience, and she added, 'Bring the lady to visit me when you can; I am starved of gossip.'

'I'd never deny you your pleasures,' Marshal said, 'though I hope she can control her tongue.'

'As Pembroke's daughter, I'm sure she can. Not that it will save her. Even stones surrender their secrets when I'm about.' It was offered as banter, but Marshal's smile was slow in coming, for her boast was too close to the truth. One would have to be a blind, deaf mute to withhold a secret from Queen Eleanor.

Yet she had, once, failed to predetermine events – her own arrest – and had spent sixteen years repenting her ignorance. But it was over now, and she would not let it happen again. Nor, from what he had promised, would William Marshal.

The storm had come up the Thames and was now sweeping westward, toward London. The summer sky wore a tattered cloak, the billowing garment pierced by shafts of lightning. The white-hot lances split trees and riverside dwellings, and struck two fishermen who had been out on the marshes, netting eels. Their scorched bodies smoked and steamed in the rain.

The storm dragged its cloak across the eastern boundaries of the city, and lightning flew at the massive, ninety-foot high fortress known as the White Tower. This was London's fortress, built by William the Conqueror. It was said that whoever commanded the Tower controlled the capital, and the claim was supported by walls fifteen feet thick, and a moat that was, in places, more than a hundred feet wide. Subsequent monarchs had added encircling walls, strengthened the gate towers, erected a palace in the courtyard. But few improvements had been made to the keep itself. Whitewashed from bastions to battlements, it remained an outstanding example of military architecture, and a damp and impregnable refuge. The lightning crackled against the ragstone walls, then moved on to shatter roofs in the city.

Standing dangerously near one of the upper windows, Isabel de Clare watched the storm darken London. She was unnerved by thunder and lightning, and had spent most of the past hour with her hands pressed to her ears, or with an arm raised to shield her eyes. However, now that the worst was over, she felt pleased with herself, and retreated to the warmth of the fire.

'There,' she said. 'I told you I would do it. Did you ever see me flinch?'

Her maidservant shook her head. She could truthfully say no, for she had been crouched well back in the top floor chamber, her eyes squeezed shut. Now she ventured, 'You braved it well, my lady. He will be impressed.'

'I hope so,' Isabel remarked, 'for *I* am. Just think, if the lightning had found the window niche—' She shuddered, and told the girl to lay more wood on the fire. 'This place could as well be beneath the river, as beside it. Mid-summer, and the walls run with water.' She walked over to the time-candle, its thick, tallow shaft ringed to mark the hours. If his estimate was reliable, and the storm did not wash out the road from Winchester, he would reach the Tower before the next ring melted.

Her husband-to-be, an unseen knight about whom she had stored a mass of information, hearsay and rumour. Every mention of him was grist for the mill, no matter how biased.

He was forty-three years old, that much was established. In appearance he was tall, and with a knife for a nose. He had curiously dark skin, and could be mistaken for an Arab. He did not care to set his buttocks on a seat, but preferred to prowl the room. Before he had become King Henry's champion, he had earned his living in tournaments and, in one ten-month period, he had unhorsed seventy-two knights. Thus vanquished, they had been honour-bound to surrender their armour and equipment and pay whatever ransom was fixed for the day. Yet he was reported to be penniless and landless. He was fond of Bordeaux wine and venison, and had no palate for fish.

He was attractive to women—among them the European paragon, Countess Marie of Champagne, with whom he was supposed to have enjoyed a torrid affair—yet he had never married. He was patronized by none other than Queen Eleanor—another affair?—yet had supported the man who imprisoned her.

He would see no man hanged, nor allow his women to wear tasselled girdles.

He had once been so severely jousted in a tournament that it had taken a blacksmith's hammer to beat his helmet from his head. On that occasion he had been declared champion of the day, and the Duke of Burgundy had awarded him a solid silver lance. He had sold it a week later.

More recently she had heard that he'd unhorsed Richard Plantagenet at some bridge near Le Mans, then told Richard he was lucky to be alive. *Richard Plantagenet*? Well, it was more wheat for the mill.

The firelight flickered on the laced bodice and pendulous sleeves of her gown. An engraved silver bracelet enclosed one wrist, the flower pattern repeated on the flattened links of a long necklace. The chain was double looped, so that it both encircled her throat and framed the neck of her gown. The firelight caught the metal and made gold of the silver.

Gradually, the heat permeated the woollen *bliaut* and drove the dampness from her hair. She settled herself in a panel-backed chair and watched the flames lick the applewood.

Forty-three? God, he was *old*. And passing for an Arab, those devils with whom the West had been so long at war. A professional soldier, disciplined and –

She looked across at the candle, then around the room. Yes, that was another thing she'd heard; he did not like slovens.

The heiress of Pembroke and Striguil had been placed under the guardianship of Richard Fitz Renier, Sheriff of London, so it was Fitz Renier who welcomed the rain-soaked Marshal and entertained him while he changed into dry, come-wooing clothes.

They had been friends for many years, and the sheriff thought it safe to say, 'She has been like a captured cricket. There's too much to know about you, Marshal. Every visitor has a tale to tell, and every women she meets – well, it depends on their dreams. You're either a chivalric ideal, or an irresponsible lecher, here for de Clare's inheritance and her – '

'In all the years,' Marshal growled, 'your mind has flourished in a cesspit. Hold this damn cloak for me. I could make a tent from it.' He finished dressing, pressed his damp hair to his skull, then drank the wine his friend had provided. 'Not that I place credence on your opinion, Fitz Renier, but is she likeable? And don't say it – '

⁸ – depends what you like. She's too controlled for my tastes, but you know I've always favoured the more un-restrained type – why are you grinning?'

'I wonder who taught you that word. It's the most *restrained* term you've ever used to describe your women. That Irish herbalist, do you remember her? Sold you that love potion, and damn near killed you? And the messenger, what was her name? The only woman in England who could out-run a charging horse? Oh, yes, Fitz Renier, you do like them un-restrained.' He laughed quietly to himself, and draped the heavy, embroidered cloak around his shoulders.

The sheriff waited his chance, then said, 'About the wedding.'

'What about it? I cannot afford to be married here. I'll take her to Pembroke, or to another of her holdings. Lady Isabel may not approve, but she'll have to foot the bill.'

'No, she won't. You're to be married in London, and the costs have already been met.' It was his turn to grin now, and Marshal's to glower. 'There's money to spare where you're concerned. A married Marshal is a sight to be seen. I doubt if we could have raised such a subscription for the king himself.' He ignored Marshal's expression, and pointed at the ceiling, 'She's directly above us. You can study the guest-list later. God speed.'

The maidservant answered the door, recognized him from the weeks of description, and hurried down the steps. Fitz Renier stood in the doorway of the lower chamber and hissed her to a halt.

'What did they say?'

'I don't know, my lord sheriff. They hadn't met. I withdrew before they – '

He shook his head in disgust and turned away, slamming the door. What did she mean, *before*? Servants were supposed to be domestic spies. She should have stayed. She should have loitered. She should have played the servant! Why else had she been given eyes and ears?

Well, she thought, they were right, he *would* pass for an Arab. He's not as thin as I imagined, and better dressed. And strong, one would need to be strong to carry that pavilion of a cloak. God, must he fidget, as though he had a thorn in each heel? Did he hop like that for Marie of Champagne, or Queen Eleanor. Be still, sir; I'm the one with the right to be nervous . . .

I shall be bedding my daughter. If I had a daughter she'd be no older than this. And not half so miserable, I hope. Look, woman, I'm smiling. See, you widen your mouth and – Yes, that's better . . .

A grey wolf, like the stories. No wonder he won his jousts; he smiled them off their horses. He might have been poisoned, his face is so contorted. But he wears his age better than the cloak . . .

One step, I swear, and she'd hurl herself from the window. The heiress to half England, and she flinches like a lunatic. Welcome me, woman, or must I think I've found the wrong room? Invite me in, it's commonly done with visitors . . .

His tongue has been ripped out. I heard he was in Palestine. The Arabs discovered he was an impostor, and tore out his tongue. Identify yourself, my lord! It's not the woman's place to guess . . .

Before he was ready, he said, 'I-had-a-wet-ride-here-from-Winchester-so-I-changed-my-clothes-you-probably-saw-the-storm.'

She brought his name to her lips, but she would not tell him who he was. 'Yes, I watched from the window.'

'That was foolish, when you're festooned with silver. It's a known thing, lightning seeks metal. I was once near a man who was struck down. Hard to say who he was, afterward.'

'Not only him,' Isabel murmured, reminding Marshal of his omission.

'I'm sorry. I am Sir William Marshal, son of John Marshal, who served under King Stephen, and of the Lady Sybil. I did send word of my arrival, but – '

'It was well received, Sir Marshal, and it was good of you to risk the storm. If lightning seeks metal, and you were wearing a hauberk and helmet . . .' She let the retort lie, and bowed him into the room. It is not often that a bride and groom meet for the first time within hours of their wedding, but by now they had recovered their composure, and their stride. Courtesy dictated an exchange of compliments, and Marshal said, 'I would normally have taken my own advice, but this journey was of a special nature. I have travelled through storms before, though I was never so well rewarded at the finish. You are, my lady, without peer, and not even the English weather will keep me from you.'

It was nicely said, and Isabel acknowledged it graciously. 'I did not think it would,' she replied, 'for your determination is renowned.' The studied phrases put them at their ease, but she could not resist adding, 'I am flattered that you should think I stand comparison with the enviable Marie of Champagne.'

Marshal frowned, as though dredging his memory. Then, placing the relationship on the right level, he mused, 'The Countess Marie? Oh, yes, she *was* attractive, in her way; to a young man's unschooled eye. But you, my lady, must accept a more worldly view. Do you mind?'

No, she indicated, she did not mind at all, and moved aside unnecessarily, drawing him into the room. 'I've some Bordeaux wine put by. There, in the alcove. I don't know your tastes, how could I, but – '

He came forward and took her hands in his, and the marriage was made as assuredly as if they had been in church, with a thousand witnesses. Fitz Renier would get his chance to grin later, but it was already confirmed by the hand-clasp of a middle-aged knight, and a woman not half his age. She had been kept aside, like the wine, for the right man. It was a courtship that lasted a few moments and, compatible or not, it would lead to the altar. And from there the marriage would survive for as long as the husband decided, or until he was killed.

But, so far, they both felt it had gone well. Isabel de Clare might have been a griffon, or self-centred, or of a diseased mind. And William Marshal might have been stunted, or a riot of boils, or a hater of women. That they were none of these was an advantage and a blessing.

There was no romance in it yet, for he was a battle-hardened soldier, collecting King Henry's promised reward, whilst Isabel de Clare was merely the heiress to lands and income, valued only for what she possessed. But the compliments had been sincere, and he thought it remarkable that she should have guessed his fondness for Bordeaux wine.

Guided and financed by Fitz Renier and Marshal's city friends, the couple were married on the first day of August in the Chapel of St John, a superb pillared chamber in the south-east corner of the Tower. During the ceremony Marshal decided, for no particular reason, to grow a moustache. For her part, Isabel acknowledged the solemnity of the occasion and dedicated herself to the advancement of her husband. She could not say she loved him, but she respected him, and was impressed by the interest he had shown in her wedding gown. This warrior knight, who had fought so long for King Henry and had dared unseat the bellicose Richard Lionheart, had not been at all ashamed to converse with seamstresses, or offer advice on the hang and stitch of her gown. She could think of no other man who would show such interest in the colour of a thread, or the jab of a needle, yet earn his reputation on the field and in the lists. No, it was not yet love, though the tide was running.

There was to be another wedding that month, according to the rumours that emanated from Normandy. Young John was reconciled with his brother, and had been promised the hand of Hadwisa, heiress of Gloucester. In fact, she had been betrothed to him twelve years earlier, but as she had grown into an attractive young woman, he did not oppose the union. If she was enjoyable company, so much the better. And if not, the income from her lands would enable him to stay out a little later at night.

However, there was opposition to the marriage, and from a powerful quarter. Baldwin, Archbishop of Canterbury, was appalled to learn that John and Hadwisa were second cousins, and that their marriage would violate the Church's law of consanguinity. He issued a dire warning to both parties, and Hadwisa hesitated, fearful of divine retribution. John, on the other hand, kept the Archbishop's letter in his purse, and re-read it until the parchment cracked. Outside bed, nothing aroused him so much as the opportunity to goad the Church, particularly when its senior servant was the pompous, do-right Baldwin of Canterbury. Until now, John had been too busy with Norman women to find time for Hadwisa, but Baldwin's letter kindled a sudden passion for the heiress. How dare the old fool come between lovers? The Church was throwing too long a shadow! Of course he would marry Hadwisa. It would be his first act on reaching England. And no pious prelate would stand in his way. He wrote to her, to keep up her courage.

In the week preceding his departure from Normandy, John remained celibate and indignant. Richard was astonished at the change that had overtaken his libertine brother, and realized that Baldwin would never deter him. *'L'amour triomphe surtout'*, was John's new catchphrase.

Chapter Four

THE MASSACRE OF JOY

August 1189 – August 1190

They did not know how they would be received when they reached England. They had hounded their father to his grave, and might well stand accused of treason and regicide. True, Queen Eleanor was at liberty, and travelling the country, encouraging the people to accept her favourite son. But there were many who regarded her as a dangerous and meddlesome woman, and these were not likely to be blinded by the flash of her silver tongue.

So it was with some trepidation that Richard and John stepped ashore at Portsmouth. Wisely perhaps, Geoffrey had chosen to come alone, a few days later.

The brothers were both dressed in full armour and escorted by two hundred men-at-arms. But, before they had reached the landward end of the quay, they found themselves confronted by a seething mass of citizens. The soldiers hefted their spears and drew together, their shields held edge to edge, fencing off the quay. Archers had roped themselves to the masts, or were crouched in the bows. It needed only a shout from Richard, or the sight of his gloved hand, and the arrows would fly.

But Queen Eleanor had done her work well, and it was soon apparent that the crowd had come to cheer, not charge. They milled about, blocking the narrow streets that wound up from the port, delighted by the Lionheart's military-style arrival. He had a fine sense of the dramatic, did Richard Plantagenet. To come ashore like this, as though he was invading his own country! He was ever the general, God knew it!

They roared their welcome – *'Richard-le-roi! Coeur-de-Lion!'* – and the giant slapped his brother on the shoulder. Raising his crested helmet high in the air, he said, 'Don't be so furtive, boy. We're at home now. Go on, salute them. They're your people, too.' He made a grab at John's helmet, but he had already moved away.

'How long are we to be detained here?' he called. 'I'm being drowned in the spray.' He snapped at the sergeants to clear a path through the crowd, then followed Richard along the shifting corridor. He heard his own name being shouted, but it was Richard they wanted, and Richard who responded. Dear Christ, John thought, doesn't he love it so? He was born for this, the mouthings of the mob, and the flags and flowers and – He would conquer a country, just to receive its welcome. Give him a battle in the morning, and a parade at noon, and he's a satisfied man. Oh, and a kiss from dear Eleanor.

Horses were urged through the crowd, so that the brothers might mount and be more easily seen. They rode into town, Richard bellowing jokes at men he had never met, or snatching at hastily-picked bouquets. John followed, his stomach still unsettled by the voyage. He glanced at Richard's broad, armoured back and wondered how it was that the Lionheart, a notoriously bad sailor, could stage such a quick recovery. The answer, of course, was that he devoured applause, and stilled his churning belly.

Fearing the worst, Richard had kept secret the exact date and port of arrival, so neither Eleanor nor William Marshal were present. But the ships had been spotted when they were still an hour from shore, and the civic dignitaries had had time to don their regalia. They were now assembled in the town square, practising their speeches on each other.

They need not have troubled, for once he was free of the portside crowd, Richard spurred ahead, through the square and along the road to Winchester. He knew his mother had already left the city, but he had associated the place with her for so long that he felt drawn towards it. In part it was filial devotion, in part a sense of duty, in part a need he could not explain. He did not feel inferior to Eleanor, nor did he regard her as a lesser creature, so he did not go as supplicant, or suzerain. He simply felt they should be together, as soon as possible.

They were lions, that's what they were, two lions roaring free in the wilderness. The other animals, the deers and bulls and wild boars, they had their own lives to lead, but they were not lions. As no other woman was Eleanor of Aquitaine. As no man was Richard of Normandy, soon-to-be of England.

Even brother John, well, God protect him, he was hardly a lion. He was more of a – what could one say? A member of the family, certainly, and yet, with the best will in the world, scarcely one of the pride. One could not imagine him reared up, fangs bared and claws extended, snarling defiance at the world. He was more of a –

Lost for an example, Richard turned in his saddle, to see John spurring in his wake. The duke laughed in his throat, a deep, indulgent rumble, and waved John level. 'Seeing you back there,' he said, 'you brought to mind a ferret at a fair. You're all pinched-in, boy. What is it, the pace I set?'

John glanced at him, looked away until he had bridled his tongue, then sibilated, 'Yes, that's it, the pace. I don't have your turn of speed, brother, no one does.'

Richard saw no reason to contradict the truth, and gave John an encouraging slap on the leg. 'Tell you what,' he boomed. 'You see that farm ahead? I'll race you to it. Five marks if I win; twenty if it's you. But watch how I hold the reins. You see the way my knees grip. And my back arched for balance, you see that?'

John nodded imperceptibly, and Richard shouted, 'Two! One! Go!' Then he was off, and unable to see John ram the heel of his hand against his helmet. The metal casque slipped back and hung by its strap from his shoulders. He let his hand rest on his head, as though locating a sudden sharp pain. 'Go on,' he snarled to himself, 'ride to hell! *Watch-my-reins, see-my-knees.* Christ, you are a bag of noise, brother. And was ever a bag so pleased with its seams?'

By which time Richard was well along the road, the certain winner of the race to the farm.

To display his love for Hadwisa, John travelled north to Marlborough, where the heiress was being held in ward for her husband. *En route,* he enjoyed an uninhibited evening with a family of gypsies in Savernake forest, and arrived at Marlborough next morning, red-eyed and dishevelled. Hadwisa's appearance held promise, and he did not regret his celibate week in Normandy. However, his own appearance was less well received, and Hadwisa's first words to him set the pattern of the marriage.

'You should not have exhausted yourself, riding through the night. My father's friends call by here every day, my lord, but now I shall have to swear my household to secrecy. You are in no condition to meet them; you must first recover, and be measured for some proper clothes, and that means hiding you away and pretending you have not yet reached us. You should have broken your journey, and not risked the dangers of the night roads. Salisbury, that's where you should have stayed. Or Amesbury. Or even Rushall, that's an easy ride from here. But to come non-stop from Portsmouth! It shows you are in earnest, but it makes more problems than it solves. I'll tell the stewards to pour you a bath.'

Again John nodded imperceptibly, and conversed with himself when she'd gone.

Richard had meanwhile turned east from Winchester, and was continuing his triumphal journey toward London. Half his escort became emissaries, sent in search of Queen Eleanor, and his progress slowed, as he waited for her to join him. Eventually she did so, and those crowds that had gathered to welcome their new king were now swollen by those older members of the population who revered his mother. They rode hand-in-hand through the towns and villages, and shared a covered cart on the country roads.

In the privacy of the cart, he told her he would do what Henry had done, and imprison her for another sixteen years. Why not, mother, when you bear it so well?

It was not something to joke about, she admonished. *He* would not survive sixteen months. Not that one could ever cage the Lionheart.

'I'd tear aside the bars.'

'I believe you would.'

'And chew the gaoler to gristle.'

'Yes, and spit him out.'

'Then I'd take an axe and chop the building to the ground.'

'Yes, you would, yes. It would be a slack profession, being a gaoler, when you were about.'

He put his arm around her, and she rested her head against the wall of his chest. They had no secrets from each other – he had not known Henry would arrest her, so long ago – and, more important perhaps, they never found the other worthy of ridicule. So he did not mind that she hummed quietly, like an exploring bee, and she found nothing strange in his sudden gasp and long, drawn-out sigh. They were lions, were they not, the only lions in England . . .

The advent of Richard and John brought Marshal from the country. He and Isabel had been installed in an attractive manor house in the village of Stoke d'Abernon in Surrey, and the two weeks they had spent there were among the happiest they had known. Ungallantly, Marshal cursed himself for not having married earlier in life, then accepted that it was not the state of wedlock that made him happy, but Isabel de Clare. Although he enjoyed the company of women, he was critical of them, but so far his wife's most apparent fault was that she rose after dawn and ignored the coming of night. They were not soldiers' hours, but then, to be fair to himself, he was not on campaign.

He left Isabel and her servants safe in the moated manor and rode to London, where he rejoined Roger Malchat and Sheriff Fitz Renier. Although Malchat had not yet been offered the stewardship of Richard's court, no one doubted he would get the job, nor that Fitz Renier would retain the shrievalty of London. They were both reliable men, well-versed in civil administration, and their knowledge would leave Richard free to organize his Crusade.

Strangely, the only one whose position was insecure was Marshal himself. Marriage to Isabel de Clare had brought him extensive lands in England, Wales and Ireland. He was now Earl of Pembroke, Lord of Striguil – a vast network of fiefs spread throughout nine English counties – and Lord of Leinster in Ireland. His holdings in England and Wales made him one of the most important barons in the kingdom, whilst possession of the Irish counties of Kildare, Kilkenny, Carlow and Wexford placed him on a level with the nobility of Europe.

But John was already Lord of Ireland, and he would not be happy to lose the fertile counties that made up Leinster. At best, he would claim the right to bestow them on whomsoever he chose – not necessarily William Marshal. At worst, he would try to keep them for himself.

In a contested claim of this kind, the final arbiter would be Richard Lionheart. The question was, who was more likely to convince him, the man who had knocked him off his horse, or his contrite, dish-eyed brother?

But there were greater priorities and, during the latter half of August, all London prepared for Richard's coronation. He arrived with his mother and they installed themselves in the palace at Westminster. A week later they left for Marlborough, where, on 29th August, they attended the wedding of brother John and Hadwisa of Gloucester. Marshal had not seen John since his arrival in England, and prudently remained in London. If John was offended by his absence – well, they could squabble about that when they argued possession of Leinster. But before all else, England needed a king.

It was, by any measure, a magnificent parade. Sunday morning, 3rd September, and it seemed that half the English army was lining the road between the palace and Westminster Abbey. Bolts of cloth carpeted the ground, and the soldiers leaned back against the cheering crowd in a desperate effort to keep them from soiling the cloth. Flags and banners had been suspended overhead, but a few had proved too heavy for their fastenings and swung down like soft-bladed axes. They were seized by the nearest onlookers and draped from the windows. There were flowers everywhere, and an extraordinary variety of dress. No colour was missing except yellow, for that was worn by the Jews, and they were not welcome at this Christian celebration.

Crosses had been nailed to the doors, or hung in the windows where they rapped the watchers on the head. Musical instruments were in evidence, and innumerable lutists roared or warbled songs specially composed for the occasion. To this cacophony was added the cries and shrieks of children, aware that, today, they were at liberty to cry and shriek; women who screamed blessings, men who bellowed their loyalty, then broke off to curse whoever had stepped in their way; all these and the grunting soldiers, struggling to keep back the crowd . . .

There was an advance guard of mounted knights, then purple-robed clerics, then the senior Churchmen, moving through the drifting clouds of incense. Hands were cupped around candle-flames, and the sun sparkled on beads of holy water and on gold spurs, a gold cross, gold swords that rested beside gold-encrusted scabbards. Marshal passed, bearing the sceptre. It looked new, for much of the regalia had been hastily refashioned after the theft of King Henry's treasure. John passed, in step with the Earl of Leicester, each carrying one of the swords of state. Then there were others, responsible for the king's coronation garments, and these were followed by the great William de Mandeville, Earl of Essex.

He was the son of the notorious Geoffrey de Mandeville, who, fifty years before, had helped prolong England's first and most bitter civil war. His acts of atrocity had culminated in the sacking of a Benedictine monastery, for which he had been excommunicated. On his death – a violent one, as befitted such a man – his body was refused burial in hallowed ground. His only friends were members of the harsh military order of the Knights Templar, but not even the Templars dared inter him. They took his body, sealed in a lead coffin, and suspended it from an apple tree in their orchard in London. And there it hung for twenty years, until the Church lifted its curse . . .

But the sins of the father had not been visited upon the son, and William de Mandeville had remained loyal to King Henry throughout his reign. He was also popular with the people, who cheered him on his way.

And then Richard was in view, flanked by the bishops of Bath and Durham, and the crowd surged forward against the sweating fence, and the plainsong was finally drowned in the wave of noise.

He was shadowed by a white silk canopy, with spears for tent poles. The shaft of each spear was gripped by one of England's senior barons; a supreme honour, and hard on the wrists. He nodded left and right, acknowledging the roar, and made no attempt to keep in step with the bishops. His long, even stride was not lost on the crowd, and they were delighted when he suddenly quickened his pace, forcing the barons to rebalance the swinging canopy. Oh, he had a sharp turn of humour.

He was not yet their king, not by an hour or so, but he had been modelled for the part. His red hair and round, open face; his thick neck, rooted in broad, tapering shoulders; his deep chest and solid belly; thick wrists and arms, long, powerful legs and a spring in his stride. God had carved him thus, in preparation for the day. And in this perfect body He had implanted the mind of a leader, and the heart of a lion. They shouted until their throats were raw, then croaked their joy.

Small wonder that the crowd became hysterical and threatened to crush the procession. They had at last been given a king worthy of their dreams. Richard of Anjou, and of Normandy – and now of England!

He would defeat the chilly Philip of France! He would reconquer Palestine, and wrest the holy city of Jerusalem from the devils of Islam! He would make England the richest and most powerful nation in the West! No, in the world! He would, wait and see, he would! Christ be praised, he would!

Their wrists aching, the four barons shadowed him along the street and into the open area in front of the Abbey. The populace were hemmed in along two sides of the square, but there was still some confusion. The fourth side of the square had been reserved for those who would attend the ceremony but had not taken part in the procession, among them Queen Eleanor, John's wife Hadwisa, and Isabel de Clare. With them were numerous relatives and friends, important visitors from France and Germany, Italy and Spain, even a few influential merchants. These had been invited at Richard's behest, for merchants meant money, and the cost of the coronation was – He drove the thought from his mind, for fear that his heart would stop. It was as well the people cheered, for they, too, must pay for their pleasure.

The tail of the procession wound into the square. Churchmen and officials clustered around the Abbey door. Eleanor and Hadwisa led the dignitaries forward, and the assemblage somehow resolved itself into a line. Standing to one side, the principal organisers, Malchat and Fitz Renier, agreed that it had not gone badly. No one had tried to assassinate Richard. The few gate-crashers had been discovered and evicted. It had not rained. The Abbey had not burned down. The regalia was all acounted for. John had behaved himself and kept his hands off the girls in the crowd. Richard seemed happy, thank God. Yes, it could have been worse.

There had been a dozen candles in the chapel at Chinon. Here, in Westminster Abbey, there were hundreds. The building blazed with light, a sensible precaution against the September weather. It would be embarrassing if the sky suddenly darkened, leaving the clergy to grope their way through the service. So the smell of burning tow mingled with incense and individual perfumes, while the congregation blinked in the acrid air.

Richard was led forward to kneel at the altar. In front of him were grouped the senior Churchmen of England and Normandy. They would all play a part in the ceremony, though the major role belonged to Baldwin, Archbishop of Canterbury.

Once, as the procession had reached the Abbey, and again now, seeking him out in the congregation, Baldwin glared at Prince John. The Archbishop had thought seriously of barring

John's entry to the church, and it was with the greatest reluctance that he had abandoned the idea. It would have angered Richard, whilst John would have revelled in the ugly scene. But just because the consanguineous creature had sauntered into God's house, it did not mean he was welcome. Neither he, nor his cousin-wife. Each was as guilty as the other, and they would pay the penalty for their incest.

Baldwin returned his attention to the ceremony, content in the knowledge that he had dispatched a strong appeal to Pope Clement in Rome. It had been sent in secret, and John did not know of it. But Baldwin was foolish to under-estimate the prince, for John had done exactly the same, and Baldwin did not know *that*. It posed an interesting problem for Clement, reading the same story by such divergent authors.

On his knees, Richard was shown the splinter of wood, said to be from the True Cross on which Christ was crucified, and the vial that was purported to contain the blood of John the Baptist. The great illuminated Bible was laid open before him, and he touched it with his fingertips as he recited the vows of a king. He swore to be honourable and peaceable all the days of his life, and to worship God and revere the Church; to show mercy and justice to all his peoples, and to whomsoever appealed to him for help; to seek out evil laws and practices and destroy them, as he would support and strengthen all laws that were made for the betterment of mankind. He spoke slowly, giving the echoes time to fade.

Marshal had completed his work, and now found himself with Malchat on his left and, on his right, Prince John. He silently cursed his friend for having arranged things so tactlessly, but before he could let Malchat know, John swayed sideways to murmur, 'I heard how you unseated him at Le Mans. I left too soon.'

There was a low hum of conversation in the Abbey, so Marshal risked a reply. Speaking to John for the first time since Henry's army had retreated to Le Mans, he said, 'You did, prince. You should have stayed, you and your friends. We needed labourers, to chop down the bridge.'

John stiffened, then nodded to himself. Very well. If that was the way of it. If this upstart, this parvenu, this earl-for-a-week, if he wished to be uncivil, then incivility would be the watchword.

'I've seen your lady, Marshal. Very pretty she is. Solace for your old age, eh? And how she draws the glances.'

'She always did. It's only now that men might lose their eyes because of it.'

John swayed away again, reloaded his tongue, then rocked back to murmur, 'Don't be too eager to gouge out eyes. Remember, I have a part of her, too. The part that rests in Ireland. I shall be king there soon, and her holdings will be at my disposal.'

'*My* holdings,' Marshal corrected. 'I shall do homage to you as your vassal, but I shall retain my authority in Leinster. It is the better part of my lady's inheritance; the part for which I shall fight most strenuously.'

It was a clear warning of his intentions, and it had come sooner than John had expected.

'Now listen to me, earl fledgling! I could go forward this instant, and Richard would give me what I wanted. I can approach him at any time and in any place, and catch his ear. Retain your authority in Leinster? You will be fortunate to retain Leinster at all!'

'Pray I do,' Marshal snapped, 'for if you're in charge we are bound to lose it!' It was a dangerous retort, and one John would remember. But Marshal was furious that the prince had chosen this time to start a squabble, and furious with himself for having contributed to it. Damn John for the troublemaker he was. And damn Malchat, for tying them together.

Meanwhile, Richard had moved to his throne, where he had been divested of his street clothes. He now stood in knee-length linen breeches and a linen shirt, unlaced at the chest. He would never again appear so humble before his subjects, but he was not embarrassed. After all, he had the body for it, and for one irreligious moment he was tempted to stretch his arms. Then one of the prelates motioned to him to be seated and guided his feet into doe-skin slippers. That done, Baldwin stepped forward to anoint him with holy oil, making the sign of the cross on his naked shoulders and forearms and deep, unflinching chest. Then they dressed him in a cap and full-length tunic, and he was presented with a sword with which to smite Christ's enemies. Spurs were strapped to his ankles, a reminder of his vows of knighthood. A magnificent cloak, stiff with embroidery, was draped around his shoulders, and he was allowed a moment in which to settle the clothes and take a firm grasp on the sword and sceptre. Then he was invited to stand before the altar again, to hear Baldwin's formal warning.

'In the name of God Almighty, do not accept the crown unless you mean to keep it for your people, and with it to keep the oaths you have made, and fidelity to the Church.'

Richard bowed his head, thinking that Baldwin's voice carried well, for an old man.

'I do accept!' he boomed in reply. 'Under God I shall keep my word and serve my people!' Pleased with the sound of his own voice, he reiterated, 'Under God I shall!'

Baldwin's stern tones had subdued the congregation, but it was Richard who silenced them. If his body had been created for parades and combat, his voice equally belonged on the battlefield, or in such a place as this. His words leapt from niche to pillar, from wall to wall. It started the hairs on the back of the neck, and made the eyes widen in alarm. One could sneer at the transparent drama of it, and there were those who did, the widest sneer settling on the lips of brother John. But no one could deny the power of the man, nor his right to be where the candles were brightest.

He was an actor without inhibition, a commander devoid of doubt. And now, as two barons lowered the heavy crown upon his head, he was the King of England, as they had all known he would be.

It was not yet over, for he had to pay a token coin at the altar, and there was Mass to be celebrated. The unendurable crown was removed by the same hefty barons and Richard was led to a chair, merely one of the congregation before God. But there were now guards around the chair, and at the doors of the Abbey, and emissaries were already riding out across the country and down to the ports. Their message was simple. Richard is crowned. England has her king.

Part of an inner wall of the palace had been demolished, in order to accommodate the twenty trestle tables. More than six hundred guests had been invited to the banquet, and all of them were anxious to see and be seen. Roger Malchat had devoted long hours to the seating arrangements, aware that the guests were, without exception, jealous of their position. If this baron was given a better seat than that one, there had to be a good reason for it. So seniority was balanced against age, title against wealth, Richard's personal friends against those who had best served England. Fitz Renier helped, but it was Malchat's doing, and the sheriff eyed him with renewed respect. The cherubic steward worked tirelessly, calling those he knew by name, flattering those he did not. He spoke quietly, so that each woman believed that her gown alone had been singled out for admiration. And each man, whether baron or merchant, acknowledged that he had been given one of the prime seats in the hall.

If this doesn't earn me a place in the king's household, Malchat thought, there is no justice.

There was some unavoidable confusion as the guests took their places, and there were the commonplace problems of spilt wine, identical gowns, the clandestine touch of adulterers. An iron bracket fell from the wall and its burning torch set some rushes alight on the floor. But the fire was quickly stamped out by servants, and then, as though he had organized the display, King Richard advanced through the smoke. He had changed from his coronation garments into a long, gold-weave tunic, around which was buckled, somewhat incongruously, his war belt and sword. But the contrast brought a cheer from his guests. He was so completely the warrior king, even at the dinner table.

He made his way past the three central firepits, mounted the platform at the far end of the hall and moved behind the thirty-foot-long high table. Then, flanked by Archbishop Baldwin and the Chief Justiciar, Ranulf Glanville, he bowed to those in the body of the hall. The gesture was not required of him, but it brought a further howl of delight from the assembly. They were in his pocket now, every one of them, and it gave John pause for thought. Richard had either found himself a cunning tutor, or was revealing a hitherto unseen gift for diplomacy. Whichever, he was the darling of the day.

Pushing down on the pommel of his sword, he settled himself in his chair and looked past Ranulf at his mother. 'Are you well?' he asked. Her expression told him she was as well as she had ever been.

Although all Jews had been barred from the coronation and the banquet, they were anxious to find favour with the new king. The first Jewish merchants had come to England with William the Conqueror and had immediately shown a natural talent for all forms of financial business. They controlled much of the shipping, and the manufacture of cloth, and they were not bound by the Church's condemnation of usury.

Saxons and Normans came to them to borrow money, but the springs of gratitude often ran dry when repayment was due. Furthermore, the settlers made few attempts to involve themselves in the community. They had their own way of life, and were content with it, and prospered. They helped new arrivals set up shop, and *they* prospered, and the chasm widened between the Jews and their Christian neighbours. It made bad blood, and it was bound to be shed.

Now, acting in innocence, or ignorance, or with an insolent disregard for the crowd, a Jewish deputation donned their finest yellow robes and brought gifts to the palace. They did not expect to be admitted, but they hoped to be received. Aware of Richard's tastes, many of them brought money or plate or jewels, carrying the gifts openly through the streets and under the noses of the impoverished citizens. The banquet was well under way when the deputation reached the palace.

They hesitated on the steps, and delivered a speech of loyalty to the stone-faced guards. Then they requested that King Richard, or one of his commanders, come out and accept their gifts. Someone in the crowd told them to get off the steps, they were not welcome at a Christian feast.

Whatever their motives, the Jews could not have chosen a worse time, nor a less likely setting, for a display of wealth and largesse. The excitable crowd had watched Richard stride from the palace to the Abbey, and had heard reports of his bellowed vows. He had sworn to serve the people of England, and seek out evil in all its forms. Fired by his words, and a day's drinking, his subjects were determined to prove themselves worthy of the giant. *They* would serve him, and *they*, too, would smite Christ's enemies. And for the want of a Saracen army, under the command of the great Sultan Saladin, there were the Jews . . .

The banquet hall was filled with smoke from the central fires, and the roar and chatter of the six hundred guests. Servants edged between the tables, replenishing wine pitchers, dragging away empty dishes, setting down more venison, another suckling pig, a spluttering side of lamb. After the initial cautious survey, the diners had changed places, and now a senior overlord imparted the wealth of his experience to some eager knight, while his wife entertained a neghbouring chatelaine, or risked a brief moment with her lover. There were no more complaints about spilt wine, for the tables were stained red, and the rush-strewn floor was awash. Enemies cracked mugs with each other, or peered through the firesmoke, hoping to salute their king. Musicians played, their music lost, whilst jugglers showed their finest tricks to wolfhounds and servants. Everybody shouted to make themselves heard, then screamed to vault the shouts. A table collapsed amid shrieks and laughter, and a dozen guests were carried from the hall, their howls of pain adding to the tapestry of joy. Had the roof of the palace fallen in, showering its heavy slates on the diners, it would have gone unnoticed by all who were not maimed. The dead would have been removed, and the dust would have settled and the banquet continued beneath the night sky. Or so it seemed.

The man who had told the Jews to get off the steps had been joined by another. He had grunted at their reluctance, then struck the nearest Jew in the face. The man had staggered, dropping his gift, and the steps had suddenly rung with coins. The sound acted like a carillon of bells, summoning the people to war. The massacre had begun.

The guard eased his way along the hall. He was a common soldier, and he had never before rubbed shoulders with so many important people. Earl and lady, baron and count, knight and heiress, they all lurched in his path and grinned at him as he edged by. Christ on the Tree, he thought, I could enjoy myself with these flapping women. They lead a treasured life, our long-nosed nobility. I swear, I could pass myself off as the Lord of Bootheel, and take half the women here. Look at them! I've touched twenty breasts in as many steps. And not one of them thinks to send some ale out to us. Hell, why should they, they don't know we're at the door. And by the looks of them, they don't know where they are either!

He reached the steps that led up to the platform and was stopped by one of the sergeants. Any message for those at the high table would be passed on.

But the din was so great that after a moment the sergeant shook his head with irritation, and urged the guard up the steps. He followed closely, dagger drawn. It would not do for the soldier to become an assassin.

At the top of the steps the guard's courage gave way, and he gazed terrified at the row of faces. The Bishop of Durham, Hadwisa of Gloucester, Archbishop Baldwin, King Richard himself, Ranulf Glanville, Queen Eleanor, Prince John, the mournful Alais of France, Geoffrey FitzRoy, other Church-men, other nobles. He chewed his lip until blood ran down his chin. Behind him, the sergeant snarled, 'Go on, curse you! You're not here to eat with them!'

The guard had almost lost the will to move. How was he supposed to alert the king – *touch him on the shoulder? Shout down at him? Lean over the table like some intimate friend?*

The sergeant was still herding him forward when Richard turned in his chair. His gaze moved from the guard's bloody lips to his hands, empty of weapons, then to the sergeant, to *his* hand, gripping the dagger. He saw the sergeant nod that it was safe, and beckoned the guard forward. 'Here. Shout your best. What? They are *what*?'

'The crowd is rioting, king! The Jews came, and the people set upon them! There's killing outside!'

Richard's reply was lost in the noise. He gestured to the guard to wait, then clamped a hand on his justiciar's shoulder. 'Get out through the front, Ranulf. There are some Jews, I don't know, I'm told they're being murdered. See to it for me. Clear the ground if you can. Go on, as a friend.'

The austere Ranulf Glanville was one of the few sober men in the hall. He did not like drink, *or* banquets of this size, *or* the howl of wine-sodden guests. But neither did he like his meal interrupted by news of murder. With a word of apology to Queen Eleanor, he made his way to the end of the plat-form and down the wooden steps. Then, followed by the guard, who had only just thought to staunch his bitten lip, he pushed his way through the hall. He shoved aside all who stood in his way, men and women. To Ranulf Glanville, a drunken lady was a contradiction in terms. It was bad enough when a man lurched and blathered, but one wished better of a woman. He had seen his own wife dress in a wineskin, and it had not improved her looks.

The palace steps were slippery with blood and littered with broken money-boxes and torn lengths of silk. Five yellow-robed bodies lay at the foot of the steps; four old men and a woman. The crowd had withdrawn from the palace, or, more accurately, forced the Jews to retreat. The populace made less noise than Richard's guests, for killing is a serious business, but Ranulf was guided across the courtyard by the light of torche and the moans of pain.

The guard who had brought the news had been joined by two more from the door, and they ran to overtake the justiciar. Their lives would not be worth a spark in water if Ranulf Glanville was struck down, yet he had still not identified himself to the rabble. It was with this in mind that one of the guards roared, 'Make way for the justiciar! Christ help you, get out of the way!'

They reached the fighting ground and saw yellow cloaks spattered with red. Men and women had been bludgeoned to the cobbles, whilst others scrabbled in search of coins, a broken necklace, a shattered brooch. The crowd did not join the Jews in their search, but waited until they had reclaimed some trinket, then snatched it from them. They were not yet in the mood for indiscriminate killing, but were happy to deal with the Jews, one by one.

Ranulf Glanville had never in his life had cause to defend the Jews, and he shared much of the Christian suspicion of this intelligent, exclusive race. But he would not see them butchered, and felt nothing but revulsion for their assailants. This was not a war, nor even a street brawl between well-matched ruffians. None of the Jews was armed, and they had made themselves conspicuous in their yellow robes. Their only crime was to have paraded their wealth, and believed themselves inviolable. They should have known better, and spent some of their coins on a bodyguard.

Flanked by two of the guards, his back protected by the third, he moved to the centre of the circle. He had the advantage for the moment, and knew he must keep it.

'For those of you who do not recognize me, I am Ranulf Glanville, Justiciar of England. Any man who raises his hand against me will be peeled alive. Your king was crowned today, and yet there is blood on his banquet hall. He has made wine and food available to you, and yet there are bodies in his yard. If this signifies your displeasure in him, he will want to know. Shall I tell him so? Because, if I do, he will come among you, I promise you that!' While he spoke, he sought out the most likely ring-leaders, then suddenly stepped forward, directing his anger at the largest of them. 'You! You tell me the reason for this. And meanwhile –' He leaned forward, wrested the man's club from his hand and threw it to the ground. The circle contracted, and other men hefted their clubs. The darkness lent anonymity to the scene. It would not be difficult to kill the four intruders, then escape into the night. And whoever slew the justiciar would earn himself a reputation, at least among murderers.

But Ranulf did not give them the time. He knew that the slightest hesitation would be fatal, but that the rabble must not feel trapped. He went forward again, snatched another club from its owner, then tossed it aside. It dawned on them that he had not yet drawn his sword, but seemed ready to tackle each of them in turn, then discard the confiscated weapons. It tipped the scales too much in their favour, and robbed them of all self-respect. They chose to forget what they had done; what they had contemplated doing to the justiciar. God knew, they were not murderers. They were citizens of London, and they had merely allowed themselves to be carried away by the excitement of the occasion. As for the Jews, well, they had brought it on themselves, flaunting their riches before those who loved their king. Oh, a Jew could afford to be generous – with the money squeezed from Christians!

Ranulf went at them again, but this time the men let their own clubs fall.

'I want this place cleared. Go home and stay there. If any of you are found in this area, we'll start tomorrow with some hangings. You've thrown enough blood on the crown, wouldn't you say?'

They abandoned the rest of their weapons, and the circle widened and broke. Ranulf and the guards remained with an island of dead and injured Jews, and the lucky few who had not yet been robbed or beaten.

'You have nothing more to fear,' he told them. 'The king's soldiers will escort you home, and I shall see to it that the injured are attended by his physicians. This has been a tragic day for your people, and more so since you came here in peace, to honour the king. But you are safe now.'

Other guards appeared, and the dead and injured were taken into the palace. Several of the Jews murmured their gratitude to the justiciar, but they also voiced their doubts. Yes, they were safe now. But did he really believe they had nothing more to fear?

There were eighteen dead in the immediate precincts of the palace, and perhaps forty wounded. The crowd had dispersed, leaving the silent yard ringed by guards. Peace had been restored, though, when Ranulf had completed his report, he advised Richard to curtail the banquet. The king refused.

'These people have come from every corner of England. This is a gathering they will remember all their lives. How can I dismiss them? A few Jews have been murdered, and it's to be regretted, but you cannot expect me to alienate the entire nobility. Anyway, you said yourself, the trouble's over.'

'No, king. I said I had cleared the yard.' Nevertheless, he resumed his seat, and gazed unsmiling at the revellers. He did not think this was something they would remember all their lives. He did not think they would remember it when they awoke next morning. They were far too drunk.

No one in the hall was aware that anti-Jewish feeling had already been rekindled in the city, or that a number of Christian priests had stationed themselves at street corners, where they exhorted the crowd to kill any Jew they found. Or that it was rumoured that King Richard had offered ten silver marks for every yellow-clad corpse. Or that several serious fires had been started. Or that the plague of hatred would eventually spread to Norwich, Lincoln, Stamford and then to York, where one hundred and fifty Jews would be burned alive, seeking refuge in the royal castle.

Ranulf Glanville had done what he could, and was not to know what others would do, when the curb was off.

The massacre was abhorred, or condoned, and then forgotten. Outbreaks of violence were not rare in England. This time it had been the Jews; next time it would be those suspected of witchcraft, or Arab merchants thought to be spies, or some local family, accused of cannibalism. For a while, Richard was embarrassed by the spread of anti-Jewish feeling, and he authorized the sheriffs of Norwich and Lincoln to deal severely with the malefactors. But he issued no public condemnation, for fear that it would merely fan the flames. He did not like the Jews, but he needed them for their money –

money for his Great Crusade.

King Henry's long war in Normandy had all but emptied the royal coffers, and what was left had been spent on the coronation. It had happened in the past, and would happen again: the King of England was almost bankrupt.

His advisers suggested a tax on wealth and property, but he rejected it on the grounds that, by the time each individual amount had been assessed and collected, he would be too old to ride a horse.

'I need something *now*. I promised to meet Philip of France before the year is out, and accompany him to Palestine. But first, I must raise an army, and equip it, and hire ships to carry it, and that means money. Also, messires, let us not forget my father's debt of 20,000 marks. Philip will not start for the East until he gets it, and I'm not such a fool as to leave him behind. I would not be halfway to Palestine before he invaded Normandy and Anjou. So, 20,000 marks, if you please, messires. *And* the expenses for my army. Come on now, there must be ways. How does *anyone* raise money?'

It was Eleanor who provided the answer. 'You seem to forget,' she told him, 'you are the king. You own more than any single man, and have more to sell than the Church.'

'I've said this often enough,' Richard laughed grimly, 'and I shall repeat it again. I'd sell London itself, if I could find a buyer. But that apart, where are these valuable assets? I have any number of forests and swamps, but the Church own most of the good ground. And with Archbishop Baldwin and John at each other's throats—'

'Forget Baldwin. Your wealth is in your head, and in the air, and on the scrolls. You badger the council, but *you* think, my sweet. If I was a bishop, what could you sell to me?'

'I don't know. I don't—Oh, yes. Yes, I do!' He slammed his hands together, and his roar of delight made her hum. 'I could sell you a title, couldn't I? *Archbishop* Eleanor?'

'And to a merchant?'

'A concession? Yes—The only man in the district to market wine!'

'And what if I were one of the nobility, and a home-lover. I am only pretending, of course, but what if I, as a baron, did not wish to go on Crusade? What would you do with me then?'

The question defeated him. 'If you would not fight for God, I'd throw you into gaol.'

'I have had my share of that,' she smiled, 'and I could not pay you, from a prison cell.'

'I could demand a ransom.'

'Perhaps. But like the tax, it's time consuming. Would it not be better if you let me – what shall we say – purchase my vows? I could give you my purse in lieu of my person. Then I would retain my honour and stay at home, and you would be so much the richer. If a baron is to keep warm by his fire, he must pay high for his logs, why not?'

'You be my council,' he said. 'I don't need the others. God's legs, I never thought of it, but I *do* have things to sell. Advancements and privileges, titles, absences, concessions – '

It was time to control his excitement. 'It is not an auction,' Eleanor warned. 'You must sell to the right man. And if that man cannot pay your price, don't exclude him. I am showing you a way to raise money, not sell England. Ranulf Glanville, for example; you may ask him to pay something for his next term as justiciar, but you must not replace him. He is the best we have, and not to be valued in coins. And another name I want borne in mind. William Marshal.'

'Yes, mother, I know your feelings for him. I shan't leave him begging by the roadside.'

She strode toward him, and his smile fled. 'Don't condescend to me, Richard Lionheart! I am not seeking a favour. I am telling you to give him what he wants, for the sake of England. Set a price, yes, fair is fair, and he can afford it now, but don't let me hear that John has entered where Marshal is barred. That *would* reduce my love for you. Am I clear?'

He shifted awkwardly, and his face reddened. He knew exactly what she meant, and told her, 'John has already approached me about Leinster. I deferred a decision until – '

'Yes, well, now it's made. But at a reasonable price, my sweet.'

'John will be incensed. He *is* Lord of Ireland now, and – '

'He'll understand,' Eleanor murmured. 'I shall speak to him about it. He'll understand.'

Richard nodded, half-shrugging as he did so. He could never mimic his mother's tone, but it so often combined warmth and warning. A word or two from Eleanor could make a man's heart sing. Or stop.

In the event, Ranulf Glanville got little for his money. Richard demanded, and received, the incredible sum of 15,000 silver marks, almost enough to pay Henry's debt. Perhaps to show his disdain for Richard's merchant-methods, Ranulf paid without demur, then promptly announced his intention to go on Crusade. He would still be justiciar, though he would be unable to administer the office. *He,* the king might care to note, would both pay for his privileges, *and* honour his vows.

The courtiers waited to see if Richard would return Ranulf's money, or rather, how he would manage to keep it. They agreed amongst themselves that the young king was loath to part with a bent penny, much less 15,000 marks. They also agreed that, if Richard could not find a way round the problem, Eleanor would.

Their faith in her was well-founded. At the next meeting of the Great Council, its members were told to divide the justiciarship between Ranulf and Bishop Hugh of Durham—for which Hugh had paid two thousand marks. It was too onerous a job for one man, Richard explained. It should have been shared out long ago.

The decision was greeted with wry smiles, though there were some who wondered how Richard would fare without his mother to guide him. And that time must come, for she was now sixty-eight years old, more than twice his age.

Having succeeded with Ranulf Glanville and the Bishop of Durham, Richard extended his sale of offices, and summoned all those who had taken the Crusading vow. Then he waited for the excuses, and the donations to arrive. King William of Scotland purchased his release for 10,000 marks; a wealthy baron named Godfrey of Luci was granted the shrievalty of Hampshire and the bishopric of Winchester in exchange for 7,000 marks. For Richard it was a dream come true, and he worked day and night, investigating claims, reviving obscure titles, affixing his seal to deeds and charters. He discovered vacancies and filled them, created new posts and elected the applicants, confiscated estates, then sold them piecemeal. Everything had its price and, if the price was met, he was prepared to part with castles and manors, fiefs and concessions, even the rights to hunt and fish on crown lands.

During October and November he became a rich man. He

could now pay his father's debts to King Philip, raise and equip an army, and hire a fleet of one hundred and fourteen ships. He asked Eleanor if he should extend his policy to Normandy, Anjou and Aquitaine. 'England is too small. But if we added our other possessions – '

'Great God,' she exclaimed, 'you *do* have the mind of a merchant! A few weeks ago you were near destitute, and now your debts are paid and you are able to mount your Crusade. A miracle has occurred, a miracle through greed, perhaps, but nevertheless. Can you not be satisfied with that?'

'It was a thought,' he said truculently. 'It seems pointless to own a stable of horses, and only ride one.'

'One is enough. Leave Normandy and the others until you need them. The war in the Holy Land may drag on, and you'll be glad you have fresh destriers at home.'

He was impatient to join Philip and start out for Palestine, but there were a few more important appointments to be made. And the business of Leinster had yet to be settled.

Roger Malchat became the king's steward, at a price, though he would remain in England.

Fitz Renier continued as Sheriff of London, also for a consideration.

King Henry's bastard, the grey-haired Geoffrey FitzRoy, was nominated Archbishop of York. Both Eleanor and Richard felt that, by accepting an important position in the Church, Geoffrey's more regal ambitions would be thwarted.

The final appointment was reserved for one of Richard's faithful officials, a Norman named William Longchamp. He was a brilliant administrator, and utterly devoted to the Lionheart. But he was also deformed, stunted and dwarfish, unable to speak a dozen words of English, and unwilling to learn. He was contemptuous of the country, its inhabitants and its customs, and never missed an opportunity to say so – in French.

Prince John immediately dubbed him 'the monkey', then translated the term for Longchamp's benefit. Longchamp replied that he, at least, had been deformed by God, whereas John had chosen to cripple himself. After that, nothing would reconcile them.

But Richard remained oblivious to these exchanges, Longchamp was elected Chancellor of England, Bishop of Ely, and custodian of the White Tower. It made him as important a man as the resident justiciar, Hugh of Durham, and it did not help when Longchamp heard Hugh refer to him as *le singe nain,* the monkey midget.

Longchamp had two sworn enemies, and would make more.

'Thirty miles,' he groaned. 'She is like a stream when the snow melts. Thirty miles, God judge me, and she never once stopped babbling. Her parents must have shut her away as a child, or forced a gag between her teeth. So, where you or I have had ten years of normal conversation, she has had ten years in which to store up. And what she says is of no great value. "Be gentle with this uncle of mine, he's an old man, and very frail . . . Can you name the trees which keep their leaves throughout the winter? . . . Will you ask the king to send me some lace from Sicily, if he stops there on his way to the Holy Land? I, myself, would ask him, but he intimidates me . . ." I swear it, leaves and lace and old men, for thirty miles!'

Prince John complaining to a friend about his wife, Hadwisa.

'In other respects, is she –'

'No,' he said. 'In other respects, she is not.'

Surprisingly, the business of Leinster was settled with the minimum of fuss. No one knew what Eleanor had said to John, but his behaviour was meek and out of character. He was still Lord of Ireland and, as such, Marshal swore fealty to him. But in return, John was required to renounce all direct claim to Leinster. Marshal could not dispose of it without his overlord's permission, but neither could John give it away to his friends.

The young prince coined another nickname – the dark-skinned Marshal was 'Saladin's spy' – but the childish phrase did not catch on. William Marshal was Earl of Pembroke and Lord of Leinster. And only an idiot would say otherwise.

On 11th December, Richard Lionheart left England for Normandy, while the English fleet set sail for Marseille. It would take them two weeks to cross the treacherous Bay of Biscay and follow the coastline of Spain. Hopefully, the French fleet would be assembled in Marseille when the English crusaders arrived.

But Richard did not go south to meet them. In early February, 1190, he was joined in Normandy by Queen Eleanor, his brothers John and Geoffrey, and by King Philip's sister, the pitiable Alais of France.

Alais was no longer a young woman, and it horrified Eleanor to think that the princess had been betrothed to Richard for a quarter of a century. If rumour was to be believed, Alais had been seduced and abused by King Henry, and she had certainly been ignored by Richard. It was a tragic fate for the princess, but Eleanor was determined that Alais and Richard *would* be wed, if not in France, then in Sicily, or Cyprus, or Jerusalem itself. She would take the woman with her, and they would follow Richard wherever he went. Follow him and haunt him, until he made Alais his queen.

Sister and brother were united, and Philip asked Richard what he intended to do. 'I am aware that marriage is a serious step, and not to be undertaken in the heat of passion. But twenty-five years, my dear friend, twenty-five years . . . I shall begin to think you evasive . . .'

'There will be a wedding,' Richard assured him. 'A few months more, when we have – By the way, I've another settlement to make with you. 20,000 marks, and my own present to you, a Damascene sword. Why not use a Moslem blade to cut off Moslem heads, eh?'

Philip sighed, and let Richard's words wash over him. It was obvious that *Coeur-de-Lion* was not yet ready for marriage.

The two kings made final preparations for their Great Crusade. They embraced in eternal friendship, vowed to fight shoulder to shoulder, swore to brave together the terrors of Islam and return the city of Jerusalem into the hands of Christendom. Who else could do it, if not they?

But their mutual suspicions detained them until August. Shoulder to shoulder, yes. Where they could keep an eye on each other.

Chapter Five

THE MONKEY

November 1190 – December 1192

The house was now empty, and at the mercy of vandals.

King Richard had gone, and Prince John, and Geoffrey FitzRoy. The last two had sworn to stay out of England for three years, or until Richard returned. But it was unlikely they would keep their word.

Queen Eleanor had gone, taking with her the luckless Alais.

Baldwin of Canterbury and the elderly Ranulf Glanville had gone, intent on honouring their Crusaders' vows. William Marshal had gone, commanded by Richard to accompany him at least as far as Marseille.

Hadwisa of Gloucester had gone, unwilling to let John out of her sight.

They had all gone, and the house was now left to whim and weather . . .

Roger Malchat re-read what he had written, shook his head and threw aside the pen. Then, for the third time that morning, he tore the parchment from side to side.

It was no good. The last attempt sounded as weak and plaintive as the others, no more than the whinings of an ill-used servant. Richard would take no notice of it, or assume that it was merely a personal lament. 'Poor Malchat. The winter in England has lowered his spirits. He sniffs the cold air and scents some kind of persecution. No, it's not worth a reply. What's next?'

The steward could imagine that being said, but he dared not make the letter more forceful. What he wanted to say – what half of England wanted to say – would enrage Richard beyond measure.

'The fault is yours, my lord king, and all blame attaches to you. This dangerous situation would not have arisen had you offered the chancellorship to a reliable man. But you gave it to Longchamp, an evil, overbearing, arrogant, contemptuous – '

That was what he wanted to say, that and more. But Richard was the last man on earth to admit he had made a mistake of such magnitude, and he would probably shower

Longchamp with a few more honours – just to show them.

Whenever Malchat was alone in his chambers in Westminster, he warmed his bald head with a green woollen cap. But vanity forbade him to wear it in public, or now, when there were footsteps on the stairs. He snatched it off, rubbed his head to remove the imprint of the wool, and answered Fitz Renier's recognizable knock.

The sheriff entered, snow on his cloak.

He had often visited his friend in these palace chambers and, since the onset of winter, he had always knocked, entered, then commented on the spartan conditions. Today he pointed at the small, triangular fireplace set in one corner of Malchat's study, and grumbled, 'I've seen candles give out more heat. You'll be a dead man before Christmas if you don't move rooms.'

'It suits me here. Besides, the cold keeps me alert.' He saw Fitz Renier gaze quizzically at the sheaf of torn parchment, and added, 'In this case it's not the cold I need, but courage. How do I tell the king that I'm convinced we are veering toward civil war?'

Fitz Renier reached up to release the clasp on his cloak, then thought better of it. 'Things are not so far gone, are they? If you mean Longchamp, yes, well, he can be contained.' He helped himself to some wine, then went over to hog the fire. 'I've known men like him before; ambitious upstarts who run power-mad for the first few months. But he's already achieved what he was after. People say he comes from a peasant family, and that's made him hungry for power. But his two miserable brothers have both been given shrievalties, the one in Herefordshire, the other in Yorkshire. And the rest of his scabrous family have been accommodated, one way or another, whilst he, himself, struts about like a Barbary ape. He's a repulsive little man, but he's got what he wanted, and he won't risk losing it. In my opinion, he couldn't start a hare, let alone a war.'

'You'd dismiss him so easily?'

'Ah, I'd like to. I'd like to jab a sword in his arse and see him leap the Channel. But it doesn't do to take these creatures too seriously, Malchat. They begin to believe in their own importance.'

The steward poured himself a mug of wine, then leaned forward on the littered desk. 'It's true what you say, but it's a partial truth. Yes, his brothers have been given the shires of Hereford and York. But are you aware that their sister, Richenda, now commands Dover Castle? And did you know that Osbert, I think that's the one, did you know he also stands to gain Norfolk and Suffolk? Or that Longchamp plans to extend and fortify the White Tower, where you once resided?' He saw Fitz Renier frown, and continued, 'You were re-elected Sheriff of London, but you no longer have custody of the Tower. So you no longer control the city.'

'I make myself heard, don't fret about that.'

'Yes, you do, and the people like you, but you have lost your castle, that's what I'm saying.' He held up a hand, to forestall his friend's denial. 'I am King Richard's steward, but what authority do I wield? None, because Longchamp excludes me from his councils. And as for our resident justiciar, I honestly believe that Hugh is frightened of Longchamp. We are being squeezed out, all of us, and I'm surprised you cannot see it.'

'Very well,' Fitz Renier grunted, 'I admit we've lost some ground. But when the others return, John and Geoffrey and Marshal and Ranulf Glanville –'

'My point,' Malchat said. 'When they do return, it will be to find Longchamp in sole command. And do you think they will tolerate that? Geoffrey FitzRoy is to be Archbishop of York; but with one of Longchamp's kinsmen as his sheriff? Again, can you imagine John acknowledging the monkey as his peer? And how do you suppose Ranulf Glanville will react, when he discovers that Longchamp has virtually usurped his position? I'll tell you how, if you cannot guess.'

'Christ's open tomb, I'm not defending Longchamp! But I have more faith than you in Hugh of Durham. He is the elected justiciar, and he has the power to chain the monkey.'

'The power, perhaps, but not the persuasion. Have you ever seen them together? Hugh pales when the chancellor is about. His skin actually grows pale. It's an ugly sight, but not one lost on Longchamp. Mark my words, Fitz Renier. We are in for trouble.'

'This damn room of yours is so cold I can see my breath. Look at that, and I'm against the fire!' He came forward to refill his mug, poured some for Malchat, then asked, 'So what are we to do? If things are as grave as you say, hmm? You and I both have fiefs in the country. Are we to strengthen them, as you claim Longchamp is doing to the Tower?'

'I have already started,' Malchat told him.

To be visited by Chancellor Longchamp was to be reduced to penury overnight. Throughout the winter he toured the southern and eastern counties of England, and it was not unknown for a baron to receive advance warning of his visit, disperse his household, abandon his castle or manor-house and flee the district. Longchamp would then come upon the place, to find it cold and deserted. If the baron was lucky, the chancellor would continue on his way, in search of another, more welcoming host.

It was not merely personal dislike that put the barons to flight. Longchamp alone was sufficiently objectionable, but even he would be satisfied with a flagon of wine and a good cut of meat. What terrified them was that, wherever the chancellor went, he was followed by a four-hundred-strong retinue of servants and soldiers. They moved like unseasonal locusts across the country, causing livestock to be slaughtered, foodstores stripped bare, an entire winter's stock of firewood turned to ash in an evening. Sometimes he repaid the hospitality, but it was never enough. More often, he gave nothing in return, leaving the baron, his family, household and garrison to live like peasants until the autumn harvest. One could tell Longchamp's whereabouts by the frenzied activity ahead.

They plunged down the embankment from the Roman road, their horses floundering in the snow-drifts, then swaying upright as their hooves made contact with the frozen fields. The Icknield Way stretched east and west into the white fog that shrouded the county. Luckily someone had known where to turn off for the manor; they'd nearly missed it in the fog.

It was Longchamp and his retinue come calling. On Isabel de Clare.

On this occasion, neither Isabel nor her neighbours had been forewarned. They had heard that Longchamp was somewhere to the east, visiting his brother Osbert, but they had expected him to pass well clear of them on his way to London. Unfortunately for Isabel, the chancellor was riding west, not south, heading for his winter court at Oxford. It was even more unfortunate that he possessed such a good memory.

Weston in Hertfordshire; a small manor and mill; part of the de Clare inheritance, now under the control of William Marshal. But Marshal was abroad, and the Lady Isabel was God knows where. So the occupants of the manor would not dare deny hospitality to four hundred weary travellers.

The cavalcade trotted across the fields. Startled rabbits ran for the hedgerows, and there was the sharp twang of bow-strings and hiss of ill-aimed arrows. None hit their target, but it was an excuse for the archers to whoop and trade insults. The walls of the manor garden loomed out of the fog. No towers were visible, though the twelve-foot-high boundary was crenellated and looked built to last.

The gateway was open and through it the horsemen could see the house itself, another solid-looking structure made vulnerable by large, ground-floor windows. There was no sign of the mill.

A practised glance told the riders that one hundred or so could be crammed into the manor. The others would have to bed down in the mill, pitch their tents in the garden, invade the nearest village. These overnight halts always presented a problem, but there were always solutions.

They saw figures running back through the gateway and reined-in. Longchamp would play the very devil with anyone who preceded him, so they remained outside the walls. It was a measure of his supreme self-confidence that he could ride in, alone and unprotected, an avowed Anglophobe. And it was a mark of England's despondency that he was allowed to.

Swathed in a heavy sheepskin cloak and perched on his high horse, he entered the garden. All those who had retreated through the gate had disappeared, and there were no watch-guards on the walls. He peered round at the bushes and out-buildings, shrugged at the craven nature of the English, and made his way toward the house.

When he reached the centre of the garden, a young woman emerged from the manor. Longchamp pulled the reins against his malformed chest and waited for the servant to approach. But she remained beside the door, her head covered with a fur-lined hood.

The chancellor hesitated, then called to her in French. 'Come here, girl. I am William Longchamp, Chancellor of England. Take my horse, or fetch one of the ostlers, don't hang back. Who's your master here, in the absence of Earl Marshal? Well? Speak out, girl, your tongue won't freeze.'

But the woman did not reply, or signify that she had understood.

In English now, and aided by a dumb-show, the exasperated chancellor shouted, 'William Longchamp . . . Me . . . The Chancellor of England . . , Yes? . . . Trap the horse . . . Come, come, come!'

The young woman drew the hood closer around her face. She said nothing, forcing Longchamp to urge the palfrey forward. *Bon Dieu,* they grow more stupid every day. What am I to find here, that they are all deaf as well as ignorant?

Worried that he might lead the animal on to a frozen pond, he kept to the centre of the garden, following what he hoped was the path. Gusts of wind brought more snow into the enclosure, and he slapped irritably at the neck of his cloak. He'd stayed up late with brother Osbert, and he was now cold and tired and in need of a good meal. The journey had been bad enough, without this.

He reined-in, removed the bird's-bill cap he wore when travelling and pointed the long peak at his chest. 'The-Chancellor-of-England . . . You come the, ah – You bring the – *le seneschal,* yes?'

In French, and with a better accent than his own, Isabel said, 'We have no seneschal, my lord chancellor, and I do not take the horses.'

Longchamp glared at her. 'I see. So you do understand. Then through what impertinence did you ignore me when I addressed you before?'

'You did not address me, my lord. I am Isabel de Clare, whom you mistook for a servant. So *you* ignored *me.*'

Long service with Richard Lionheart had taught the chancellor that anger was often a good disguise for embarrassment. 'I don't have the eyes of a hawk, you know. In this weather . . . If you huddle so coyly in the doorway . . . Besides, I had no reason to believe you were here.'

'Nor to believe I was not.'

'Even so, you should have come to greet me.'

'Oh? Why's that, my lord? I had no reason to believe you would visit us. Besides, you thought I was a servant; when you rode through the gate, *I* thought, well, this is gypsy country.'

He knew she was lying – he'd seen the members of her household run back to warn her of the cavalcade – but worse, she knew he had seen them, and was unrepentant. She was being too audacious, this pretty little vixen. She had learned French better than she had learned her manners.

He heard a sudden creak and a crash, and twisted in the saddle. The solid garden gates had been shut, and four men were lowering a heavy bar in place. Even now, it did not occur to Longchamp that he might have ridden into a trap, but he turned back to howl at Isabel, 'What is this? I never saw those men! I want the gates opened!'

She had to decide then whether or not to go on with it. Two months earlier, she had written to Marshal, asking what she should do if Longchamp and his retinue ever visited their lands. She would abide by Marshal's wishes, and relay them to every constable and seneschal in their employ.

His answer had been immediate and unequivocal.

'Those men?' she shrugged. 'Gardens need gardeners, my lord, even in winter. They have been out there most of the day. And they close the gates in the evening; it's a common habit. Now, will you dine with us? That was, I imagine, the purpose of your visit. Well, it could hardly have been otherwise, could it, since you did not know I was here? So far as I'm aware, this humble manor has never been honoured by such an important guest, perhaps because it is so out of the way. Had we been nearer London, we could doubtless have expected you more often. But isolation is the price we must –'

She stopped abruptly. She had made no attempt to conceal her sarcasm, and he suddenly realized she had been holding his attention for a reason. The four men who had closed the gates were now grouped around the horse.

He stared down at them and felt the first tremor of fear. The woman had insisted that they were gardeners, but they were all young and deep-chested. They *might* have been gardeners, and they *might* have been working with the hoes and picks they carried like weapons. It *might* have been one of their duties to seal off the garden, though they had done that with the ease of the vanished wall-guards. And they *might* also be waiting to take his horse, rather than his life.

It seemed to depend upon Longchamp.

He directed his uncertain gaze at Isabel. 'I do not like the manner of this greeting, Lady de Clare. You invited me to dine with you, yet you shut out my companions.'

'No man has that many friends, my lord chancellor. Not even you. And they are not shut out, for they never tried to come in.'

'But apparently you will not feed *them*.'

'I will not starve my household for months to come, I'd put it that way. You are welcome to eat, I've said so, you and any twenty of your – companions. But, as the chatelaine of Weston, I don't give banquets in mid-winter. If I did, well, as I told you, the countryside is full of hungry gypsies.'

Longchamp nodded. This had never happened to him before. The houses in his path were either abandoned, or their occupants resigned to his visit. No one had had the temerity to number the plates.

Nevertheless, he would forgive her insolence. She was an ill-mannered cub, and too free with her tongue, but he would offer her one last chance to redeem herself. He would present her with a simple choice, aware that it was, in fact, no choice at all.

'So, you put your household, even your gypsies, before servants of the Crown. Very well. If you will not feed my companions, you will not feed me. But I am sure you would not deny succour to the Chancellor of England.'

Isabel looked up at him, then brushed snow from her face. 'One moment,' she murmured, 'I'll have the gates opened – '

'Yes, that's better.'

' – then you will be able to leave.'

The group remained silent, while the white flakes eddied around them. Then Longchamp let his twisted body sag in the saddle as he leaned toward Isabel. She braced herself for his anger, but she was unprepared for the intensity of his scream.

'Stupid! Stupid! You are the only one, you stupid – Do you think you have gained anything? – you haven't, you stupid *salope! Catin!* God see me – the Arab will find nothing! *Espèce d'ordure,* you think you've won, oh, no, but what you have lost! There'll be nothing left for him when he comes! Nothing! *Ils seront déserts, ses fiefs!'*

He felt a hard object drawn along his calf, and lurched sideways to discover that his right boot had been slit from rim to ankle. His skin was untouched, but the snow was already exploring the crack. The gardeners gazed at him impassively, paying no heed to the uproar that came from beyond the gates. Then one of the men reached up and caught hold of the bridle, while the others walked back through the garden to lift the heavy beam. Isabel turned away, sickened by his words, and by the spittle that had flown from his lips. Her maidservant ran from the manor to guide her indoors.

Within a matter of days, the vast territories of Pembroke and Striguil had been made ready for war. The scores of scattered manors, similar to Weston, were also on the alert. Word had been sent to Leinster, and Marshal's commanders there kept watch for Longchamp's invasion. No one doubted that he would implement his threat to make a wilderness of the fiefs.

He had not stayed to attack the manor at Weston, but had forced his retinue to follow him through the night on a bleak, fifty-mile journey to Oxford. His fury was so great that his fine Norman palfrey had to be put to death *en route,* its flanks slashed to ribbons by his spurs.

Had he wished to suppress the story of his eviction, he might have razed Weston, slain its inhabitants, and sworn his followers to secrecy. But he could not have silenced four hundred tongues, nor prevented Isabel's neighbours from witnessing the massacre. So, varied accounts of the incident spread throughout the country and across the Channel. Some told of how the duly-elected chancellor had been lured into a trap, fought his way clear and laughed in the face of de Clare's vile curses. Others spoke of the lady's extraordinary courage, and festooned the tale with romantic trappings. In these Isabel was depicted as all in white, a vision in the snow, sternly dismissing the cringing upstart.

. . . She had come forward to kiss him, but had stabbed him instead . . . He had made revolting overtures to her, slinking crabwise through the fog . . . She had bewitched his horse, causing the noble beast to topple over on the road . . . He had sucked blood from his lips, and spat it in her face . . .

There were enough stories to satisfy everyone, and make them reach for their swords.

With the departure of the crusading fleets, and particularly King Richard, his brothers had hurried north from Marseille. They had both vowed to remain on that side of the Channel, but had had no intention of doing so. Deeply suspicious of each other, they had gone their separate ways, John to his Norman fief of Mortain, Geoffrey to stay with friends at Tours. They had heard of Longchamp's activities with increasing concern, and had daily grown more restless.

By December, John decided it was safe to move. King Richard was at Messina, in Sicily, his face turned toward the Holy Land. And even if he did look over his shoulder, surely he would not recognize his brother from a distance of one thousand miles?

But one could never be too careful, so John and Hadwisa left Mortain under cover of dark.

Marshal was also at Messina, and it was there that he heard the news of Longchamp's eviction. Fortunately, it was a balanced account, and soon followed by Isabel's own version of the incident. He immediately sought King Richard's permission to return to England.

'I've heard the stories,' Richard dismissed. 'They're pure invention. Chancellor Longchamp is a fine administrator. He's not the kind to parade about at the head of an army. Someone is sowing dissension. If I do let you go, it will be to discover who it is.'

'May I ask something? How many times have you heard these – what you call inventions?'

'How many times a day do I draw breath?'

'Exactly. Times beyond number. And so have I. Every messenger speaks of Longchamp's arrogance, of the way he has advanced his family, and always of his locust army.'

With a dangerous spacing of his words, Richard said, 'Let me be clear. Do you say my appointee is at fault? That I am at fault for having put him there? Just what *do* you say, Marshal?'

'That there's an ominous consistency to the stories, and that I wish to see things for myself and protect what is mine. My wife tells me she is under threat – what was Longchamp's phrase? – that he would make a wilderness of my lands. I believe what she says. What I am not so sure about, lord king, is whose words you would take. Whatever the situation in England, I shall send you as fair a report as I can manage. I hope it will be of value to you, or will you discard it as yet another invention?'

'Do you know,' Richard warned, 'you have become quite

the bull since we ennobled you? If anyone could hear us now, they'd be hard put to say which of us was king. Send your report, and leave it at that! If I read it, then it's read. If not, send another. And if the trusted William Longchamp does lead an army, he'll have good reason for it. That man served me in Aquitaine and Anjou and Normandy, so why not in England?'

'No one says he is not serving you. What's said is that he's cutting too thick a slice for himself, and depriving others. Now, my lord, do I have your permission –'

'Yes, go!' He let Marshal reach the door before calling after him. 'God's legs, you're a quarrelsome man, Earl Marshal.'

'I? Oh, yes,' he replied straight-faced, 'I love a dispute.'

'Well, I don't,' Richard insisted. 'Leastwise, not between friends.'

Marshal nodded. 'I'll keep it in mind.' He paused, then asked, 'Is that why you recalled me?'

'Not entirely. I want you to wish me God speed. I may be away from you for a year or more, who knows? And you're wrong, I do respect your word. I have a real affection for you, Marshal. You could be warmer toward me sometimes, but –' He lifted his shoulders and grinned, his expression unusually sensitive. He was the boyish gambler who had ignored good advice and put his pennies on the wrong horse; the swain who is once again refused admission to the lady's house, and told to wait in the street.

'I will read your reports, if I can find the time, though I'm out to slay God's enemies, not go blind over paperwork.'

With characteristic vanity he extended a hand for Marshal to kiss. Then, with a display of emotion that was equally a part of his nature, he abandoned formality and clasped Marshal in an embrace.

'God speed,' Marshal said. 'He will make you triumphant. We'll hear that Jerusalem is ours again by summer.'

'And that not a single Moslem is left! You'll learn of my victories soon enough. I'll herd those pigs into – well, whatever is beyond their lands. *Deus Vult!* That is our cry. And *Coeur-de-Lion!*'

Still held in the king's embrace, Marshal allowed himself a brief smile. No one but Richard would think to put forward his own name, as an alternative to God.

That winter was one of the most severe in living memory, and Longchamp was unable to make good his threat. Many of his ships were frozen to their moorings, and it would, anyway, have been suicidal to attempt an invasion across the Irish Sea. So Leinster remained safe, as did the snowed-in fastnesses of Pembroke. Even the Roman roads became impassable, and there was never enough food available to feed the army. Marshal's English castles remained the most likely targets, but Longchamp acknowledged that in order to reduce them he would need the help of scaling towers, catapults and rams. He told his military architects to design sledges, capable of bearing the weight of the great mangonels and belfries. They did their best, but the idea was abandoned when they convinced him that at least fifty oxen would be needed to draw each sledge-borne tower.

Thwarted by the weather, the chancellor continued to pit his authority against the resident justiciar, Hugh of Durham. Hugh had always been stronger in the north of England than the south, a situation that was to Longchamp's liking. London, Winchester and Oxford were the real centres of government, and the crookback chancellor scurried between them, holding councils, and issuing edicts, his feet rattling, as someone remarked, in a pair of Richard's cast-off boots.

Isabel de Clare had moved from the manor at Weston to her impregnable castle at Pembroke. She spent a cheerless Christmas without her husband, though she had heard that he was on his way from Sicily. She prayed for his safe return, and spent much of her time at the window, for she knew he would not be with her until the new year. But it gave her pleasure, and there was little else to do.

The festival was made more sombre by news of the deaths of both Ranulf Glanville and Archbishop Baldwin. These elderly Crusaders had succumbed to the heat and aridity of the East, though they had reached the Holy Land, honouring their vows, and that was something.

She lit four candles on Christmas night, a tall, translucent offering in celebration of the birth of Jesus Christ, and three smaller waxes for Ranulf and Baldwin and Marshal. She expected no reward for her piety, but three days later she was accosted by one of her guards, who told her there was a drunkard in the bailey.

'He says, well, it may be a bad joke, my lady, in which case he'll get his deserts, but he says he is King Richard's steward. Claims he's travelled across England, right through the snow, to be with you, and he brings presents and greetings from Fitz Randolph.'

'Fitz Randolph? Do you mean Fitz Renier?'

'That could be what he said. It's difficult to know. There's three men holding him up.'

Her smile widened, and she asked if the visitor was bald; well-fleshed and bald.

'Again, my lady, he could be, but he's buried in cloaks and his head's covered by a woollen cap. I wouldn't trouble you with him, except he insists he's the king's steward.'

'Treat him like glass,' Isabel said. 'I think he is.'

'Masshat,' the guard murmured, 'something like that.'

'Malchat. Roger Malchat. That's him. And in heaven's name forget his cap. He believes it's his secret. No, on second thoughts, mention it to him. Discreetly. He's probably forgotten to remove it.'

She then changed into her finest gown, doused herself with perfume and clanked beneath the weight of jewellery. If Malchat was too drunk to see or smell, no matter. His visit was well-meant, and he was welcome. He had traversed an entire country to be with her, so he had earned his drink.

In the middle of January, 1191, Marshal reached England and joined his wife at Pembroke. A few days later, John and Hadwisa stepped ashore, and immediately rallied their supporters in the West Country. The young prince summoned his own councils, elected his own chancellor and issued his own decrees. With Hugh in the north, Longchamp in the south-east and John in the south-west, England was a ship with three captains. The situation had to be resolved, and there were only two men who could do so; the ailing Pope Clement III, and the crusading King Richard.

Longchamp was aware of the promise Richard had extracted from his brothers, but he did not dare move against John. The prince now controlled the bordering counties of Cornwall, Devon, Somerset, Dorset and Gloucester, and he had been enthusiastically received by the people. It never occurred to Longchamp that his own unpopularity was the main reason for John's new-found favour. The people had thought the prince selfish and lecherous, but what was he, beside that venomous Norman upstart? Just a twenty-three-year-old, seeking a young man's amusements. Yes, they had been rather harsh on him, come to think of it. John was irresponsible, but that was all. He was not evil, like the crippled monkey. He was in need of guidance, whereas Longchamp was in need of a dripping throat, or a nice tight noose.

Nor did the chancellor attempt an all-out assault on Marshal, though he repeated his threat like a litany. He would have his revenge, when the time was right. Pembroke would be a desert, Leinster a playground for carrion crows. You will know Marshal's castles, he predicted, by the flatness of the ground . . .

Instead of violence, a war of letters ensued. Each of the protagonists appealed to the Pope and to Richard, and the English courts were treated to the near-comical sight of Longchamp, waving a letter of authority, only to have Hugh of Durham produce another, with a more recent date. A week later, the chancellor would be back with a fresh mandate, superseding Hugh's.

The appeals and justifications continued until March, and then the humour of the situation was quite lost on the councellors. Limping into the chamber at Westminster, the chancellor took his place at the head of the table and let his hooded gaze slide from face to face.

'I hope,' he said, 'that you have tied your futures to me. I don't know your innermost thoughts – do the English have them? – but I would advise you to despair of John. He should not even be in this country. He dishonoured his vow to Richard, and that may show you the measure of the man. But he is here, and I shall not start a civil war to drive him out. As for Hugh, wherever *he* is, you may also despair of him. As from today, he wields no power in this land. He is no longer papal legate, so the Church need not answer to him. Nor is he anything more than justiciar-in-name. His power here is – terminated.'

He waited for the murmurs of surprise and disbelief to die away, then used his less twisted hand to lay a heavy leather wallet on the table. From it he produced two letters, prolonged the tension by lifting first one, then the other, then raised the first again and said, 'Church before State, I think. I shall recite each letter in turn, and later they will be available to you. The date on this is 3rd February. The seal is that of the Lateran Council, serving the Pope. The name above the seal is, of course, Pope Clement's. Now, let's see, how does it go?'

It went very well for Longchamp, as he knew it would, since he had read both letters several times before.

'Pope Clement, to William Longchamp, Bishop of Ely and Chancellor of England; greetings. We are happy to abide by and comply with the wishes of our dear son under God, the blameless and heroic Richard, King of England, who pleads with us to confer upon you, William Longchamp, the authority of the Church, and to charge you to represent the Church in England and bear the title of papal legate.

'Such authority will also extend to Wales, and to those regions of Ireland over which our dear son under God, the brave and noble Prince John holds sway and jurisdiction.

'This seal is given under our hand . . .'

'. . . and so on and so on.' He let the parchment fall. 'High-flown language, though I'm sure you can unravel the meaning. If not, I'll make it plain. I am the head of the Church now. It will be my duty to appoint God's senior servants and to control the sale and purchase of ecclesiastical lands. And with any luck the prelates will learn some French.'

He might as well have said that he had inherited half the wealth and property of England, for it was true.

The counsellors stared at him, unable to reconcile the dwarfish foreigner with the news he had imparted. Longchamp as legate? Oh, no; oh, no. Chancellor, yes, they could accept him as that. And even as Bishop of Ely. But not as supreme head of –

'It has been a good day for letters. Here's the other. Written a week earlier, though it had farther to come, 27th January, and King Richard's seal. He was still in Sicily then. By now he is probably on his way again. He writes in French, of course.'

Though nobody had stirred, Longchamp could not resist adding, 'A translation has been made, for those of you who

, . .' and left it at that.

'Richard, King of England, Duke of Normandy and Anjou, to William Longchamp and all my loyal subjects; greetings.

'We decree and command all those who love us and are faithful to us to be obedient to our trusted chancellor, as you would be to ourselves.

'We expect you to serve him in everything, and do whatever he tells you in our name, and be wholly loyal to him, so earning our love.

'Witnessed by myself at Messina . . .

'. . . and then the date and so forth.' The letter fell beside the other. Longchamp stirred the sheets with a finger. 'Self-explanatory,' he said. 'The translation is merely a courtesy. But you see what I mean when I tell you to despair of John and Hugh. It's put plain enough in the king's own hand. Obedience . . . Service in everything . . . Your whole loyalty . . .' He let his triumphant gaze tour the council. *'Cela saute aux yeux, n'est-ce pas?* It makes your eyes come wide, no?'

Word reached them that Richard and Philip had quarrelled again about the wretched Alais of France. Queen Eleanor had followed her son to Sicily, as she had promised, though the young woman who accompanied her was not Alais, but the Princess Berengaria of Navarre. Eleanor found it necessary to remind Richard that he had met Berengaria in Spain, some years earlier, and had been taken with her.

'You wrote poems and dedicated them to her. You even set them to music; you were always good at songs.'

'Did I? Well, I wouldn't do it now. Look at her, mother. She's so passive, so – matronly.'

Near desperation, Eleanor said, 'She is a fine, attractive woman. And she adores you.'

'Perhaps, but I don't control the tide. All of us adore things we cannot have.'

They were on the waterfront at Messina, and the wind was lifting the spray. Eleanor raised the hood of her travelling cloak and turned her back on the sea. 'Things,' she queried, 'or people? I had hoped to avoid this, my sweet, but the French seem much amused by your antics with Philip. They say you won't leave him alone. Is there anything in that?'

'I don't know what you mean.'

'Oh, I think you do. I think you know precisely what I mean. Are you enamoured of him, Richard? Is that why you resurrect old quarrels, in order to be with him?'

'He's a cold fish, and the French are anyway notorious liars. I'm saddened that you would take their word against mine. They are the ones who are stirring the pot, not me. Enamoured of Philip? That's plain madness. I don't even like the man. He's a cold fish, did I say that? Well, he is, and I'd no more think of – befriending him, than – '

'Very well, that will do.' She put a hand on his arm. There was no point in continuing the discussion. She had her answer. King was quite clearly in love with king.

'I want you to visit Berengaria,' she told him. 'The princess has just ended a sea voyage, so you cannot expect her to look her best. I'm sure I don't.'

'Oh, yes,' he insisted, 'you do. Nothing impairs your looks. I would not mind if Berengaria was your mirror image. I could get on with her then.'

Yes, Eleanor thought, that's the tragedy of it.

Nevertheless, he agreed to meet his intended bride, and they hurried from the windswept quay.

The queen felt very sorry for Alais, finally discarded by the family who had brought her so much misery. But Eleanor was determined that Richard should marry and sire a son. Berengaria was young and, as he had so callously remarked, matronly. She would make an ideal mother, if only Richard could be enticed into her bed.

Eleanor stayed in Messina until she had wrung from her son the promise of marriage. She was shrewd enough to offer something in exchange, and assured him she would safeguard his interests in England.

'There'll be a deep layer of dust on your throne when you return, sweet. I'll see that no one tests it for comfort.'

She had spoken to him of other things and, as a result, she was accompanied homeward by the gentle and unassuming Walter of Coutances, Archbishop of Rouen. In his purse he carried three letters, all bearing the king's seal. Eleanor was satisfied with their contents, for she had helped Richard compose them.

Now firmly established as head of Church and State in

England, Longchamp twitched his muscles. Ranulf Glanville was dead. Hugh of Durham had faded into the shadows. John glared from a distance, but was powerless to act. Marshal was chained to his own lands, waiting for the attack that might or might not come. The Council at Westminster were a mere chorus, chanting Longchamp's songs.

Opposition to the chancellor centred around John, though the disaffected barons were still faced with the same problem; how to remove the Norman upstart without pitching the country into civil war? If that happened, and Richard learned it was at his brother's behest –

John winced at the thought. He had done well out of Richard, and he knew from experience that the Lionheart set him apart from other men. It was poor John, stupid John, John-led-easy. But this was not the mill-house at Sablé-sur-Sarthe, and Richard would not shrug off the destruction of his kingdom.

Nevertheless, he pondered the problem, often staying up late to plan assassination attempts with his supporters. Safe in one of his West Country strongholds, John paced the room, hand on head, his bejewelled rings sparkling like an imitation crown. 'It can be done. If we perfect the method. If we learn where he'll be, and when, and if we can somehow draw off his bodyguards. How many does he have these days?'

His old friend Belcourt said, 'I saw him in Oxford not long ago. He had thirty men with him then, though they were each as huge as your brother. He calls them his Goliaths.'

John sighed and straddled one of the benches. 'It *can* be done,' he said listlessly. 'We'll dig a hole in the street and line it with sharp stakes, I don't know, but there must be a way.'

The ideas became more fanciful, and they discussed hiding on a house-top, then dropping a rock on him as he passed beneath. Or nailing shut the doors of the Council chamber and setting fire to it when he was inside. Or finding out who supplied his wine, and poisoning the entire stock. Or sending to Aquitaine for a box of scorpions.

They did not once suggest that John should seek an audience with the chancellor, then step forward, draw his sword, and plunge it into Longchamp's heart. After all, the topic was assassination, not suicide.

Word reached them that Richard and Berengaria had sailed

to Cyprus where they had been married in the Cathedral at Limassol. Two hours after the ceremony the newly-wed king had ridden off to pursue some private feud with the Cypriot Emperor.

'Or,' John said, 'we could wait until he goes hunting, then set a trip-string in the forest. If we knew in which direction he was headed, we could get there first and either set some snares on the ground, or tie a thin cord between the trees. His horse would step into the loop, or stumble over the cord and come down, hopefully on top of the vermin. If he wasn't crushed by the weight of the animal, he'd break his neck on a tree, or be blinded by a thorn bush. And we'd dress in green, so they'd never find us in the forest. How's that?'

'He doesn't hunt,' Belcourt said.

Hadwisa was growing tired of her husband's nocturnal schemings. She knew they would never amount to anything, and that John would no more attempt to assassinate Longchamp than he would murder King Richard and seize the throne. It lifted her husband's spirits and lessened his feelings of guilt, but it also interrupted her sleep.

He came into the bedchamber in his high-heeled boots, muttered an apology as Hadwisa raised herself against the carved headboard, then grunted when she asked how the plans were progressing.

'What did you cook up tonight, my lord, a tunnel into his rooms?'

'Make light of it if you wish, but someone has to work for his downfall.'

'Why not leave it to him?'

He had drunk too much, had his best ideas rejected, and was in no mood for her levity. 'Look,' he snapped, 'I know I have intruded on your sleep, but – '

'I wasn't asleep. I also have a plan. I thought you might care to hear it.'

He rammed a toe against a heel, and one boot crashed to the floor. 'You're wonderfully loyal,' he yawned, 'but you cannot understand the situation.'

'Humour me,' she said. 'Pretend I can. I don't have the mind of a skilled strategist, and I am not adept at late-night tactics – '

'Very well, say your say.' He rid himself of the other boot, then turned to face her, patient and long-suffering. He supposed all wives were the same, pathetically eager to help.

'You want Longchamp destroyed, but you have no wish to die, yourself. Is that right?'

'Brutally put, but yes, close enough.'

'Then let him destroy himself, my lord. You remember the vow you made to your brother, to stay out of England?'

'It was convenient to do so at the time. I doubt if he took it seriously.'

She shook her head. 'I don't ask you to justify it; I ask you to recall it. You made the vow, and, for whatever reasons, chose to ignore it. So we came from Mortain to England.'

His belt thudded on to the planks. 'I know my life story better than most. I *know* where we came from.'

Undeterred, Hadwisa continued, 'But Longchamp did not move against you. He knew you should not be here, but you were, and are, too strong for him. My question is, how would he react if Geoffrey FitzRoy came over? If, say, someone wrote to Geoffrey, suggesting that his Archbishopric of York was in danger, and that it was imperative that he spring to its defence. Do you follow me?'

'And Longchamp had him arrested! He'd do that, he said he would!'

'You follow me. But it would make the chancellor even more unpopular, laying hands on a senior prelate, whose only wish was to continue in God's service, And *you* would be most indignant, would you not? The brother you love so deeply, seized like a common felon?'

Hadwisa had snuffed all but one of the candles, so John was forced to lean forward and peer at her. He could not believe that this was the same woman who spent her days prattling about flowers and foodstuffs, needlework and the niceties of backgammon. He felt that perhaps he had underestimated her.

'Yes,' he nodded defiantly. 'If that stinking creature laid a finger on my brother, I'd raise all England against him! How did you think of it?'

'Long, quiet nights,' she said acidly, 'alone, and in the dark.'

Eleanor and Walter of Coutances reached England and separated at the port. The elderly queen turned westward, anxious to see John and Marshal, while Walter went in search of Longchamp.

He found the chancellor at Oxford, and attempted to deliver the first of Richard's letters. But Longchamp did not acknowledge him, and kept him waiting several days. Then when Walter was finally granted an audience, in the first week of August, the chancellor treated him like a hired messenger.

Speaking of him as though he were not in the room, Longchamp said, 'He's brought a letter from the king, is that what he says?'

'I have,' Walter replied, 'and I am over here, quite visible.'

'Give it to me then.'

'It's to be read aloud.'

'Surely I should decide whether –'

'By me.' He prised off the seal and read:

'Richard, King of England, Duke of Normandy and Anjou, Defender of Sicily, to William Longchamp; greetings.

'We do charge you to welcome and cherish our revered Archbishop Walter of Coutances, and henceforth to seek his advice in all matters of government.

'He is experienced in the affairs of England, and will do much to lighten your burden. Care for him as you would for us, and pray that we may be victorious and return to you soon.

'Witnessed by myself at Messina.'

Without a word, Longchamp stretched out a hand for the letter. Then, still silent, he ripped it to shreds and stamped on the scraps that fluttered underfoot.

Matching silence with silence, Walter withdrew from the chamber, left the palace and set out westward to rejoin Eleanor. He was well-pleased with the reception, though he did not stop trembling until he was ten miles on.

They had been waiting for him for two weeks. All along the south-east coast, Longchamp's men kept watch for his ship. They did not know which route he would take, or where he would land, only that he was coming. And when he came, *Bon Dieu*, he would find the reception tougher than the crossing.

As it transpired, he stepped ashore at the worst possible

place, beneath the cliffs and castle of Dover. This was the fortress that Longchamp had given to his most zealous supporter, his sister Richenda. She had prayed that Geoffrey FitzRoy would land there, so that she might repay her brother's generosity, and had insisted on taking her turn as watch-guard. She was bitterly disappointed that she, herself, had not sighted his ship, but she was one of the first on to the beach.

He did not see them until the vessel was close inshore, and by then it was too late. The light craft grated on the pebbles, and was immediately boarded by Richenda and her men-at-arms.

There was no violence at first, though the chatelaine seemed hard put to restrain herself.

Shrill and excited, she cried, 'Geoffrey FitzRoy, you are not wanted here. You have broken faith with your brother, the king, and with his chancellor, William Longchamp. The rumour is that you're bound for York, but we think you are here to claim the crown of England!'

'It would be a tight fit,' the grey-haired Geoffrey told her, 'with Richard's head already in it.'

'Ah, but what if he should die? What if he falls prey to the Moslems, what then?'

'Then I imagine we shall adhere to tradition, and bury him.'

'And you will seize the throne!'

'That has all the cadence of a promise, my lady. I wish I shared your conviction. So I shall seize the throne, eh?'

'You'd like to, but you won't while Longchamp's around! He's the only one whose loyalty stands the test. You won't get past him, not in a life of trying. He has your measure, don't think he hasn't! Oh, yes.'

'How fervent you are, for so early in the morning. I trust you grow more tranquil as the day goes on. Now, I am delighted to be met, Lady Richenda, but the rumour's true, and it's a long way to York.'

He nodded politely to her, then started down the swaying gangplank, the hem of his robe held clear of the water.

Richenda stared at her guards. She was furious to see that several of them were grinning in Geoffrey's direction. Adhere to tradition, and bury him. Yes, they'd like that. And admonishing her for her fervour. Hell, it was about time someone told her to be less shrill.

'You seem to forget!' she snapped. 'We are here to arrest him, *not spend the day on his ship!* Get ashore, get after him. Look, burn you, look! He's taking one of your horses!' Shouting at him to stop, she ran nimbly down the plank and up the shelving beach. Geoffrey ignored her cries, rammed in his heels and sent the palfrey clattering toward the narrow cliff path.

One of Richenda's mounted sergeants spurred forward to head him off, and the two riders collided at the foot of the path.

'Hold up, you. You've got business with Longchamp.'

Geoffrey did not reply in words, but slipped his right foot from the stirrup and lashed out at the sergeant, catching him in the ribs. It was a clumsy blow, but solid enough to make the man snatch at the saddle, and it gave Geoffrey time to draw clear. Behind him, he could hear Richenda screaming amid the chink of pebbles, and then the path angled up into the cliff, muffling the noise.

There was, of course, no question of riding to York. The roads would be barred, and the strident chatelaine would soon dispatch her search-parties. It had to be somewhere nearby, somewhere that could offer him sanctuary.

He reached the clifftop, frowned in an effort to orientate himself, then sent the stolen horse thundering along the road toward the priory of St Martin. The monks there would surely take pity on an Archbishop, even though he was not dressed for the part.

Before noon the soldiers had learned of his whereabouts and ringed the priory. Richenda demanded the fugitive's surrender, and there were heated exchanges between the chatelaine and the elderly prior. But the courageous old monk refused to part with Geoffrey FitzRoy, unless Geoffrey's safety could be guaranteed.

'He is the Archbishop of York and, in the eyes of God and the Church, a far greater man than the chancellor. But that is beside the point. We would grant him sanctuary if he were a shepherd, or someone off the ships. If he is guilty of some crime, then he must be brought to trial. But he has told us his story, and I believe it. You wish him harm, Lady Richenda, so I am bound to resist you. Fetch someone who is impartial, and then we'll see.'

It was a brave speech, but the prior did not know Long-champ's sister.

Frightened to commit her own soldiers, she hired a group of mercenaries and four days later they burst into the priory, discovered Geoffrey at prayer and dragged him from the altar.

He was kicked and pummelled from the building, and those monks who went to his aid were hurled aside. A horse was brought forward, and he was told to mount up. The prior remonstrated with the invaders, but he, too, was pushed away.

'Don't meddle, old man. We're not of your cut, and your threats of damnation don't work with us. You bleat that this is Geoffrey, Archbishop of York. We say he's a bastard who cannot even name his mother, and a traitor to England. Now, do you mount up, FitzRoy, or will you sniff the horse's wind?'

'I am already used to the smell,' Geoffrey said. 'It's been in the air since you came. If you wish to take me out of here, you'll have to drag me every step of the way.'

They loved him for resisting, and tethered him behind the palfrey. Then they rode out, while Geoffrey stumbled behind, like a captured slave.

The barbaric scene was witnessed by farmers on the road and by the inhabitants of Dover. Twenty miles to the north-west lay the cathedral town of Canterbury, a permanent reminder of an earlier martyr, Thomas Becket. It was Geoffrey's father who had instigated the murder of Becket, and the similarities were ominous. Both men were archbishops. Soldiers had invaded the cathedral then, as they had now invaded the priory. Becket had been dragged from the altar, as had Geoffrey. And Becket had then been struck down . . .

The mercenaries hauled their captive through the town and up to the castle. Richenda did not receive him, but waited to hear that he had been flung into one of the dungeons. Then she sent a triumphant message to Longchamp. She knew he would be pleased.

Word reached them that the Crusaders had landed in Palestine and captured the citadel of Acre. However, the victory had been marred by a further quarrel, this time between King Richard and Duke Leopold of Austria. It seemed that Richard had taken exception to the presence of the Austrian standard, claiming that Leopold had played no part in the assault. A squalid tussle had ensued, when Leopold's banner had been hauled down from the wall and thrown into a ditch. Five days later, the Austrian contingent left the Holy Land . . .

Had Longchamp been taller and stronger, he would have attacked the messenger. As it was, he made the man repeat Richenda's message, then screamed at him to get out. The chancellor knew, even then, that he was finished in England, but he could not bring himself to accept it. He had worked too hard for it to end like this. The things he had done for his family, and now, oh, God, what Richenda had done to him! He had never told her to arrest the bastard Geoffrey. Never! Apprehend him, yes. Demand that he swear fealty to Longchamp and King Richard, yes, all that. But to hire bloody brigands . . . To invade the priory and drag him out . . . To parade him at a rope's end, then lock him in some stinking dungeon . . . Oh, no, it was beyond belief.

Why not hack him to pieces at the altar and have done with it? Why not, when Geoffrey FitzRoy was already a martyr? Aah, Richenda . . . Stupid, stupid . . .

The net was drawn in by willing hands. All England was united in condemnation of the chancellor, and John immediately summoned the leaders of Church and State. He exuded charm and courtesy, yet remembered to cover his actions with a fine dust of indignation.

'How dare that deformity lay his filthy paws on Geoffrey FitzRoy! He has gone too far now. We have him at our mercy, though he can expect none from me. He must be seized without delay, and my brother released before we have another Becket on our hands. And I advise you to keep us apart, the monkey and I, or there may yet be bloodshed!'

Eleanor was at Pembroke when she heard of Geoffrey's capture. She was delighted to see Marshal again, and flattered to discover that Isabel was jealous. The two women got along well enough, though the dowager queen was eventually obliged to take Isabel on one side.

'The advantage of age,' she said gently, 'is that one may speak one's mind with impunity. I can say things to you, my dear Isabel, that you would only dream of saying to me. Here, come and sit down. I'm about to lecture you in your own home.'

'You are free to say what you like,' Isabel told her, 'and this is as much your home, while you are here.'

'You see?' Eleanor smiled. 'You obey the dictates of courtesy, and rightly so. But you would rather ask me when I'm leaving, hmm?'

'No, my lady. You will leave when you're ready. It's immaterial to me.'

'But there'll be no pangs of remorse when I go.'

'I shall be sorry, yes, but –'

' – you'll be glad to have Marshal to yourself again. And, for my part, I shall be glad to leave him with a woman I so much admire. I can think of no one who would have stood up to Longchamp as you did. It sets you apart, among the chatelaines of England.'

'You have disarmed me,' Isabel said. 'You're better at this than I am.'

'I am better at this, my dear, than anyone. But listen to me for a moment. What I have to say will not make you feel less possessive toward Marshal, but it might lessen your suspicions toward me.

'In my life I have borne five sons, of whom all but two are dead. Those two, Richard and John, are beset with problems, and always will be. But they are my sons, and I shall continue to support them.

'However, I am not blindly maternal. King Henry sired a bastard in Geoffrey FitzRoy, and I have often though: Geoffrey more capable than either Richard or John, So, although he is not directly a son of mine, he has Henry's blood, and perhaps the best of it.' She smiled again and asked, 'Do you know where this tale will end?'

Isabel demurred. 'You support Geoffrey for his abilities?'

'Yes, I do. And I thwart him for the same reason. In my opinion he should not be king; I am not so selfless as to put the result of my husband's infidelity before my own true sons. But yes, I find Geoffrey intelligent and resourceful, and so he earns my support. As does a certain William Marshal of Pembroke and Leinster. I have two real sons and a bastard son, so why not an adoptive son?' She raised her hands in a gesture of self-reproach. 'Perhaps I am blindly maternal, after all.

'But you must understand this, Isabel. We are not vying for Marshal's favours. I have known him since he was nineteen. He has known you since you were nineteen. But there

is a world of difference, and it's not to hurt you that I say
he holds a special affection for me, and I for him. God
knows, there must be some warmth in the room after twenty-
five years.'

They sat quiet for a while, and then Isabel nodded. 'I
understand better, my lady, and I know you need not have
troubled to tell me these things.'

'I wished to. But I hope you are not now going to say
you will never again be jealous of me. That would be un-
natural.'

'No, I shall still be jealous. But less obviously so.'

'Good,' Eleanor commended, 'excellent. I shall adopt you as
my daughter-in-law.'

The axe fell.

Longchamp retreated to the White Tower, and remained
there until he heard that Geoffrey had been released from
prison, and Richenda arrested.

London was suddenly the stamping ground for prelates and
nobles, and John presided over a council of revenge at Westminster. Longchamp was brought into the chamber, where
Walter of Coutances presented him with Richard's second
letter.

In this, the king decreed that the chancellor should be fully
obedient to Walter, and accept him as supreme authority in
England. Longchamp procrastinated, at first accusing Walter
of having forged the letter, then demanding the right to appeal.
His mouthings gave John the opportunity to strike, and Walter
was told to get on with it and present the final letter.

It said, quite simply, that since Longchamp had ignored the
two previous warnings, he was to be deposed as Chancellor
of England. His lands were to be confiscated, and he was to
be held for trial. Walter of Coutances was given the authority
to redistribute titles and holdings, and immediately dispossessed Longchamp's brothers and sister. John prowled the
chamber, continually warning the barons to restrain him, lest
he murder the monkey.

In the confusion of the meeting, Longchamp managed to
escape. He fled to Dover, disguised as a woman, and there
suffered the greatest indignities of his career.

Those servants who had remained loyal to him had
succeeded in hiring a fishing boat, and the monkey-turned-

woman huddled on the beach, waiting for it to drift inshore. While he waited, a group of fishermen came stamping across the pebbles, slapping their hands against the October weather. They stank of fish and wine and seaweed, and one of them veered across to the woman and thrust his cold hands between her legs. Longchamp's scream of dismay brought his servants running through the surf.

The disgusted fishermen recoiled in horror, then decided to warm themselves with a brawl. They beat Longchamp's men into submission, caught the imitation woman by the skirts and dragged him into town. Witches and warlocks were known to masquerade, so the fishermen were none too gentle with him. He did not help his situation by screaming in French – for all they knew, the language of Satan. Dazed and bleeding, he was thrown into the town dungeon, to await the test of fire, or water.

Eventually, however, he was identified and, with rare compassion, John allowed him to continue his flight. 'If he's brought back here,' the prince threatened, 'I shall kill him! Better he should seek some warmer clime, and be chancellor over the monkeys.'

Geoffrey FitzRoy was free by then, and embarrassed by his half-brother's pageant of affection. He had always thought John cunning and selfish, and was bemused by this sudden display of fraternal devotion. Nevertheless, he sustained himself in the knowledge that, whenever the prince hugged and kissed and comforted, it was time to beware. In that, at least, he was reliable, was brother John.

Chapter Six

KING'S RANSOM

September 1192 – December 1193

The date by the Moslem calendar was 22nd Shaban, 588 A.H., reckoning the years from the *Hegira*, the Exile, when the prophet Mohammed had fled from his persecutors in Mecca. By the Christian calendar it was Wednesday, 2nd September, 1192.

The Great Crusade, the Moslem *Jihad*, their Holy War, was over. King Richard lay wasted by fever, imploring his commanders to let him return to England. He had reached the Holy Land on 8th June, 1191, and in the subsequent fifteen months the Crusaders had captured Acre, Tyre, Caesarea, Haifa, Arsuf, Ascalon – all the coastal strongholds. But they had not reclaimed Jerusalem, nor did they hold much more than a three-mile-wide coastal strip.

There had been magnificent victories and, at one time or another, the Frankish kingdom had been visited by four kings, four queens, and legions of the nobility. But the might of the West had been weakened by disease and by the strange climate in which the heat of the day blistered the flesh, and the cold of the night cracked stones. Men lost hair from their heads and groins, and those Frankish overlords who had settled in Palestine were afflicted by impotence.

But this was not the end of it, for the West brought its own contagions. They were vain men, hungry for power, jealous of their position. Intrigue was as necessary to them as bread and water, and their vices blossomed in the arid air. The Emperor of Germany, the red-bearded Frederick Barbarossa, had been drowned on his way to Palestine. King Philip of France had arrived, stayed less than four months, then departed. Duke Leopold of Austria had withdrawn in high dudgeon as a result of his squabble with Richard, and it had been left to the King of England to rally the remaining Crusaders.

In June, 1192, Richard had led a small group of horsemen to within sight of Jerusalem. But he, himself, had refused to look at the walls and minarets and the great, golden Dome of the Rock. His army was exhausted, and he knew there was now no hope of taking the city. Weeping openly, he told the riders, 'It is sufficient torture to have come this close. I do not care to view something I can never have.'

A few weeks later he was smitten with fever, and he now lay in the damp citadel of Jaffa, pleading to be absolved from his vows.

'You may go,' the barons told him, 'when we have something to show for our labours. Sign the treaty that Sultan Saladin proposes, then we can all go home. Christ knows, most of the soldiers have already deserted us.'

It was not as the Lionheart had envisaged. England had been bled white in order to finance the Crusade. Saladin still held sway over the vast Arab empire, and the Moslems had lost nothing but a hundred miles of coastline. Philip Augustus was back in France, and it was rumoured that, in exchange for Normandy, he would help John secure the English throne. Then, together, they would turn against Richard.

'Fetch their emissaries,' he mumbled. 'Warm the sealing wax. Let's get it done with.'

The soft-spoken sultan regarded it as a very generous settlement. The truce was to last for three years, and the Unbelievers were to be allowed to keep their coastal gains. Moreover, their pilgrims were permitted access to the Christian church in Jerusalem, and to Christ's birthplace at Nazareth. The Moslems would scarcely notice their presence in the Holy Land. And, if they broke the treaty, it would be simple enough to tip them all into the sea . . .

Des Roches had lost none of his bulk. The thick-set knight who had helped Marshal defend the bridge near Le Mans had survived the rigours of a Norman winter and a Syrian summer, and had not taken in his belt by a single notch. There were more scars on his face – the results of a Saracen ambush near Caesarea – and his sight was impaired by a cataract in his left eye. The eye had become filmy and for some reason the eye-lid drooped, as if to hide the infirmity. It gave des Roches a sinister appearance, and an air of even greater authority. The right eye was opened wider, seeing what the left could no longer see. Those who had been educated were reminded of the Cyclops, the one-eyed giants who had once inhabited the volcanoes of Sicily. Others merely saw him as a big-bellied knight who would finish any trouble that was started.

And that was how the gate guards of Pembroke saw him as they escorted him into the dark snow-covered bailey.

He sheltered in the guard-house while one of the men tramped up the torchlit steps and into the keep. Soldiers who had ended their watch, or were waiting to go on, huddled around the banked fire, or sent dice clattering across the communal table. Des Roches leaned against the wall, studying the faces to see if there was anyone he recognized. Anyone would do, for he only wanted an excuse to tell them it was colder where he'd come from.

But one glance at their gigantic visitor had been enough and they kept their eyes averted. They hoped that Earl Marshal would receive the monster, whoever he was, for it'd be a damn difficult job to throw him out.

There was a roar from the yard. 'Des Roches! William des Roches!'

Now the guards did look up, saw their visitor respond and clamoured their greetings. So that's who he was! Someone slopped wine into a mug and pressed it to him, while others straightened their tunics, or surreptitiously buffed their helmets on the hem of their cloaks. Not a month went by without Marshal making some mention of his old friend, usually when he was displeased with the garrison.

'By Gad,' he would groan, 'if I had des Roches with me, I'd turn you loose, the lot of you. I employ nearly two hundred to safeguard this place, yet the River Tower was empty this morning when I went by. It is normal practice to make the guard-change on the walls, or in the towers, not down here in the yard. I don't wish to see it empty again, do you understand?'

Or, more simply, he conjured his friend as a judgement on them all. 'I pray des Roches does not see this place. He'd mistake it for a dung-heap, I swear he would. Scour the rust off those hinges, or you'll be paying for new ones. Yes, you three! Get on with it!'

But there was no acrimony now as the Earl of Pembroke strode through the snow, shouting for his friend.

Des Roches squeezed between the doorposts and bellowed his reply. 'I haven't shrunk, have I? Or do you mistake me for a horse?' They ploughed toward each other, the visitor critical of the unswept yard, his host aware that he should have had it cleared.

Isn't that always the way, Marshal thought. It had to snow just before he arrived. And what's this? Is he blind in one eye?

Well, well, the Arab's grown a moustache. He could hide an army in it. Now whose idea was that, I wonder; his, or that young lady he married, quick, what's her name, Isabel, yes, Isabel de Clare.

They collided in a wordless embrace. The wall-guards snatched a glance at their paragon, then turned their attention to the moonlit snowscape beyond the walls. He was big, no doubt about that. *And* he had a voice. And, judging from the scabbard, a sword like a ship's oar. They made a mental note; William des Roches; not to be crossed.

The knights stumbled apart, breathless. When Marshal had refilled his chest, he said, 'You're in time to celebrate Christ's Mass with us, *confrère*. And to eat us empty, I hope.' He was about to take des Roches by the arm and escort him inside to meet Isabel when he saw the man hesitate.

'Before we go in, there is something I must tell you. Is there a private room we can use?'

'Well, I – Yes, anywhere. But if you want a fire – '

'No, that can wait.' He pointed at the deserted smithy, in effect little more than an open shed, lined with broken farm implements and racks of blunted swords. 'That'll do.'

Marshal nodded, detoured to collect a torch from the wall, then rejoined des Roches at the entrance to the workshop.

'We may have to celebrate elsewhere,' des Roches told him. 'In a week or so, all England will be stirring.'

Marshal jammed the torch into a knot-hole in the planks, and both men withdrew into the smithy. 'It must be serious, if you expect the country to awake in winter.'

'It is serious. The most serious thing that could have happened. King Richard has been captured.'

'King Richard has – *What*? That's not possible!'

Des Roches sighed. 'Nevertheless, it *has* happened. And I was with him at the time.'

'With him where?'

'In Vienna, Austria. A damn sight colder than this. I was also with him in Syria. We left there in October – the ninth or tenth, it doesn't matter – and we were blown off-course to the island of Corfu. *Sea Slicer,* that's his ship, it was damaged by the storm, but the king had heard such alarming rumours about John – By the way, are they true? Does John intend to seize the throne?'

'It seems so,' Marshal said. 'He's gone from bad to worse these last months. Not even Queen Eleanor can control him. But let me hear your story first. *Who* captured him?'

'I'll get to that. We were in Corfu, but Richard was so anxious to press on to England that he wouldn't wait for *Sea Slicer* to be repaired. So he hired – and can you credit this – he hired a pirate vessel to take us up to Ancona or Venice, from where we'd go overland. But October is not the time to sail the Adriatic, and anyway the corsair had as much knowledge of weather and navigation as I have. Less! Oh, he put us ashore firmly enough. On the rocks of Dalmatia! It's some comfort to me that the fool drowned, but, as you may know, Dalmatia sits across the water from Italy, and it's a long ride to England.' He lifted one of the broken plough-blades, fiddled with it for a moment, then returned it carefully to its place. 'Did you hear of the business with Leopold of Austria?'

'When Richard threw down his flag?'

'That's it. I mention it because Austria now lay directly in our path. But again, the king would not be delayed. I advised him to wait for a merchant ship, but he's a bad sailor at the best of times, and I think he'd had enough of the waves. So we bought some horses, and disguised Richard as – '

'How many of you were with him?'

'Just two,' des Roches said, letting his breath hiss out like smoke. 'Myself and a squire.'

A dozen questions clung to Marshal's tongue. Why had Richard travelled without a bodyguard? Where was the squire? Had John been informed of his brother's capture? Had Philip been told? Indeed, was Philip the gaoler, or was it the vengeful Leopold? And what force had been assembled that could defeat the Lionheart and des Roches?

But he managed to restrain himself, and waited for the knight to continue.

A curious guard appeared in the entrance, saw his suzerain and hurriedly withdrew. The torch in the wall seemed ready to expire.

'We disguised him as a Templar. I can't remember where we found the uniform, but we dressed him in a white cloak with a red cross on the shoulder, and a leather cap with a good wide brim. Then we rode north, through Slovenia and into Austria.' He turned his good eye on Marshal and emitted a harsh, self-accusative laugh. 'It was pitiful. Did we really think *Coeur-de-Lion* could be mistaken for a soldier? Can you put horns on a horse and make a bull of it? I don't know . . .' He slumped against the wall, the last of his strength ebbing with the torch-light.

'We'll go in soon,' Marshal encouraged. 'But tell me how he was captured. And who – '

'That? Oh, that was easily done. We reached Vienna, and Richard strode into a tavern, booming French at the top of his voice, demanding food and wine, removed his cap – and that was that. One moment the place was half-empty, the next it was full of Duke Leopold's men. Thirty or forty of them, coming in the front doors, and through the back. I had Richard's cap in my hand, I remember, trying to make him put it on. His hair – Well, Christ support me, he might as well have been wrapped in the banner of England.'

He remembered something else, and smiled. 'Through some odd oversight, *I* was left at the table. Ironic, eh, old Marshal? I had to leave the steaming food and follow them to the castle, all but begging to be arrested.'

'But they let you go.'

'Myself *and* the squire. They needed us to spread the word. Yes, and to relay Leopold's terms. I saw him briefly, at the castle, and I can assure you he is as angry now as when Richard displaced his flag. He claims he has been insulted as never before, so he demands a ransom that has never before been equalled.'

'A ransom? From England? We'd have trouble filling a saddle-bag.'

'Well . . . We will need quite a few saddle-bags if we're to get our king back. Quite a few.'

'How much does Leopold want?'

Des Roches squinted out at the snow, then looked back at Marshal. 'He wants one hundred and fifty thousand silver marks, I regret to say. A mark is half a pound in weight, so we must somehow amass, let me see, I'd already worked it out, yes, close on thirty tons of silver. Saddle-bags? A pack-train, more likely.'

Marshal let his head swing in despair, while des Roches

D.L.   E concluded, 'But it should be enough to satisfy even the Lion-heart's vanity, hmm?'

Richard had always known he had enemies, as a lion has fleas. But he had prided himself on his ability to deal with them, either by tolerating them as the parasites they were, or by scratching them off. His confidence had never deserted him, for he had never imagined he could be harmed, or locked in a cage.

But he was caged now, his whereabouts unknown, and his enemies made ready to bite.

Leopold of Austria regained all the esteem he had lost at Acre, though he was soon forced to relinquish his prisoner.

Frederick Barbarossa's son, Henry of Germany, was another of Richard's enemies, and Leopold's overlord. Delighted by Leopold's *coup*, he nevertheless demanded that his vassal duke surrender Richard to him. So the prisoner ceased to be the property of Austria, and was taken to Germany.

Philip of France was also elated by the news. At last the boorish giant had been brought down, fair punishment for his insults, and for the way he had discarded poor Alais. He offered to purchase the prisoner from Emperor Henry, at any price the German cared to name. But one did not snare a lion every day, and Henry declined.

Geoffrey FitzRoy greeted the news with equanimity. He had never forgiven Richard for having hounded their father to his grave. However, since his maltreatment at the hands of Longchamp and Richenda, Geoffrey had become a celebrity in England. He had not died like Thomas Becket, but he had suffered like Becket, and he bathed in the reflected glory of Becket's martyrdom. He was now regarded as head of the Church – almost a king with a mitre, in place of a crown. So he was content to bide his time.

And then there was John.

Born on Christmas Eve, he was just twenty-five years old. But it was in the last three months that he had matured beyond recognition. Longchamp's expulsion, together with Richard's absence in the Holy Land, had wrought an extra-ordinary change in the high-heeled prince. He was no longer John Lackland, the boy-led-easy, the playground for soft-limbed courtiers. He had mastered his mannerisms and kept his hand from his head. He coined no new nick-names, but addressed his peers by their full titles, and gave lessons in courtesy. He bathed regularly, dispensed with jewellery, offended no one.

Hadwisa was paraded on his arm, her every attempt at humour rewarded by his chuckle. She heard him commend her in public, credit her with a rare sense of intuition and speak of her as his inseparable companion.

'Whatever slight virtues the Lord God has thought fit to bestow on me will be brought to fruition by my Lady Hadwisa. I would be lost without her, though I don't intend to mislay such a treasure. And be warned,' he laughed, 'I'm a jealous man.'

He was well aware that he had become popular by default, as the only alternative to Longchamp, but he was determined to retain this unexpected gift. However, it was not enough that England accepted him as somewhat better than the monkey. They must be made to love him for himself. And, later, perhaps to worship him?

It was with this in mind that ten days after the news of Richard's capture, he made a solitary journey to Paris. There, he swore fealty to Philip of France. John agreed to help the king invade Normandy, if Philip would then support a revolt in England. And, as a gesture of good faith, John promised to divorce Hadwisa and marry the shopworn Alais.

'In all honesty,' he said, 'I cannot take another lecture on the size of cooking pots, or the way to mix dyes. Hadwisa is well-informed, I'll grant her that, my lord king, but the boredom of it all . . .'

By the end of January, John was back in England, making plans for the insurrection that would sweep him on to the throne.

The table was large enough to accommodate all six; Queen Eleanor, Marshal and Isabel, Roger Malchat and Sheriff Fitz Renier, and the massive des Roches. A full night had come and gone, and they were still there, plotting their course of action. Others, who were unable to attend in person, had sent messages of encouragement, most of them including suggestions as to what might be done. These were often as fanciful as John's assassination schemes, but nothing had been rejected, or laughed out of court.

Indeed, there had been no laughter at all that night, for it was hard to wring gaiety from the imminent destruction of England.

They had recently learned of John's visit to Philip, and of the incredible bargain that had been struck. Whether or not Hadwisa knew of it they could not say, but they spared a thought for her in her world of cloth and cookery.

His voice dulled by lack of sleep, Fitz Renier attempted to sum up their discussions.

'We are faced with two choices. We can arrest John as a potential traitor, or, if that fails, declare war on him. Or we can raise the ransom and bring Richard back as our re-established king. To my mind, the first is too desperate a course to follow. Forty years ago, this country was racked by civil war. Most of us were mere children then, but even now I have memories of those God-forsaken times. "The years when Christ slept"; that's how someone described them, and we dare not put Him to sleep again.'

A terrifying picture edged into Marshal's mind. The scene was so vivid, the faces so clear, that a small mew of alarm escaped his lips. It was the sound a child would make when monsters stalk the bed . . .

The castle of Newbury had been under siege for weeks. Its castellan was elsewhere, pursuing the war against King Stephen. But the king had out-flanked him, and the royal army had surrounded his home. Inside the battered walls was the castellan's five-year-old son, too excited by events to miss his father.

The foodstocks had run out, and it was evident that the garrison must surrender or starve. The constable of the castle pleaded with Stephen and it was agreed that, if the castle was not relieved within three days, the gates would be opened. The five-year-old was lowered from the walls and given as a hostage to the besiegers.

The image shifted, moving forward half a week . . .

Newbury had not been relieved, though its castellan had sent word to the constable. There was to be no surrender. Help would arrive. Meanwhile, the gates were to stay shut.

Now the child was in the enemy camp. He could see the king, with his thin black hair and straggly moustache, and he heard someone snap, 'Do what you said you'd do. How else will you earn respect? Haul him up where they can see. Great God, you're England's king, aren't you? Then act the part!'

He saw a group of barons move under a tree and throw a rope at one of the branches. It occurred to the child that they were trying to knock down fruit, or dislodge something trapped up there. He'd seen the local boys bring down squirrels that way, and he was pleased when the king took him by the hand and led him toward the barons.

He remembered speaking . . .

'Everybody eats squirrels. I'll try, if you like.'

'What did you say, boy?'

'If you want to get the squirrels—'

'No, no, it's not for that.' The king stopped, and there was further argument. The barons had only succeeded in throwing the rope over a branch, but nothing had fallen from the tree. The child accepted that this particular exercise was finished and looked round for some new diversion. He saw a man named Arundel, or perhaps that's where he came from, leaning on a long, painted spear. A small pennant hung below the spear-tip, and the boy tugged at Stephen's hand.

'Can I have that?' Then, remembering his manners, 'My lord Stephen King?'

The king seemed glad of an excuse to interrupt his argument. 'Have what, boy? What do you want?'

'His spear. Arundel's. Just to throw.'

'You couldn't even lift it. It's not as light as it looks. It's quite a—Sweet Jesus, I'll not go through with it! Pull down that rope! Can't you see, he doesn't know! We'll take that castle, but not this way. Not this way, Arundel! Get over here! Give me your spear, oh, for God's sake, let him touch it. He's a child!'

And then the image splintered, like a dropped mirror . . .

A fragment showed the king, his face buried in his hands, weeping about something or other.

Another shard reflected the tall, hollow-faced Arundel, frowning as he watched the boy stagger beneath the weight of the spear. 'Take care,' he said awkwardly, 'or it'll come down on you.'

In a further chip of memory the constable of Newbury was reclaiming him and snarling like an angry dog. 'We saw what you were about, you bloody butchers! You were going to hang him. Five years in this world, and you were going to hang him! A thing like that—It should remove all doubt from your minds as to why we oppose you. Stay still, William

*Marshal. Oh, go on then, if you must, bow to the king. Very
well, now stay with me. I'm taking you home.'*

And, ever since, he had never hanged a man, nor signed
his name to a sentence of death by hanging, nor permitted
any tree to bear such fruit on his lands. As Isabel had discovered, when she had been unearthing what she could about
her future husband, he could not abide the feel of rope, or
the sight of a tasselled girdle . . .

At which point Fitz Renier said, 'The second choice is less
dangerous, but almost impossible to achieve,' and Marshal
realized the nightmare had passed in the blink of an eye. He
shifted in his chair, felt the blood course into his buttocks, and
leaned forward to hear the sheriff's conclusions. The dawn
light turned them as grey as they felt.

Earning their weary admiration, Fitz Renier continued,
'There are various ways in which we might raise the money.
Or at least part of it. Both Geoffrey FitzRoy and Walter of
Coutances have promised to squeeze the Church. Others of
us will contribute all we can, and we will borrow a further
sum from the city states of Italy. The King of Spain might
help us; after all, Queen Berengaria hails from Navarre. And
then there's – '

'Forgive me,' Marshal intruded, 'but I may have – ' His
thoughts outstripped his words, and it was a while before he
appended ' – a solution, or as you say, a part of it.

'Amongst us all here, who are the greatest landowners on
this side of the Channel? I'd suggest Lady Isabel and myself.
With Pembroke, Striguil, the five or six counties of Leinster,
those and the fifty smaller holdings scattered throughout
England. And how did King Richard raise the money for his
Crusade? Yes, you see it, don't you?

'There are those who cannot be enticed to part with a penny,
if it's for love or loyalty. But if it is for land? And, dare I
say, if it is offered by Earl Marshal and Lady Isabel de Clare?'

He summoned the first smile of the night – now of the day –
when he told them that he, himself, would rush to buy from
such a distinguished couple.

They were too sensible and too exhausted to remonstrate
with him. It was a brilliant solution, for Marshal could ask
a high price for even indifferent fiefs. And the profit from
those, together with donations from the Church and loans
from abroad, might just tip the scales at thirty tons of silver.

Anyway, it was better than drowning the country in blood.

Three hundred German-speaking scouts were dispatched to find Richard. Their efforts were crystallized in a troubadour named Blondel, who, it was said, rode from castle to castle, singing a ditty composed by the Lionheart. Eventually, after many months and adventures, his song was heard by the captive king, who responded with the next refrain. It taxed the credulity, but it was a pretty tale, and England was sorely in need of a legend.

By the time they had discovered his whereabouts, Queen Eleanor and her party had raised more than half the ransom. But they also learned that John and Philip had already matched the gigantic sum, and were offering it to Henry of Germany – on condition that Henry kept Richard a prisoner for life.

The castle of Durrenstein was like most of the others in which he had been lodged during the past twelve months; too ornate for his taste, and too cold for comfort. But he was thankful that the game of hide-and-seek was over, and that England knew his address.

On a personal level, he was particularly glad to be rid of the gibbering Leopold. The weeks of captivity in Austria had been intolerable. Every day, Duke Leopold would summon him into the Great Hall, then scream new threats, or prowl around him, gloating over his trophy.

'One hundred and fifty thousand silver marks,' he'd chant. 'Your kingdom will be drained!

'Or perhaps they will not want you back, had you thought? Three years you have been their king, but how much time have you spent with them in England? Three months? Not more. Why should they pay for a stranger, a man who insults those better than himself? No, I do not think they will reclaim you, *Löwenherz*. I think you will stay here and regret how you treated our flag.'

But he had been proved wrong. Emperor Henry had taken charge of the prisoner, moved him from Austria to Bavaria to Carinthia, and finally incarcerated him in the Gothic castle at Durrenstein. Richard's chambers overlooked a narrow, rock-strewn river, but not even the *Löwenherz* was prepared to make a rope from clothes and belts and curtains, then risk the eighty-foot descent.

Henry visited his prisoner in March and June and again in August. They were traditional enemies, the Hohenstaufen and the Plantagenet, yet each was pleasantly surprised by the other's manner. Henry was twenty-eight years old, the same age to the month as Philip Augustus, but he was blond where the French king was dark, and took a larger size in clothes. On his third visit, the emperor invited Richard to accompany him on a bear hunt, and told him of John's treacherous offer.

'He's hand in glove with the Frenchman, and Philip has made several inroads into your duchy of Normandy. I have met them both, of course, and personally I detest them. I'm sorry to speak so of your brother –'

'Why not?' Richard said equably. 'Everybody else does.'

They swung apart to avoid a twisted spruce tree, then brought their horses close again as they crossed open ground.

'Will you accept their offer?' Richard asked.

The young emperor parried the question with a question. 'Can you give me a good reason why I should not? From what I hear, your mother – a remarkable woman, we're agreed on that – but even so, she is finding it difficult to raise the money. England is a market-place these days; everything is for sale.'

'I'm surprised,' Richard commented. 'I thought I'd already sold it.'

They had both lost interest in the hunt, and slowed their horses as Richard said, 'Yes, I can give you a reason, my lord Henry. If you take money from Philip and John, England will immediately lose Normandy, Anjou, God knows what. Philip is far too clever for my brother. He'll outwit him at every turn.'

'I believe you,' Henry nodded, 'but that is your concern, not mine.'

'Yes, it is. At present. But if Philip is not stopped, you may soon find that the kingdom of France extends from your western borders to the borders of Scotland. Philip knows John by now; he knows which tunes to play, and the steps John will dance. And, once the Frenchman has seized Normandy and our other possessions, he'll invade England itself. God's legs, you're aware of all this; that's why you hesitate to take their money.'

He glanced across at Henry, but the emperor's expression betrayed nothing. They skirted more trees and reached another clearing. The hunt was out of sight, somewhere to the left.

'Is that it?' Henry queried. 'Is that why I should refuse them?'

'I'm not finished.' He glanced back, saw the eight armed riders who were there to prevent his escape, and raised his hand in mock salute. They did not find it amusing. They wanted to be up with the hunt, not playing watchdog to the giant.

Completing his answer, he said. 'Today, Germany is a great power. So is England, whilst France sits uncomfortably between us, shouldered by her neighbours. But if I'm kept locked away, Philip will swallow my kingdom, and then *you*, Hohenstaufen, you will feel jostled. You may detest Philip all you like, but he has more sense in his ear lobes than my brother has in his half-grown body. John believes he is cunning, as he believes he can manipulate me, but he'll be quite lost in the hands of the ambitious Frenchman.'

'You think your brother a complete fool, don't you, my lord Richard?'

'I know him for one.' With a dismissive gesture he said, 'John is a boy. He follows the jugglers wherever they go.'

'David was a boy, in the story. But he brought down Goliath.'

'He was a master of the sling-shot, that's why. John has mastered nothing, unless it's to walk in raised boots.' He returned to the problem again. 'Money's attractive; I'm the first to admit it. But if you take silver from Philip, he will destroy England, and you will have given birth to a monster. *There* will be your Goliath, wearing the crown of France.

'You watch his progress in Normandy. He's moving his left arm now, to nudge me. But imagine we are a year hence, and think of your own border territories. What if he moves his right arm, eh, my lord?'

'Let's start back,' Henry said. 'We've lost the hunt anyway.'

'Eighty-nine thousand,' Malchat said, 'and that's where it's stuck. Almost all of Marshal's smaller fiefs have been sold off, and we cannot ask him to chip at Pembroke or Leinster.'

Des Roches growled something about the next war being with Spain, then glanced quickly at Eleanor, to see if she had taken offence. But the dowager queen was too much the realist to argue.

'I'm as disheartened as you, messires, but I see it as Spain does. They owe Richard nothing. He had no wish to marry the Princess of Navarre, but only did it to please me, or stop me pestering him. And, since then, he has ignored Berengaria, as he ignored Alais. Small wonder the Spaniards refuse to help.' She clicked her tongue and nodded over the sad, undeniable truth. 'Every time we put Richard with a woman, England gains another enemy.'

Malchat said, 'There's no hope of our raising the total sum this year. But we know that the emperor is worried by Philip's advances in Normandy, and I think Henry can be persuaded. If we collect another eleven thousand marks, we'll have a hundred thousand, two-thirds of the ransom. We'll take that to him – under the heaviest guard the world has ever seen! – and pray that he accepts it. The balance to follow in six months or so. My lady?'

'Yes, I'm for it. It will at least prove we have raised something, other than a wail of alarm. And that much silver spread out on the floor will look most impressive. Any man would be sorry to see it taken away again. Yes, arrange it, Malchat. We'll buy my son piecemeal.'

Berengaria had been taken to Sicily, where she had been all but ignored by King Richard.

She had accompanied him to Cyprus, though they had not travelled together.

Richard had married her there, and she had watched him ride off within hours of the wedding.

From Cyprus, they had continued eastward to Palestine, again in separate vessels.

For eighteen months, she had remained in the Holy Land, following in his wake like a leper, who must keep her distance.

And then she had been sent home, whilst he had made his way via Corfu and Dalmatia, into Leopold's clutches . . .

Berengaria was the Queen of England, but she had never reached her kingdom. Taken ill with fever on the journey, she had settled on Eleanor's lands in Aquitaine. 'It would be best for you to stay there,' Eleanor had told her gently, 'until Richard is released. You are not yet strong enough to deal with John and his rebels.'

Berengaria took that to mean that Eleanor did not think her completely recovered from the fever and the elder woman did not disillusion her.

Back in France again, John cheered the king's incursions into Normandy. In fact, Philip had gained very little, for he faced strong Norman resistance, and his own warlords were loath to take part in such a treacherous attack. It was not the act of a *chevalier,* raised in the ideals of honour and heroism. Besides, if Richard *Coeur-de-Lion* was released, there'd be hell to pay.

The prince stayed clear of the battlefields, though he soon knew the layout of every court in France. His derisive humour appealed to the more indolent courtiers, and he introduced a number of English fashions, particularly that of dining after dark. Before long he had been elevated to the head of the table, the charming foreigner who knew more anecdotes than a troubadour.

'Listen to this,' he told them. 'It's a true story. I read it in a translation of the Memoirs of the Arab prince, Usamah of Shaizar.' He waited for them to register appropriate admiration, then went on, 'Usamah wrote a great deal about us, that's to say the early Crusaders, though he did not know what to make of them. Animals, that was his conclusion. The Crusaders were as courageous as lions, and as strong as oxen, but as mindless as animals. The Moslems have always thought themselves superior to us, with their medicines and writings and coloured fountains and delicate palaces. But they should have come here,' John said, waving a hand at the ill-lit chamber and the courtiers, slouched around the table. 'We could have taught them the true virtue of loyalty and obedience. Where was I?'

Somebody said, 'It's a true story,' and the prince nodded. 'So it is, if Usamah's to be believed.

'He was at Nablus, a town we held in Palestine, and he became friendly with a Crusader who lived there. Anyway, the Crusader invited him home one day and, when they got back to the house, the knight went in and called to his wife. "I'm home, my sweet," or something of the kind.

'But she was not in the main room. The knight apologized to Usamah, went through to his bedchamber to change into one of those Arab robes they all wear out there, and – ' He raised a hand and waited for a servant to refill his glass. The courtiers were hunched forward, their faces expectant.

'Yes. He went in, and there was his wife in bed. With another man.'

His audience loved a good story, and became immediately involved in it. A few hands hovered over sword hilts. *They* were the knight. The wife was *their* wife. And if they found *her* in bed with someone –

Mimicking the cuckold, John growled, 'What's this? Who are you?'

And in a calmer voice, 'A Crusader like yourself, sire.'

'That may be, but why are you in my wife's room?'

'I was travelling through the town, and was overcome with weariness. The street door was open, so I came in.'

'But why in here?'

'I saw the bed. I could scarcely stand, I was so tired, so I lay down for a while. I must have fallen asleep.'

'But my wife was in the bed! Look, she is beside you!'

'Ah, that,' John mimicked coolly. 'Yes, well, you see, she was asleep when I arrived. And since the bed quite clearly belongs to her, I could not prevent her from using it, could I? As an honourable man, I could not turn her out.'

They were silent for an instant, and then the room reverberated with laughter. 'What – ' they gasped, 'what did he do, the husband, what did he do?'

'As Usamah tells it, he said, "If this happens again, fellow Crusader, you and I will fall out." '

'He said *that*? Didn't he – Oh, my God! "You and I will fall out!" ' They hugged themselves with delight and crashed together, shoulder against shoulder. The remark would be a by-word with them for months to come. Any small rift would be healed with the magic words 'You and I will fall out!'

They were still convulsed when a messenger sidled past the table and handed John a letter. He thought it odd that the parchment was almost entirely encased in wax, as though to give it the greatest possible protection.

It was difficult to open, and he gouged at it irritably with his dagger. The cold wax flaked off, and he found the edge of the sheet.

'You must have other stories like that, prince. By God, I'm going to read this Ushmer.'

'Usamah,' John said absently, sawing with his knife blade.

The letter opened like the petals of a dark, waxy orchid, and he read the ten words written on it.

'No,' he said.

He shook his head, as though rejecting an unreasonable petition, and again said, 'No.' He pressed the heels of his hands against the table top to stop them trembling. This time his denial was louder, the tone of his voice rising, and his companions fell silent.

'No, it's not possible. It is not possible. It is not!' And then he was on his feet, still saying no to the truth.

The message was perfect in its simplicity. It was untitled and unsigned, but it could only have come from Philip, and could only be meant for John.

It read, *De prendre garde à soi, car le diable étoit déchaîné.* Look to yourself, for the devil is loose.

Chapter Seven

THE DEVIL IS LOOSE

February – May 1194

Philip was not one to be stirred by pity. Men made their decisions and acted on them and took the consequences. But, yes, he supposed that if he found a dog with a broken leg he would move it out of the gutter, or put it out of its misery with a sharp knife.

But one could not very well kill a prince merely because he quaked and mumbled and gave offensive proof of his terror. Indeed, one could not do very much with him at all, except to keep him out of harm's way.

'You are in no immediate danger, can you not understand? Richard has gone to England – '

'He'll be back. Rely on it, he'll be back.'

'Doubtless he will,' Philip snapped, 'to retake those few Norman castles I captured. *I,* my shivering friend, not you. Given the choice, which of the two of us do you think he would prefer to hang? You force me to say this, John, but your safety lies in your incompetence!'

'I tried,' John retorted. 'I had any number of supporters in England.'

'Almost all of whom have been arrested and disinherited. You were as successful there as you have been here, which is the long way of saying you failed.' He moved to the head of the palace steps, reminding himself that he had come to hearten John, not destroy him. He would try again.

'Look, *confrère,* what I am saying is this. Richard will be carrying a list of those who turned against him when he was in prison. We will both be on that list, but your name will be buried at the foot of the sheet. You haven't *achieved* anything, don't you see? You've been like a worrisome rat, scuttling behind the walls – '

'Please,' John protested bitterly, 'no more praise!'

'You have made a few noises and gnawed a few holes, but you have scarcely endangered the building. You stay here, where you're safe. I'll get word to you if Richard returns.' He started down the steps of the Louvre, the Parisian palace on which he had lavished so much care and money, then turned back again to tell John, 'Even so, it might be as well if you rehearsed your story. He will demand *some* explanation for the rat-holes.'

John watched him go, clamped a hand to his head and muttered to himself under his breath. The mannerisms were back.

The people felt justified in taking a holiday to mark Richard's return. They'd paid enough for him, after all, and they were determined to see him for themselves. So the journey from the coast to the capital became a long, leisurely parade, exactly what Richard enjoyed.

He had been met by Eleanor and once again they rode side by side. But this time they were not allowed the privacy of a covered cart. Their special reunion would have to wait until they reached London and found a room that could be bolted from the inside.

The general opinion was that the king looked well, considering he'd been in prison for over a year. But it would take more than a German cell to dampen the spirits of Richard Lionheart!

Nevertheless, many of the spectators were disappointed that he had not escaped. They knew that Eleanor had the ability to turn into a bat whenever it suited her, so why had Richard not become a lion, and pounced on his gaolers? Well, no matter, he was here now, in fine, regal form, and they could look forward to months of bloody vengeance.

The populace would be in no danger, for his quarrel was not with shop-keepers and craftsmen and peasants. It was with the barons who had supported John Hideaway, John Softsword, Prince Treason. They were Richard's target now, and everyone knew he was an expert archer.

It felt strange, knowing that one's overlord might be hanged within the week, but it did not come often to the impoverished subjects, and they made the most of it. Let him kill every baron in the land, and good-riddance. When that happened, they'd take another holiday.

'Give me a name,' Richard said. 'Anywhere that still declares for John.'

There were not many, though one of John's most important castles, Nottingham, continued to defy the efforts of Marshal and Fitz Renier. It had been under siege for several weeks, but they had made no impression on its great, grey stone walls. Back in London to greet the king, they said Nottingham.

'Very well,' Richard agreed. 'Nottingham it shall be. We'll make an example of it, eh, messires? I'll pretend it's garrisoned by Moslems.' He winked at them, and they felt a surge of compassion for the rebels. It would be no pleasure playing the Moslem to Richard's Christian.

The return of the Lionheart sent the barons running for their armour.

Only a few had openly declared for Prince John, and most of those had been imprisoned and dispossessed. But there were many more who had decided the king's reign was at an end. Some were convinced that Henry of Germany would keep him a prisoner for life. Others believed the emperor would sell Richard to his eager enemy, Philip Augustus. And there were a handful who simply rejected the story of Richard's capture. No one could seize the Champion of Christendom; he was either at liberty, or he was dead.

So, guided by their ambitions, they had looked to John as the next King of England. Fortunately for them, however, they did not take up arms against Eleanor and her party, but remained in their castles, waiting to welcome the prince.

And then, instead of John, Richard stepped ashore, and the barons thanked God they'd kept their mouths shut. After that, they ran for their armour and hurried to join the king on his march to Nottingham.

No sooner did they reach the growing army than they sought audience with Richard and assured him of their unswerving loyalty. They had always known he would return to them. Their faith had never wavered, not for an instant. Praise God he was safe. Praise God he was unharmed.

He welcomed them and helped them to their feet, then told them to find a place in the line. They went, sweating with relief, determined to be in the forefront of the assault. They were worried men, these undeclared traitors, and guilt made them remarkably obedient.

The royal army reached Nottingham on 25th March, and camped alongside Marshal's small besieging force. His troops were glad of the respite, though they were unimpressed by their come-lately allies. If the army had rallied a few weeks earlier, Nottingham might now be in royalist hands, and the besiegers would be at home with their families.

But their efforts did not go unrewarded, for the king toured the camp, stopping to speak with constables, sergeants, even the common soldiers. Marshal and Fitz Renier singled out eight squires, and Richard knighted them on the field. Then, with supreme disdain for the rebels, he strode within arrow-shot of the castle, turned his back on the walls and addressed the original contingent. The men stood enrapt, hearing the king tell them – the Lionheart tell *them* – that they had earned his love and admiration, and would be offered a place in his personal troop.

A crossbow quarrel whirred through the air and buried itself in the ground, ten feet to his left. He glanced at it, then walked across and straddled the short, thick shaft. The soldiers cheered his courage, ignoring the fact that the crossbow was notoriously inaccurate. Only blind luck would send the next shaft along the same path.

Richard said, 'Men who fight for the stability of England deserve recognition. Give your names to Fitz Renier, and I shall keep you with me, as my special guard. You'll be able to tell your friends that you are around the king, day and night. You understand, I cannot afford to pay you much, though the honour is beyond price.'

More arrows and quarrels flew from the castle, and he moved unhurriedly out of range, to be swallowed by cheering soldiers.

The only ones who did not stamp and shout were Marshal and Fitz Renier, for Richard had just stolen the men they had trained and equipped. There would be no compensation, for the king would merely shrug and say, 'They volunteered, didn't they? They were free to stay with you, if they'd wished.'

The castellan of Nottingham, Ralf Murdac, peered down from the battlements, unwilling to believe what he had heard. 'Yes, yes, I can see it's an army! But it is not led by King Richard. What do you mean, set free? He can't have been set free! Henry would not – Of course I'd know him if I saw – He's where? Christ, man, hold the spear steady, so I can look along it! No, I still ca – Aah, *Jesu*, yes, I can. You're right. That's him. I can see him now.' He spat over the wall and climbed down from the watch-tower. 'Now we *are* under siege,' he muttered grimly. 'He's brought his machines with him.'

And so he had. Arblasts, the great crossbows mounted on platforms; spring-loaded espringales, another form of cross-bow, but one which loosed a longer, spear-like missile, power-ful enough to transfix a horse, or pass clean through a wooden wall. There were four-wheeled mangonels, in which rocks, or bundles of burning, tar-soaked straw were piled in a metal bowl, then catapulted over the walls; these and massive, sling-shot trebuchets, hurling down showers of flints. There were sixty-foot-high assault towers, and portable hoardings, behind which the archers and infantry could crouch before they made their final run at the walls. They were all there, with the ladders and grappling hooks and battering rams, all for use against the Moslems of Nottingham.

In the preceding weeks, the rebels had made several sorties from the castle. In one such counter-attack, a number of them had been captured by Marshal's troops. When Richard heard of this, he told Marshal to make over the prisoners to him.

Suspicious of the king's intentions, Marshal said, 'They have already been questioned, and they're not worth ran-soming. They gave me their word they would take no more part in the action, so I was about to turn them loose.'

'Good. Then when you do so, send them in my direction.'

'Why do you want them, king?'

'I'll use them to threaten Murdac, that's all. Now, send them along.'

'Use them?' Marshal pressed. 'In what way?'

'In any way I choose, Pembroke. As it pleases me. Do as I tell you, so we can still be friends.' He was smiling, but there was a dangerous tremor in his voice. He strode off, shouting something at the catapulters, and a dozen flaming bundles hissed through the air. Three of them failed to clear the castle wall, burst against the grey stones and fell back, scorching the grass. Wedges were driven under the front wheels of the mangonels, and the next fireballs disappeared over the battlements.

Richard returned with an easy 'Come along, Marshal. Lend them to me. I want things ready when we stop the barrage.'

Keeping his voice low and level, Marshal insisted, 'I must

know why you want them, king. They are in my charge and, now that they've given their word – ' He got no further, for Richard's suasive manner fell like a mask. He clenched his fist, struck Marshal hard in the neck and stormed past, bellowing for the prisoners. They were brought forward by members of the original contingent, ignorant of the dispute, and Richard directed them toward a second group, who were digging post holes in the ground.

Enraged by the blow, Marshal stared at the workmen, his worst fears confirmed. His neck still bore the imprint of Richard's mailed fist.

The barrage ceased. The post holes were completed, and gibbets set up in a line before the castle. The prisoners' arms were pinioned behind their backs. A noose was tightened around each man's neck, the other end of the rope being taken by three or four soldiers. The king then tilted his head, cupped his hands around his mouth and shouted up at the walls. 'Ralf – Murdac . . . This – is – Richard – of – England . . . Show – yourself – and – see – my – last – offer!'

Marshal moved forward. He saw Richard turn and say, 'Bar that man!' The members of Marshal's contingent hesitated, but many of the newly-pledged barons were eager to perform. They blocked his path, though they did not dare manhandle him, or lift their swords. 'Be sensible,' they said. 'This is no time to turn pious, Pembroke. No, stay back! Do you want Murdac to see us fighting amongst ourselves?'

'Once only,' Marshal said. 'Get out of my way.'

The prisoners waited, ropes around their necks. The hanging crews waited, looking to Richard for guidance. The barons waited, as Marshal hefted his sword. And Richard squinted up at the walls, waiting for the rebel leader to appear.

Then there was a sudden spasm of action. Fitz Renier and the one-eyed des Roches appeared beside Marshal. They were three against seven, but it was the seven who flinched. Richard studied the empty wall, turned to his hangmen and, as Marshal howled with anger and barged forward, motioned for the prisoners to be lifted from the ground. Eight ropes were hauled taut, and the men choked and kicked, and their bowels opened. With that, Marshal's control evaporated, like steam in a fire. Gripping his sword with both hands, he slashed left and right, while des Roches punched with the butt of his sword, and Fitz Renier clapped a baron across the head with

the flat of his blade. The strangled bodies jerked and grew
still and were dropped by the terrified hangmen. The barons
retreated before the madman, or flopped down, cut and
stunned. Standing beside the gibbets, Richard gaped at the
mêlée.

It was left to des Roches to grip the blade of his sword in
his link-mail mittens and bludgeon his closest friend to the
ground. Had he not done so, Marshal would have struck at
the King of England.

Too astonished to do more than swivel his head, Richard
stared about him at the litter of bodies. The eight hanged men
lay crumpled under the gibbets, each in the grip of a hempen
snake. Four of the barons were still on the ground, two
knocked senseless, two with deep cuts in their shoulders. And
their assailant, William Marshal, lay within five paces of the
king, his sword trapped beneath his body.

The entire army had come to a halt, and all eyes were on
Richard.

And then Murdac's men let fly from the battlements, and
more men were brought down. The hiss and thud of arrows
sent the besiegers scuttling for cover. Des Roches and Fitz
Renier dragged Marshal unceremoniously behind the nearest
hoarding, then carried him out of arrow-shot. Soldiers
ran forward to shield the king and collect the injured barons,
and the catapulters loaded their machines with flints and fireballs. Royalist archers and crossbow-men drove the rebels
from the embrasures in the battlements, while smoke rose
from behind the walls. The fireballs had ignited something in
there, a wooden roof perhaps, or one of the buildings in the
bailey. All the catapults and slingshots were now in action,
and lines of men were dragging forward two of the great,
swaying assault towers. It would not be long before the
grappling hooks went up, and then the ladders, and then the
ramps pushed out from the topmost platform of the towers.
The first assault troops were clustered impatiently behind the
hide-covered structures, following them in toward the walls.

If Ralf Murdac had survived the flints and crossbow bolts,
the arrows and fireballs, he had yet to face the swords and
spears, flails and spiked clubs, and Richard's own favourite
weapon, his murderous, double-bladed axe . . .

Marshal took no part in the assault. His neck was bruised
where Richard had punched him, his scalp torn by des

Roches' *coup de grâce*. He lay behind the lines, while his companions debated the situation. They could not say how Richard would react. He might forget the incident, or take Marshal's outburst as confirmation of weakness, madness, even treason. And Marshal, himself, might not let the matter rest. The prisoners had been in his care, but he had allowed the king to take them and hang them in cold blood – as an example to the recalcitrant rebel.

Both des Roches and Fitz Renier knew the forty-year-old story of King Stephen and the siege of Newbury, but they did not dwell on it. They decided to put as much distance between Richard and Marshal as they could and, before the warlord had recovered, he was placed in a cart and sent to one of his few remaining English manors, Badgeworth in Gloucestershire. Des Roches went with him, to protect him from robbers, and from himself.

Three days after the arrival of the royal army, Ralf Murdac and his commanders sued for peace. They opened the fire-scarred gates and emerged to kneel at Richard's feet, begging forgiveness. The victorious king hummed-and-hawed, then allowed them to keep their lives, on payment of a crippling fine. They would remain in the dungeons of the White Tower until the debt was honoured. Then they would be banished from England and all her possessions.

Many men would have found the sentence unendurable, but the rebel leaders gave their word and crawled forward to kiss the king's hand.

The surrender of Nottingham marked the end of John's parboiled insurrection, and left the Lionheart free to prowl his lands. Once, during the siege, he had asked if Marshal was dead, or what, and Fitz Renier had told him the Earl of Pembroke had been taken ill and and was being attended at home. He did not say where, and Richard acknowledged the news with a grunt. It was impossible to say what would happen when the men met again.

The king made plans to tour the country, accompanied by Eleanor and the court. The dowager queen was now seventy-two years old, and ready to retire from public life. She had seen Richard crowned and married, captured and released, and had witnessed his victory at Nottingham. John's revolt had been crushed, and England was once again under the firm leadership of the king and his counsellors. Eleanor was tired, but she agreed to keep her son company on his triumphal tour.

When the people of England had seen their king, he decided to return to Normandy and seek out brother John. The boy would have to be schooled this time, no doubt about that. And schooled with a stick.

Nothing that Richard did was done in silence, so the hedgerows around Barfleur were lined with men. They had been hired by John, paid by Philip and brought here by the imminent arrival of *Coeur-de-Lion*. Their task was simple, or, at least, simple to say. Kill the king as he rides inland from the port. One hundred marks for the man who slays him. And, if it takes five men to do it, one hundred marks apiece.

The remainder would receive fifteen marks; enough to keep a man alert, enough to make him greedy for the other eighty-five.

They were a disparate lot, these Frenchmen, mercenaries and friends of John, but they were the best that could be assembled at short notice. They were led by John's longtime companion, Belcourt, and a ruthless mercenary captain named Guido Bruni. The joint commanders had as much in common as a herring and a hog, and the ambushing force had already separated into two competitive teams.

The mercenaries were adept at this kind of work, and saw no reason why John's fancy friends should grow rich on their efforts. The thing was best left to those who knew what they were doing. It took skill to surprise a man and drag him off his horse, then slip the knife in below his ear, or under his belt. Skill that could only come with practice.

For their part, Belcourt and the French knights found the presence of the mercenaries extremely distasteful. It was one thing for *Coeur-de-Lion* to be killed, but another for him to be butchered by some foul-mouthed brigand. If the king was to die, it should be with honour, at the hands of a knight or noble, not in the claws of one of Bruni's animals.

So the ambushers had parted, the mercenaries watching one road, the knights crouched on another. It was to be the first attempted assassination of King Richard of England. And it was, without question, the most ill-conceived and ineptly-executed essay of the time. No blunder was overlooked, no mistake avoided.

To their credit, the ambushers had chosen the right day. However, they were both on the wrong track.

Had they worked in unison, as John and Philip had intended, they would have been on the narrow road that ran due south from Barfleur to La Pernelle. But their mutual antagonism had driven them apart, the mercenaries to the west, the knights to the east. They now watched the paths to Valcanville and Reville, leaving Richard free to ride between them on his way to La Pernelle.

The king and his entourage were well past before Belcourt's scouts brought the news. The French knights immediately dashed for their horses and galloped south-west, in an effort to head off the royal party.

Five miles on, they saw the banners of England and Normandy. Emitting half-forgotten war cries, they thundered to the attack, only to lose all momentum in an overgrown orchard.

The sixty or so mercenaries had also learned of Richard's passage and set out in pursuit. They did not usually work on horseback, and their skill with a knife was not matched by their control of a frisky destrier. They passed Belcourt's men, still lost among the fruit trees, glimpsed the pennants and standards, and allowed their horses to carry them forward.

Too late, they realized that the flags did not belong to Richard's party, but to his loyal Norman barons, who had come to welcome him to his duchy. Four hundred mounted men, with twice as many foot-soldiers.

Howling with frustration, Bruni's men dragged at the reins, as often as not pulling the horses on top of them. Those mercenaries who managed to avoid the Norman cavalcade plunged away among the trees – and on to the swords of Belcourt's wandering knights.

Belcourt himself had been knocked from the saddle by a low branch and, by the time he had remounted, his knights were dispersed throughout the orchard. But he had seen the banners, then heard the shouts from beyond the trees, so he knew the battle had been joined. Yelling encouragement, he went forward again, unaware that he was inciting his men to attack the mercenaries. Blows were exchanged, then cries of recognition, then further howls of panic as the Normans advanced into the orchard.

They fled side by side, Belcourt and Bruni, followed by the remnants of their troops. The puzzled Normans collected a few strays, hanged the mercenaries and kept the knights for ransom. It was some time before they would believe their captives' story. But, since all the prisoners said the same thing . . .

The assassins regrouped. They were not finished yet, not by a long way. True, they *had* allowed the king to pass unchallenged, and *had* lost themselves in the orchard, or let their horses run away with them. And, yes, they *had* attacked the wrong group. Twice. But they were not done for yet.

Reluctantly, Belcourt and Bruni agreed to rejoin forces, and they set off in a wide, westward arc, hoping to come upon Richard just north of La Pernelle. That stretch of the path was unprotected by hedges, so they decided to charge the king's entourage from the side and sweep it off the road. Such phrases gave them fresh heart, and Belcourt thought of himself as the broom of France.

They rode fast, in an effort to out-distance the welcoming force, and eventually raced to the brow of a long, low hill, from where they could see La Pernelle and the open track.

And there was King Richard, with various bishops and barons, a small troop of knights and the usual contingent of clerks and household servants. And, beside him, smiling at something he had said, *his mother! Eleanor of Aquitaine.*

Half the assassins deserted immediately. Belcourt looked round to see them streaming away down the slope. He raised a hand in silent admonition, then let it fall again. He wished fervently that he had gone with them, wherever they were bound.

'Well?' Bruni grunted. 'What do we do about that?'

'I admit, I did not expect the queen – '

'We'll never get near him, not when he has his mother to guard. He'll hack us down before we've – '

'Maybe, maybe. I was thinking of John. He won't want his mother killed, and one can never be sure in a skirmish.'

'How you spout,' Bruni sneered. 'You're terrified to move, that's the truth. You know how Richard is about her. He'd kill us before we'd reached the road. Well? What *do* we do?'

Below them, one of the entourage called, 'Men on the hill, lord king.'

'I saw them,' Richard said, gazing up at the line of horsemen. Some were dressed in hauberks and gambesons, and carried shields emblazoned with the simple devices of the French nobility. Others struggled to control their destriers, and wore rough, workaday clothes. But he was pleased to see that, rich or poor, noblemen or commoner, they had turned out to greet him. He responded to their stiff, weary salute, then took Eleanor on into La Pernelle . . .

John looked to see if it was a joke, and realized it was not. 'And then you *waved* at him? You went there to kill him, and ended by *waving*? Nails of Christ, I don't know what to say. I promised Philip – I told him you could be trusted. I said you – Oh, never mind what I said.' He stared at Belcourt, shook his head, then stared anew, looking for the flaw in his friend.

'You know where we are now, don't you, Belcourt? I mean, the position we are in. We must ask King Philip for – how many took part in the fiasco?'

'A hundred and twenty, thereabouts.'

'A hundred and twenty,' John repeated tonelessly, 'or thereabouts. So, at fifteen marks apiece, we must ask the king for one thousand eight hundred marks. Or thereabouts! And don't forget the ransoms. You lost eighteen of his knights in the orchard, isn't that what you said? So he has them to pay for. And then there are the dead to be explained away, and the horses replaced. Better and better. And for me, the best of all.' He stabbed his chest with a finger. 'The prisoners will talk. They will tell the Normans who hired them, and the Normans will tell Richard. Will have told him! By now he must *know* it is me!'

'If it had not been for your mother,' Belcourt started, then gave up. He felt he had said and done enough. John seemed to share his opinion, for he waved his friend away and went off mumbling.

Now Richard's here, Normandy will revert to him in a week . . . And then he'll come for me . . . For Philip as well, but he can take care of himself . . . He'll come here to Paris and . . . No, wait, Philip will not allow that . . . Ah, yes, I can see what will happen . . . Philip will wish to save his lands, so he'll make a treaty with Richard . . . And give me to my brother, tied and bound . . . Well, you'll have to hurry, sweet Augustus, for I'm already on my way . . .

As good as his mumbled words, he went down to the stables, collected two fresh palfreys and set out through Paris, in the direction of the setting sun. Philip had long ago told him to rehearse his story, and John expected to be word-perfect by the time he surrendered to the Lionheart.

It was an age that prided itself on its chivalric ideals and traditions of courtesy. Fair women were prized and protected, immortalized by poets and jongleurs, depicted as gentle and dignified creatures, sometimes too perfect for mere men, often as man's witty and worldly companion.

But it was also an age in which queens and chatelaines were valued for their wealth and inheritance, then were discarded with the sound of wedding chimes.

King Philip's sister, Alais, had been unluckier than most, for she had been put aside even before she was wed.

Isabel de Clare had been one of the more fortunate heiresses, for her love was requited and she had borne Marshal two strong-limbed sons. So far as she knew, he had remained faithful to her, and he seemed eager to be with her whenever he could. On occasion, he was absent for weeks and months at a time, but they exchanged letters, and she had her family and friends. All in all, she deemed herself well rewarded.

She was particularly pleased now, for both Fitz Renier and des Roches had asked her to do all she could to keep Marshal in England, whilst Richard was abroad. Something about an unresolved argument at Nottingham.

It could not be said that Countess Hadwisa felt well rewarded. She was aware that John had never really liked her, either as a woman or as a friend. He had married her hastily enough, in defiance of the Church, but that was only to secure her inheritance. Since then – apart from that one short period when he had wooed the English court – she had been left to her own devices. She was neither a fool, nor insensitive, and she had known then that his laughter was hollow, and that the presents he had heaped upon her had been paid for with her own money. But at least she had been on his arm, his wife for all to see.

And then he had gone to France, to help Philip foment rebellion during Richard's imprisonment. News of Richard's release had left John cowering in Paris, and he had been there ever since. And not once had he suggested that Hadwisa should join him, not once in, what, fifteen months, nearly sixteen?

Small wonder the ladies of England had stopped glancing at her belly. No seed takes that long to flourish.

But the most tragic of all was the gentle and passive Berengaria of Navarre, the forgotten Queen of England. Her marriage had been a mockery, salt steeped in vinegar, and the news that Richard had arrived in Normandy did little to sweeten the taste.

According to the messenger, sent down to Aquitaine by the sympathetic Eleanor, the king had come ashore at Barfleur last Thursday. The unfortunate emissary did not know why that information should have made Berengaria weep so bitterly, but then neither did he realize that last Thursday had been 12th May, the second anniversary of her unconsummated marriage.

He waited, fidgeting with embarrassment, unable to meet the accusing gaze of Berengaria's servants. He wanted to shout at them, 'It has nothing to do with me! I didn't start the tears!' But he decided there was less risk in silence, and contented himself by kicking at the uneven tiles on the floor.

Some while later, a clerk came in to tell him he was to stay the night. In the morning he would conduct Queen Berengaria to her husband.

'And don't uproot the floor, unless you're prepared to re-pave it.'

By the time John had located his brother, he had no need to act. His arduous, erratic journey had taken him from Paris to Evreux, north toward Rouen, then south-west, following the rumours to Lisieux. He had been recognized twice on the way and, during his second bolt for freedom, had been forced to abandon his other palfrey. Since then, he had continued without a change of horses, and with an almost empty purse. Bone tired and caked with dust, his clothes and body rancid with sweat, he was the picture of contrition. There was no need to adopt a penitent expression; his appearance was sorry enough.

As he neared Lisieux he met men who had actually seen King Richard. On the outskirts of the town he stopped a priest, who told him *Coeur-de-Lion* was staying at the Archdeacon's house; follow Tower Street as far as the square, the house is on the north side.

He went on and was accosted by Norman soldiers. They did not know him beneath the grime, and he did not identify himself for fear of being murdered on the spot. Instead, he claimed he had an urgent message for the king, then allowed them to take his sword and dagger and lead him across the square.

More guards escorted him inside, and he felt a sudden rising sickness in his throat. *He will not believe me! I'm too tired, I cannot handle him like this, I've let myself be trapped!* He fell against the wall, and the guards scowled at him.

'Straighten up, man! If you've brought the message this far, you can deliver it. He's not a real lion, you know. He won't bite your head off.' They nudged him forward. 'Get along, before he retires for the night. If we have to wake him, well, then he'll bite!' Another jab between the shoulder blades, and he was pushed along the corridor and into a small dining-room.

Smoke wreathed under the roof, but he could see the huge figure seated at one end of the table, a booted foot propped on a bench. Exhausted beyond reason, John blinked and caught hold of the doorpost. He heard one of the guards say, 'I'm sorry, my lord king, but he claims it's urgent. He must have ridden half a week to get here, by the smell of him.'

And then Richard's voice, undeniably Richard's, though John had not heard it for almost four years. 'Bring him in. I'll hear what he has to say. And find another mug for him. The local wine, not my own stock.'

John was propelled into the room, threw out his hands and swayed forward on the table. Richard glanced at him and dipped his head, indicating that he should get on with the message. Then his eyes rolled upward and he raised his head again, chewed meat showing in his open mouth.

'Alone,' John managed, 'with your per –'

'Yes,' Richard echoed, as though the word was foreign to him. 'Yes, alone.' He moved his arm without taking his eyes from John's face. 'Leave us. All of you. Everyone, get out!' Then he swung his foot from the bench and stood up, the smoke drifting around his red hair. The guards and servants withdrew, closing the door firmly behind them. The fire crackled and spat, like crones in anticipation.

The brothers gazed at each other until finally terror and fatigue sapped the strength from John's legs. He slithered down, his fingers clutching at the edge of the table, and finished up kneeling on the floor, his head bowed.

It broke Richard's heart.

Here he was at last, his stupid, wayward brother, hunched down to await the whip. With a deep moan of affection and disappointment, Richard moved around the table and lifted John from the ground. He caught the weakling in his arms, pulling him to his chest. 'Oh, John, look at you, boy! Look what's become of you! You're like a curled leaf, blown in by the wind. Look at you, how the dust lies on you. I did not know you at first, and the guards, they thought you a common messenger. My brother, pushed in by soldiers . . .' It was as much as he could take, and he held John to him and sighed out his sorrow.

There was the staircase in the mill-house at Sablé-sur-Sarthe, and the naked whore, the skin of her thighs soft to his touch . . . And below him his brother, massive in the doorway, his sword dark with blood . . . What had Richard called him then? 'Foolish and stupid, doting on rumour . . . But a traitor, no, never a traitor, for you lack the conviction of treason' . . . And he had gone down the stairs and fallen at his brother's feet and been forgiven . . .

He felt the heat of Richard's breath and, like the child he was supposed to be, clutched at the king's dark tunic. The movement made Richard moan again. John *was* a child, the only child the Lionheart would know. John Softsword, the ever-infant brother. And Eleanor, the only woman he could love. What were they all, but a group of actors, forced to play a family.

'Don't cling on so, boy. I won't harm you. It took courage to face me, I know that, as I know who misled you these past years. I can't hold you responsible for what they made you do, the Philips and the Frenchmen of this world. They see how vulnerable you are and – What's that you say?'

Remembering his story, John lifted his face from the tunic and murmured, 'If I had not supported him . . .'

'Yes?'

'He said – He said he would have you killed in prison. He vowed he would send a man into Durrenstein and have you assassinated . . . If I did not do his bidding in Normandy . . .'

There was some doubt in Richard's mind, but John's dust and tear-stained face banished it for ever. 'I never heard of that threat.'

'You wouldn't. It was kept secret. That was another thing, if I spoke of it, he would have done it. That's what he said. And then, when you were released, he turned his threat against' – *Quick! Who? Think of a – yes!* – 'against Queen Berengaria. That's why we sent men to attack you when you came ashore. God knows, I took no part in it, but Philip would not be dissuaded.' He felt Richard nod and release him, and he lowered himself on to the bench. He was utterly exhausted, but any man can find the energy to hear his reprieve.

A courageous servant knocked on the door and appeared with a mug and a flask of cheap, local wine. Richard took the mug from him, then told him to bring better stuff than that. 'My own stock, I thought I'd made it clear.'

'But, lord king, you said – '

'Fetch it!'

The servant vanished again, shutting the door.

For a long time Richard gazed at his brother. Then, in a quiet voice, he said, 'You think yourself clever, don't you, boy? But I know you for what you are, what you will always be. You blame Philip for your recent transgressions, and for the most part you're right. But it was not to save me, or Berengaria, that you sided with him.'

'I promise you – '

'No, no. You'd be well served by my death, and I doubt if you've ever met Berengaria. You sided with Philip – ' He paused, but knew it had to be said. 'You sided with him because you love him. That's why, isn't it? Tell me the truth, boy. That's why.'

John shrugged to control his astonishment. He had expected Richard to accuse him of throne-hunting, or fratricide, or joining Philip for money, or security, but never for – love?

'Don't frown so deep,' Richard said. 'There's no shame in it.'

'There's no truth in it!'

'Aah . . . We are brothers, you know. And I heard how you discarded Hadwisa. You are, what shall I say, more like me than you like?'

'I wish the wine would come,' John diverted. 'I'm so tired.

I will do anything you say. Punish me how you will, but for God's sake don't accuse me –'

With sudden vehemence, Richard snapped, 'It is not you who should be punished! It's Philip! I offered him *my* friendship once, but he spurned it. It seems he has done the same to you. I *wanted* him for a friend. The West could have been united, if only he had, if only he'd – been kinder.' He twisted away and stood glaring into the fire. Under his breath, he murmured, 'More amicable.'

So that's it, John acknowledged. And Philip never said a word. Richard loved him and was rejected, and now he wishes the same for me. Well, well. The Angevin brothers, cooing over the Capetian. But why not, if Richard is determined to believe it?

'You have broken through me,' he said. 'As you know, I am one for the women, but yes, I did come under his spell.' He gave what he hoped was a bitter laugh. 'Though with scant result. He roped me with you, Richard, in what he said.'

The king turned from the fire, his face reddened by the heat. 'He spoke of me?'

'Not with any great favour, and I'd rather not repeat –'

'Yes! Tell me. What did that fish have to say? I want to know.'

'I must warn you, I have no strength left. If you get angry, I cannot resist you, so keep in mind; I am repeating, not inventing. They are his words, not mine.'

'I've told you, you won't be harmed. What did he say?'

John made a show of raking his memory, then invented. 'He said you insulted him with your protestation of affection. You are like a wild beast, he says, gross and noisome, uncaring where you squat.' For balance, he added, 'I'm as bad, in other ways. I hiss where you belch, and he advises us both to find – more suitable animals. For me the leveret. For you the tusky boar.' He lifted his dust-caked shoulders and, with a final effort, looked directly at his brother. 'Can you still doubt why I left him?'

Richard shook his head, as though to dislodge the words from his ears. *So Philip is insulted by my approaches. I'm gross and filthy, am I, and best suited to mount a boar? Well, we shall see about that! As I root his petty kingdom out of the ground! As I toss him to Hell on the tusks he gives me! Oh, God's legs, we shall see about that!*

His fury imbued him with almost comical strength. He brought his fist down on the table with such force that the wood lifted, throwing John to the floor. He writhed in pain, and Richard hurried to collect him.

'You stay by me, boy, and you will witness the death-throes of France!' He was close to tears, the lion-called-swine.

Chapter Eight

MIDSTREAM

June 1194 – October 1197

Well, Eleanor thought, what else did I expect? Why else did I tell her Richard had arrived, if not to bring her up here? I'm becoming so devious in my old age, I have to trick the truth from myself.

She had had two years in which to ponder the problem of Berengaria, but even now her emotions were tangled. Richard was what he was; her son and Berengaria's husband. An absent king, and yet the most exotic figure in Christendom. A lion in battle, and a deserter from the marriage bed. A giant of a man, who preferred soldiers to civilians and men to women. All women, that is, save Eleanor.

Not for the first time, she wished a physician could do what God had failed to do – make an incision in Richard's scalp, and in John's, and transfer some of the Lionheart's courage and Softsword's lechery. Physicians were fond of making the cruciform cut and tapping a hole in the skull to let out madness, so why not extract virtues, or useful vices? If only that could be done . . .

Her feelings about Berengaria were no less mixed. The woman was too passive, as Richard had maintained. She had allowed her husband to push her aside, when she should have clung to him, claiming her rights. Who was to say she could not have changed him, had she persevered? But, in fairness to Berengaria, no one had ever told her what change was required. She did not know the nature of his disease, so how could she effect a cure?

Nevertheless, Eleanor welcomed her to Lisieux, and made light of Richard's absence. 'He is conducting the campaign against Philip, and it goes well, I'm glad to say. He's already driven the French out of Verneuil and Evreux, and, the last we heard, he was at Loches. He's also reconciled with John, who has gone to hold Rouen for him. As soon as this present offensive is over, we'll make the king behave like a husband again. It's time he came home to you.'

She nodded encouragement, but noticed a stubbornness in Berengaria's manner. The young queen did not smile so willingly, nor let the smile linger. I'll hear your reasons, she signified, but they will make no difference. You know what it has cost me to come here. I have buried my pride and exhausted my patience. I am like a camp-follower, a whore dogging the troops. You are also a proud woman, Eleanor, so you must know what I have suffered. But I am here now, and I shall not be put off again.

All that was clear in her expression, that and the fear in her eyes. She *had* submerged her pride, and let the world see her trailing after her husband. But what if he refused to meet her? What if she insisted on following him to his camp or castle or wherever he was, and was then refused admission? But, no, he would not be so cruel. He would not shame her again, as he had by ignoring her in Sicily, deserting her on her wedding day in Cyprus, leaving her to traipse after him through Palestine. If she appeared before him now, and spoke of her love for him, if she let him see for himself how she still adored him, then surely he would not turn her away.

But her eyes showed how uncertain she was.

'I would rather not wait,' Berengaria said. 'I have no home unless you mean the house you lent me in Aquitaine.'

'England is your home. As queen –'

'England? It's a foreign country to me. I have never been there, and it was you, yourself, who told me not to come. You said I was not strong enough to deal with John and his barons, do you remember? At the time I thought you were referring to my recent illness, but since then I have begun to wonder. Are you keeping me from him, Eleanor? Is there some reason why I should not see my husband? Or is it as I have long suspected, that he does not wish to see me?'

'My dear –'

'Or perhaps I have been deposed, but not yet informed. We hear so little of importance, in Aquitaine.' Again a small smile quickly herded away. 'Tell me,' she said. 'What does prevent me riding to Loches, or wherever he is?'

'Nothing,' Eleanor replied. 'You are the Queen of England, and that includes Touraine. But, whilst he is involved in this campaign – Well, everything takes second place to Richard's love of war. Later, when he has driven the French from his duchy –'

'He will drive them from somewhere else.' She moved forward with the firmness of desperation, and caught Eleanor's hands in hers. 'We are alone now, Lady Eleanor, and it is time we spoke our thoughts. You have been gentle with me in the past, and I know you wish to keep me from harm. But, whatever kindnesses we feel for each other, we have nothing in common as women. Indeed, we are as different as two women can be! You do what you wish, but I *must* speak my thoughts!

'You have eaten, Lady Eleanor, but I have not yet been fed. You are more than seventy-two years old. You have had your marriages, and your kings. You have been the Lady of France, and the Lady of England, and nine times a mother! *Nine times!* And what have I had, but a presence beside me at my wedding, and then *nothing*! I love Richard. I live for him, and dream of him, and he is never there!

'*You* brought me to him. *You* fostered the marriage. *You* made me his wife! And now I – I *command* you, take me to him, or tell me why you will not!'

Wincing with pain, Eleanor said, 'These old bones are brittle, my lady. I deserve some torture, no doubt, but not my fingers crushed.'

'Will you take me to him, or not?'

'When you arrived, yes, it was my intention that you should see him as soon as possible. But what you have just said has shocked me to my senses. You are right, my dear, I have eaten. Twice, really; once with King Louis of France, and again with Henry Plantagenet. And I did give birth to nine children, that's also true. *And* I put you with Richard.

'But to answer your question afresh, it's yes and no. Yes, I will take you to him – we'll start today, if you like – but if I do so, I will not speak my thoughts. You'll have to deal with him as best you can, and make of him what you may. Or I will tell you what you should have heard two years ago, even before your marriage, then let you decide if you wish to go on with it. One or the other, whichever you choose.' She massaged her hands, and watched Berengaria's expression harden.

'I have not travelled this far to play a game, Lady Eleanor. Aquitaine is famous for games and songs and stories; I have no need to set foot outside the house. I have come here with one purpose in mind. To see Richard and learn why I have been discarded. That's what I want to know. And you will tell me.'

Whenever I hear my age spoken aloud, Eleanor thought, I begin to feel it. 'I think you should be seated,' she said. 'Here, these chairs are not too hard. It's French work, as you'll see by the –'

'Under God, Eleanor!'

'Very well . . .' It was her turn to take Berengaria's hands, and somehow match her courage. 'Richard Lionheart does not love you. No, please, let me continue. I am the only woman he has ever loved, in the terms you understand. I do not think he has ever shared his bed with a woman, and I am the only one who can, well, afford him some comfort.' She felt Berengaria's recoil, but Eleanor's brittle old bones had become fetters of iron.

'Hear me out, I beg you. You will never hear worse. His preference is for men; it has always been. Christ knows, he is not an animal, but he has told me, oh, he's told me so much . . .

'He can talk with men. He is not afraid of them. Well, what man ever frightened the Lionheart? But there is something in him that sets him away from women. It's a poor analogy perhaps, but there are men who don't like children, and women who don't, I daresay. I don't pretend to know the cause, or the cure, but I know my son is averse to all women except me.'

'All women?' Berengaria murmured slowly. 'Then it is not personal distaste for me?'

'Oh, my sweet, no! It is not you! You are as fine a –'

'But it is, Eleanor. Don't you see? It has been, for two abject years. It was made so by you and the others who knew of this – aversion. What else was I to think, tell me that? What else, but that he found me unappealing, witless, a drudge? Yes, it is me, because you made it so. For two years and more, you let me believe it, when I had nothing else to believe! Oh, I had my suspicions; after all, I viewed him from afar in Sicily and Cyprus and the Holy Land. I saw him surrounded by his soldiers, but, do you know what I thought, what was *my* preference? That even if he was not with me, he did not sniff after other women. Isn't that sad, Eleanor, that I thought him entirely faithful.'

This time Eleanor did not resist as the young queen withdrew her hands.

'And I shall always wonder . . .' Berengaria said. 'If I had not smothered my pride and come up here . . . How much longer would it have gone on? How many more years would you have kept me in ignorance? How much more of my life would have been wasted before I learned the truth? Two years, would you say? Five? No, not five, for I'd be an embarrassment to England by then. My guess is another two at the most, before you worked to have the marriage annulled. And you would, wouldn't you, Eleanor? There is not one thing in this world you would not do – for the Lionheart.

'It's strange,' she concluded. 'What you have told me – Though it is two years late, it does not diminish my love for Richard. But it makes me like myself somewhat better. Aquitaine is full of young men, and they think well enough of me. I haven't been unfaithful, you'll find no trace of that, but opportunities abound, thank God they do. Oh, and one more change has come over me. I now pray that you are soon consigned to Hell, Eleanor. You can marry Satan, and be a thrice-crowned queen.'

The next day, Berengaria, Queen of England and Princess of Navarre, started for her principality and obscurity. Neither England nor its king had any need of her, and she had no further need of them. Instead, she joined the innocent ghosts of history, Alais and Hadwisa and the legions of discarded women who haunted the hallways of the West. Berengaria continued to light candles for the salvation of Richard's soul, and she was given to periodic bouts of tears. But Richard never went to see her, and her pain was lessened by the knowledge that he never would. Why should he, when he had an army to choose from?

A few weeks later, the dowager Queen Eleanor retired to the abbey of Fontevrault. This had always been her favourite religious foundation, and she had done much to endow it. She did not die soon, in accordance with Berengaria's wishes, but lived on for another fourteen years, watching the world from the window of her cell. She had been the most important and influential woman of the age, the patroness of poetry and song, politician and Crusader, confidante and chatelaine, the mistress of a dozen men and the queen of two nations. She had been praised more lavishly, and despised more vehemently than any woman in the span of a hundred years. Eleanor of Aquitaine had always been remarkable, and would doubtless dominate the ghosts . . .

The border war continued. Richard drove the French from Loches and the fortresses of eastern Touraine, then swung north to gain a decisive victory at Freteval. The bulk of Philip's troops were routed, and the king himself was forced to flounder chest-deep across a tributary of the Loire. He left behind most of his personal treasury, together with his seals of office, a complete set of silverware and a trunkful of incriminating documents. These showed how long and hard he had worked to undermine Angevin authority in Normandy and the border counties.

But there was one puzzling aspect of the letters. In them, the French king often referred to Richard, though never in disparaging terms. He spoke of 'my proud enemy', or 'the ambitious *Coeur-de-Lion*', but never of 'the sweating boar, the king-cum-swine'.

There were two interpretations one could place upon his words. Either, he was more courteous with his pen than his tongue, or brother John had been lying. Whichever, it gave Richard pause for thought.

Prince John was still at Rouen, and fast wishing he wasn't. King Philip's flight from Freteval was now a thing of the past, and he had re-established his troops for a further attack on Normandy. He chose Rouen as his first objective, and the joint garrison commanders, John and a Crusader earl named Robert Pernel, were called to the walls to view the invading force.

Like Marshal and a few others, Pernel had never wavered in his loyalty to the king; first to Henry, then to Richard. He had accompanied two Crusading armies to the Holy Land, then returned to hold Rouen for his king. During Richard's imprisonment at Durrenstein, Pernel had successfully defended the Norman capital against three French assaults, but even he was impressed by the size of the present invading army.

Beside him on the city wall, John said, 'We have less than a week's food in store. And, at the last arrow count, we were down to sixty a man. I don't see how we can keep them out.'

Pernel scratched at the skin around his throat. It was dry and flaky, the result of an infection he had picked up in the East. Out there, Arab physicians had supplied him with an unguent that relieved the itching, but he had long since exhausted the supply. Here, in the West, nothing seemed to work, so he settled for the temporary relief of a good scratch.

When the itching had lessened, he turned to glare at John. The prince had been with him for almost two months, long enough for Pernel to cultivate a deep and abiding hatred of his compeer. John had shown he had talent – for seducing women, unearthing wine, or finding gamblers to play backgammon. But his greatest gift was to cast shadows, and demoralize the defenders.

'Tell me,' Pernel said. 'It's an achievement in itself to get you up here, on the ramparts. But why is it that, each time we meet, you find it necessary to tell me we lack this, or are weak in that? There's only so much water, you announce, or so many seams of grain. What will you do when the bins and quivers *are* empty? You'll have nothing left to say.'

'I know how you feel about me,' John retorted, 'and it's half what I think of you. What's your favourite litany, Pernel? "I shall hold this place until King Richard arrives, no matter what"? It should be embroidered on your tunic. But meantime, we run short of food and weapons. And now look – we cannot see the horizon for French banners! Or will you sing your song to them, and watch them all run away? You're out of time, Pernel, everybody says so. You belong in the past.'

'Everybody? Then they must have elected you as their spokesman, for they don't say it to me.' He studied the vast crescent of standards, then observed, 'You see there? The King of France . . . There's his emblem . . . He never came before, and it might be in our favour . . .'

'What might? If Philip gets his hands on me, I'd favour a quick death, that's all. What do you mean, it might be in our favour?' He scowled nervously at the invaders. They were drawn up out of arrow range, but he could see scaling towers and catapults under construction. Half a day at the most, and then the rocks would fall on Rouen.

'I mean,' Pernel said, 'if you cut off the head, the body dies. You must have heard that. If we seize Philip, we can dictate our own terms. We might even bring the war to an end.' He glanced at John again, then allowed himself a sudden, harsh laugh. 'Don't look so gloomy, prince! No one will ask you to go out. You're best employed here, as the prophet of doom, counting the flour-sacks.'

John replied with an obscene gesture, then hurried down the inner steps. But both men were aware that he had offered no argument.

Pernel stayed where he was, a hand around his own throat. There was much that he regretted in life, but, more than anything else, he was sorry he had not brought back a larger supply of unguent from the East.

Richard was still quartered at Loches when the travel-stained rider reached the castle. The scene was reminiscent of John's earlier arrival at Lisieux, but this time Richard recognized his brother on sight.

The prince's left hand was bandaged, and his hair had been scorched to the roots above his left ear. One side of his face was swollen, half-closing an eye. He hobbled badly, but only because he had lost the heel of his boot. This seemed to upset him as much as his injuries, and he quickly lowered himself into a vacant chair.

The main hall at Loches was a damp, rectangular chamber, its walls lined with peeling plaster. Today, it was crowded with knights and vassal barons, all of whom had responded to the king's clarion-call. Fresh trouble had broken out along the eastern border of Aquitaine, and Richard was determined to suppress the insurrection before it gathered strength.

John's arrival – and his condition – put an end to the council of war, though the barons did not disperse. They knew John had been ensconced at Rouen, and they wanted to learn why he was here, looking like this. They were intrigued by his injuries, for they could think of no creature on earth that was fast enough to out-run Softsword.

Slumped in his chair, John mumbled, 'I came straight to you, brother. I wanted you to hear it from my own lips first.'

'Get him some wine,' Richard said. 'And a physician. God's legs, boy, you've been wrestling with a demon. If you would rather wait until you're rested – '

'No, you must hear what happened.'

Richard nodded, then was left to prompt. 'Well, what's transpired?'

John squinted at the barons. He had not expected to deliver his speech in public, but he could see they would not be dismissed. There were several of the assembly he knew, but none he liked, so he addressed himself directly to his brother. 'Prepare yourself,' he said, 'though my looks should have warned you. Rouen is lost.'

There was a growl of dismay from the barons, and Richard asked the question that was already on their lips. 'Where is Pernel? Is he following you?'

'That stinking turncloak? He is *why* we have lost Rouen!' He sensed the barons move forward, and knew they did not believe him. Robert Pernel had a scabrous skin, but he did not stink more than most, and he had never been disloyal in his life. And who was the squirming Softsword to level such an accusation? More details, sire, and they had better be convincing . . .

Richard was equally astonished by John's outburst. 'You blame Pernel for the loss of Rouen? How's that?'

'Very simple. And keep your officers back, brother. I never speak well under pressure.' He waited for the barons to withdraw, then said, 'I heard what happened at Freteval, but it's a pity you didn't drown Philip while you were about it. As it is, he dried off and came against Rouen with the largest force I've ever seen. As soon as Pernel saw the king was there in person, he set out to capture him. At least, that was his claim, and he supported it by taking two hundred of our best men with him.'

'Pernel made a sortie, to capture Philip?'

'Well grasped, brother, but it's not what I said. I said, it was what he *claimed* to be about. In my opinion, he had quite a different plan in mind. I think it was his intention to leave me caged in Rouen, whilst he made his peace with the Frenchman. I would have been Pernel's dowry! How perfect, don't you see? He weakens the defence by two hundred men. The French take the city, and me with it. And, when you are told of the loss, you also hear that Pernel has been captured, and so appears blameless! How perfect, or it would have been, had I not escaped.'

One of the knights could stand it no longer. Robert Pernel was his hero, and he would not allow the Crusader to be disgraced by a creature like Softsword. With a shout of anger he ran forward and cuffed John on the shoulder.

'Liar! Pernel would never do that! He would not do it, I tell you! But you would! You'd do it, and worse!'

With a quick glance to make sure Richard was moving to the rescue, John lurched to his feet and engaged in a squalid shoving match with the knight. The king barged between them, hurling the knight back amongst his peers. 'Keep your places!' he roared. 'This is not the yard.' Then he resettled John in his chair, and again called for wine and a physician.

The terminals of the chair were carved to resemble a currant bush and an apple bough, and Richard threatened to crush the fruit as he leaned over his brother. 'What you say distresses me. This is not the Pernel we know. He has fought off so many attacks against Rouen, and he never turned against us in his life. But we'll leave that aside for the moment. Tell me how you came to be mauled like this, and all swollen out. You say you escaped –'

John hooked a smile on his lips and raised his bandaged hand in a plea for patience. Fear and fatigue were positive ingredients in his make-up. He had experienced them so often that, like a habitual drunkard, he knew how they would influence him, and how he would behave.

Fear, for example, could always be masked by anger or irritation. And fatigue was as much the residue of battle as of flight. Thus, a man who fights to a standstill is indistinguishable from a deserter who runs until he drops. Particularly so if they are both bruised and bloodied.

'Mauled, you call it? Swollen out? Is that all you'll allow, brother Richard? A bitter, step-by-step defence of Rouen, which is not a favourite city of mine, let me say, and that's the best you can do?' He thought it expedient to include the barons in his tirade, and twisted in the chair, pointing his bandaged hand at the knight who had cuffed him.

'You messire! You're very quick to strike a wounded man. But what if he strikes back, eh? What if he has fought his way free to bring you the news, and is tired of your far-away criticisms? *You* were not at Rouen, were you, or have you some magic powers, that let you see at such a distance?' He fumbled for his dagger, and tried to break Richard's grip on the chair arms. 'Almighty Christ! I will not be called a liar, and assaulted at will!' He struggled in the chair, but Richard restrained him without difficulty. Nevertheless, his indignation impressed the barons. Softsword was not one to draw a dagger when he could draw a measure of wine, but he seemed sincere enough in his fury. Perhaps there was some truth in his story. It was hard to believe, though stranger things had happened. And Pernel would certainly be well-rewarded, if Philip had laid hands on John. It was an unlikely tale, but not impossible. Every man would turn his cloak, if the price was right. Even Pernel.

Richard waited until John had sunk back in the chair, then turned to his barons. 'There will be no more outbursts, from any of you. My brother insists that Robert Pernel has weakened the defences of Rouen and allowed Philip to capture the city. When I heard it, I was disinclined to believe it. But now I am not so sure, and I'll tell you why.' He placed a hand on John's shoulder and stood over him, part protector, part gaoler. Then he gave his warlords his own extraordinary reasons for swallowing the bait.

'Prince John is a young man puffed with vanity. He always was. He admires his reflection, and lifts himself on his heels. We all know what he is, the way you know I am a born soldier, the way I know you – ' singling them out ' – you like dice, and would bet your entire family on a single throw. And you; you dislike conversation, yet talk to your horses. Others of you will ride miles for a wrestling match, or a woman with black skin, or a river stocked with salmon. Each to his own. But with John – Well, look at him.

'Look at the prince. Is this how he thinks of himself, bandaged and with a face like a bladder? He won't like to hear it, but look at his silly heels, snapped short. Do you really believe he would go this far, just to further a lie? He's my brother, and I love him, but I do not give the boy that much credit.'

There was a growl of voices and the shuffle of feet, but no one responded. Once again, King Richard had taken John by the hand and led him out of the maze. He knew John – as John – was quick and cunning, and master of deceit. But *brother* John, ah, that was a different animal. He was just a vain and foolish child, albeit a child of twenty-six. Richard would always find excuses for *brother* John, and would always step between him and his accusers. He had to, for he could never accept that Plantagenet blood, his brother's blood, was tainted. If John was at fault it meant that Richard's brother was at fault, and that brushed too close to the king. It would also mean that the Lionheart had been hood-winked all these years, by a boy in silly heels.

The wine arrived, brought in by the physician. John sipped it gratefully, whilst his wounds were dressed. He ignored the assembly, and took silent pleasure in the wine and the way things had gone.

The barons had not wanted to believe him, but Richard had persuaded them, or rather, deflected their aim. He had accepted John's story, and given his reasons. If the barons were to challenge it, they must also challenge their king. But it was obvious that none of them would step forward and cuff the Lionheart.

'You're fortunate,' the physician remarked. 'None of your teeth have come loose, and your hand is only skinned. Soak a glove in cold water and hold it to your face. It will reduce the swelling. As for your scalp, if you daub it with this ointment, the hair will grow again. I don't know how you did this, my lord – '

'Fighting my way from street to street, that's how.'

'Oh.'

And again, for the benefit of the unbelievers, 'Step-by-step.' He did not add that his injuries had been sustained in an effort to bore a path through the panic-stricken townsfolk, who had just learned that both their garrison commanders had disappeared.

After Rouen, King Philip made other gains in the north. Aumale fell to him, and Vernon. Further south, a second French army threatened the citadel of Châteauroux. Treaties were made, lasted a few months, then were broken. They took on the aspect of breathing-spaces, and both sides used them to reinforce their armies and review their tactics. The Capetian and Angevin empires teetered between expansion and annihilation, but the border remained like a string, pushed in from this side, pushed out from that.

More riders had arrived from Rouen, each with a different story. Some said they had seen Robert Pernel leave the city at the head of three hundred men, but others claimed he had gone out alone, or with fifty, or not gone at all. John encouraged the confusion, though it was finally accepted that the Crusader *had* made a sortie, and *had* been captured. It was also agreed that Rouen had been subjected to a heavy barrage of rocks and fireballs, and that no one could remember Prince John fighting his way anywhere, step-by-step. Naturally, with the city falling about their ears, they could not swear he had deserted them, only that they, themselves, had not seen him in the mêlée.

Once more afflicted with doubts, Richard had waved them away. Why was it, he wondered, that all John's stories raised contradiction in their wake? If he said he had had cold meat for dinner, there would be fish-bones on the plate . . .

But John knew Richard too well. If the king was to be finally convinced of his innocence, he knew he must prove himself on the field.

It was no easy task for Softsword to harden his blade, but, during the fading months of 1194, he led several successful raids in Touraine and along the borders of Aquitaine. The way he told it, he had stopped the French in their tracks.

He was aware of Richard's suspicions, and encouraged him to verify the stories. No victory was as glorious as John's description, but Richard acknowledged his brother's need to exaggerate. He had probably exaggerated King Philip's insults, and Pernel's treason. But, so long as one took what John said with a pinch of salt, he *could* be believed. It was an enormous relief to Richard, knowing that his brother was not the liar people maintained. He was a boy with an unfettered imagination and a craving for attention, and there was nothing so terrible in that. With proper guidance, young John might yet turn out to be a worthy Plantagenet. After all, it was not beyond the bounds of possibility that he would one day wear the crown of England. In another thirty or forty years . . .

They heard of further French advances.

'You know who we need?' Richard asked rhetorically. 'What do they call him, the Arab. William Marshal. He must have recovered from his affliction at Nottingham, and he knows Normandy as well as anyone. Send for him. And his companion, des Roches. England is safe for the time being; nothing will happen there. It's here we need the strength, and Marshal's just the man to take John under his wing.'

One of his attendants had the temerity to say, 'It was not an affliction at Nottingham, lord king. You two fell out over the hangings, if you remember.'

'No, I don't remember.'

'You took his prisoners, and hanged them as an example to the rebels. If you want him to rejoin you, you should send him some assurance that you still love him.'

'He knows it,' Richard snapped, 'else he would not still be

alive. Now that you've refreshed my memory, I remember him coming at me with a sword. Hardly an act of affection, would you say?'

The attendant waited, braving the king's gaze. Then, with a characteristic change of mood, Richard twisted a clawed signet from his finger. 'Here. Do you think he'll regard this as love enough?' He held up the massive ruby, engraved with the three leopards of England. It was a priceless gem, and easily recognizable as the property of King Richard. For one thing, no other Western monarch took such a size in rings.

The attendant nodded, and agreed to deliver it to Marshal.

Knights and nobles continued to arrive from the fiefs of Poitou and Aquitaine. Eager to join Richard in the defence of their lands, they reaffirmed their loyalty to him, told him how many men they had brought, then pitched their tents around Loches. The fact that they exchanged stone fortresses for flapping tents was, in itself, a measure of their fidelity.

They rode in at all hours of the day and night, and, one evening in mid-December, the king was informed that two men were waiting in the ante-chamber.

He had just returned from a victorious skirmish on the border, and was in an expansive good humour. The French force had been chased off without difficulty, and one of the *chevaliers* had taken an arrow in his buttock. This had caused paroxysms of mirth amongst the English, who conveniently forgot their own saddle-bound scars. They had trotted back through a bitter east wind and, when he had reached the castle, Richard emptied several flasks of wine in an effort to combat the cold and damp. He was now seated at the head of the dining-table, flanked by his brother and senior commanders.

He cut a wedge of salt-cured pork, washed away the unpleasant taste with more wine and told the servant to bring in the visitors. 'If any more arrive, keep them until morning. But I'll see these two.'

He thought it might be Marshal and des Roches, then realized that the emissary could only just have reached England. The sky above Loches threatened snow, so it would be worse in the north, and the messenger might be delayed several days at the Channel port of Barfleur. But, even with the country turning white, the Arab and his massive, half-blind companion should be at Loches by Christmas.

He chewed another piece of pork, threw it back as gristle on to his plate and turned to welcome the visitors. The first man was tall and cadaverous, the other stooped over, as though he spent his life writing in a poor light. They were both considerably older than the king, yet wore helmets, hauberks, the full outfit of war.

Coming forward from the shadows, the first man mouthed, '*Ayay uh Ahuse,*' then waited patiently for his companion to clarify, '. . . Aimer of Chaluz, my lord king.'

'*Eyeoun uh –*'

'. . . He is the Viscount of Limoges.'

Aimer gibbered something else and, while his companion repeated it, Richard stared at the hollowed cheeks and the hideous, misshapen mouth. And, inside the mouth it seemed, a divided palate.

Clarifying Aimer's words, the scholarly-looking knight said, '. . . My Lord Aimer would have joined you sooner, king, but he was taken with fever.'

For an instant, Richard's expression hovered between curiosity and repulsion. Then some sound Aimer made amused him, and he commented, 'It must have been a grave bout, Limoges, to leave you speaking another language. *Ayay?*' he mimicked. '*Ayay uh Ahuse?* I'll never master that!' He leaned back in his chair, one red-robed arm curled over the back rest, his smile seeking a response among his guests.

Aimer spoke again, and the translator replied, '. . . It may cause you amusement, king, but you should thank God you are not afflicted.'

'I do!' Richard agreed. 'My speeches would scarcely have the same ring, would they!' Again he tried to copy the impediment. '*I-yam-ee-ying.* You understand? I am the king. Did you understand that?' He laughed spontaneously, drunk and delighted.

Aimer looked at him, the viscount's eyes chiselled from an effigy. He uttered more sounds.

'. . . My Lord Aimer wishes you to know that he came here in good faith, to offer you his support against the French . . . He did not come to be ridiculed, and does not see how this . . . how this improves you in the sight of your guests.'

'It doesn't yet!' the king roared. 'But it will when I've

learned the language! Don't look so pious, whatever-your-name-is. Come here and teach me. I swear, I never heard such a thing!'

'. . . Nor will you again. Do you think that Lord Aimer, or any of his house, will serve you after this? No, by God, we will not . . . You fight on without us, and the devil guide you! You are no monarch of ours, Richard Plantagenet, not from today! . . . You are not halted in your speech, but there is a serious deformity in your mind!' The words were rapped out as clarification of Aimer's mouthings, and then the men turned and strode from the hall.

The senior barons, who were so often noted for their cruelty, sat huddled in embarrassed silence. Several of them had day-to-day dealings with Aimer of Chaluz, and they knew him to be a quiet, melancholic man, with a sympathetic manner that had evolved from his own affliction. But, as they had just heard, he could also be enraged.

There was not yet absolute silence in the hall, for Richard was still chuckling at the novelty of Aimer's words. As his laughter diminished, John excused himself from the table and hurried after the visitors. The appalling treatment the king had meted out had given his brother an idea, and he felt sure the Viscount of Limoges would be receptive. The details eluded him for the moment, but the foundations were there, and Aimer was just the man to help him build on them.

Marshal moved the ring into a circle of candle-light, so that Isabel and their sons could see it. The two young boys looked up at their parents and saw by their expressions that it was not the time to snatch and grab. Marshal told them the ring belonged to King Richard of England, and that it was now the property of the House of Pembroke. Then, as Isabel explained to the children that the animals were not dogs, but leopards, more like large spotted cats, Marshal asked the messenger, 'Are you quite sure he intends us to keep it, his own signet?'

'He does, Earl Marshal. As I told you, it's a token of his love, though I daresay he'll want it back if you refuse to join him. And don't concern yourself about its power. It has none. One of his advisers told him of a good way to raise money. You know his appetite for coins. Well, somebody suggested that, if he changed his seals, he could out-date all earlier grants and titles. With respect to you and the Lady Isabel, even you will need Richard's new seal on your deeds of property. For which you will have to pay a fee. But, even if the leopards don't growl, it's still a rare gift, the ring.' He had been made sufficiently welcome at Pembroke to risk adding, 'It occurred to me to sell it, and say I'd lost it on the way.'

Marshal matched his smile and replied, 'That wouldn't have done. I'd have found you and cut off your hands. Then you could have said you'd fallen under a plough.'

'My lord, it was only a joke! I would not have done it!'

'That's why you're able to clap.'

The boys had seen enough of the ring and started shouldering each other. Isabel separated them and took them across to where one of her maidservants waited by the fire. 'Put them to bed for me. If they behave, give them a piece of honeycomb. If not, let my Lord Marshal know.' With feigned severity, she asked her sons if they would abide by the arrangement. The elder was five-and-a-half years old, the younger just turned four. They nodded solemnly, aware that they could enjoy a brief wrestle and still cajole the maidservant into parting with the honeycomb. They knew her; she was soft and easy to manage.

Isabel rejoined her husband and the emissary. 'When will you leave?' she asked.

'In a day or two,' Marshal said. 'We'll collect des Roches on the way.' He managed to make it sound like a statement for the messenger, and a question for his wife. She nodded slowly, resigned to the inevitable.

They had been together for the longest, unbroken period since their marriage. Almost ten months had elapsed since he had been dumped in the cart and brought down from Badgeworth to Pembroke, his neck bruised where Richard had punched him, his scalp split by des Roches' mercy blow.

He had recovered quickly enough, but when Isabel heard about the hangings at Nottingham and of Marshal's subsequent attack on the king, she implored him to stay out of things for a while.

'I cannot detain you, no one can, but I beg you to let Richard go on without you. God knows, you deserve a rest, even if it's against your will. The war in Normandy will continue, whether or not you are there, and it's senseless to risk another confrontation with the king. Wait until he sends for you. I fear he'll do it soon enough.'

Marshal was then forty-eight years old, and ready to enjoy the first long respite of his career. As a young man he had seen service with several overlords, earned a reputation as one of the champion jousters and errant knights of the West, then gone on to serve King Henry, first as a soldier, later as the king's right arm – and legs.

With the death-flight of Henry had come the duel at the bridge, and eventual reconciliation with Duke Richard. Loyal to whomsoever was the justly-crowned king, Marshal had supported the Lionheart, accompanied him to Sicily, then returned to keep the balance between John and the hunchback, Longchamp. And, after Longchamp's expulsion, he had sold off his own lands to raise King Richard's ransom, and had gone to drive the rebels out of Nottingham.

Isabel had not needed to plead with him. He did deserve a rest, and had welcomed it.

But the glow of the ruby was like a beacon, blazing on one of the turrets at Loches. The king had sent for him, and he would go. The beacon was a signal, and the three leopards clawed at his sleeve, but he would have gone anyway. Not that he would tell that to the king, for Richard would be furious to think he had squandered a priceless ring on loyalty.

The messenger was quartered for the night, and the Lord and Lady of Pembroke took glasses and a wine jar to their rooms. When they were settled, and gazing at the fire in the corner hearth, Isabel murmured, 'This time we have had to ourselves . . . It's not something I shall ever forget . . . But whilst we were here, we heard about Queen Berengaria, and your patroness, the dowager Queen Eleanor . . . They have both retired from the world, from King Richard's world really, forced out by his inattention . . . Men can do that to their women and, for the most part, the women have no choice but to accept it . . . But I tell you, William – No, that does sound odd, I've had too much to drink, or too little – I tell you, Marshal, I shall not allow events to prise us apart . . .'

He was so quiet that she glanced at him, worried that he'd fallen asleep. But he was there, looking at her, his wine ignored. 'Go on,' he murmured, 'though I know what you're going to say.'

'Yes, perhaps you do, I think *you* do, for you have never made me feel discarded. But what I want to say – Go to

Normandy. Support the king. But if he commands you to stay on there, then command me to join you. I shall not tread down your heels, don't worry. But neither shall I be a widow-by-distance, a foreign wife, call it what you will.' She thought of something that had happened long ago, in the White Tower of London, and added, 'You know I don't flinch from thunder and lightning. Nor will I flinch from the snap of tent cloth. It's more natural for me to be with you, than a hundred miles away.' She paused, aware that she had no real control over what he did, or where he went, or how long he was away. She was his property, to be coveted, or abused, or ignored, as he saw fit. He had always treated her well and, to some extent, encouraged her to speak her mind. But tonight she had gone further, and made demands, and she awaited his rebuff.

'One year,' he said. 'It may be less, or more, I can't say. I don't know the extent of Richard's success. He might capture Philip in the week. Or he, himself, might be struck down. But I must allow him a year, is that fair?'

'Your sons will be twice as boisterous,' she smiled. 'Yes, it's fair.'

'I'll teach them to ride Norman ponies.'

Trusting the advice of her physician, who had so far been correct, Isabel said, 'Three ponies. You'll need three.' It was a reasonable statement from a woman who would, in her life, present Marshal with ten children.

And it was reasonable that he should receive the news with equanimity, since he had always intended to sire a large family. His smile was sufficiently warm and self-satisfied, but he would have been unbearably conceited, had he known that five of his ten children would be sons. And that each would, in turn, become Earl of Pembroke and Lord of Leinster. And that, as their father's name foretold, they would all earn the title, Marshal of England. Marshal the Marshal, for those with a turn of wit.

During the next three years, the nations devoted themselves to war. The struggle became more intense, for both sides were well-matched in manpower and determination. Philip Augustus continued to surprise his Angevin enemies, but Richard Lionheart remained unconquered on the field. The guile and quick-thinking of the former were balanced by the personal magnetism of the latter. Philip and his *chevaliers* would appear where they were least expected, ambushing a column of Norman knights, or overcoming one of the border watchtowers. But they wisely avoided pitched-battles, for they knew who would be leading the Angevin forces.

In the spring of 1195, King Richard was delighted to hear that Leopold of Austria had been thrown from his horse, broken a leg, and that the leg had become infected. In keeping with the times, a clumsy physician had amputated the limb and the duke had promptly died from loss of blood. With no sense of pity whatsoever, Richard thought it admirable that the Austrian should have been punished for draping his flag on the walls of Acre, and for daring to imprison the Lionheart. Serve him right. Let it be a lesson to all would-be upstarts.

Sometime later, England was delighted to hear of the death of the monkey, William Longchamp. Let that be a lesson, they thought, to all foreign upstarts.

On their arrival from England, Marshal and des Roches had been given an unrestrained welcome by the king. During the winter they had stayed with him at Loches, their backs pounded by their exuberant monarch. He had made no mention of the business at Nottingham, though, when there were prisoners or felons to be hanged, he had first sent Marshal on some errand to Tours or Chinon.

With the warm winds of spring, Richard had given Marshal and des Roches command of the troops in Touraine and Aquitaine. He, himself, had taken charge of the army in Normandy, and created a senior post for brother John. They managed to recapture Rouen and drive the French from a number of border villages, but they were unable to engage Philip on the field.

For more than a year now, nothing had been heard of Robert Pernel. Several of his friends had sent word to Philip, asking the king to allow them to ransom the Crusader, but he had done no more than admit that Pernel was alive, and a resident of Paris. He left it to the barons to decide whether the Crusader was there by choice, or as a prisoner. It was another example of his ability to sow dissension among the Angevins, and there were renewed squabbles between those who saw it as proof of Pernel's treason, and those who insisted the man was being dishonoured.

It was des Roches who found a solution, in the form of a senior French count who had been knocked senseless in a border skirmish. The man was a distant relative of King Philip, and des Roches informed the king that the count was alive, and a resident of Touraine.

Never one to overplay his hand, Philip immediately agreed to an exchange of prisoners. Robert Pernel and the French count were escorted to a ford on the border, east of Tours. Then, when both sides were satisfied, the two men splashed across the Loire, nodding to each other as they passed.

By now it had become apparent that the French were making more progress than their enemies. They had won no decisive battles, but the Angevin empire was being eroded, village by village, fief by fief. As yet, there was no cause for alarm, but it worried the leaders.

It worried King Richard, who led more reckless charges against the *chevaliers*. He could be seen with a dozen arrows lodged in the chinks of his link-mail tunic, and others that had pierced his boiled-leather boots. His reputation as a warrior was unsurpassed, but he was one lion loose on the continent, a devil loose, according to Philip, and no one lion or devil could patrol the entire Norman border.

It worried des Roches, who terrified the French by his appearance, but kept secret the fact that he was now totally blind in one eye, and afflicted in the other. He had long ago decided that he would not creep away to die, sightless, so he strained his good eye to the utmost and herded the enemy from Touraine. If he died in a headlong charge, well and good, but please God, not in an infirmary.

It worried Marshal, who had his family with him, and he, too, reaffirmed his reputation as a warlord. He had three sons now, as Isabel had promised, but he had not yet found the time to lift them on to their ponies. Recent French advances into Aquitaine convinced him that his wife and children must be sent back to England. He would ask his old friends, Fitz Renier and Malchat to assume the responsibility for their safety. The garrison at Pembroke could be trusted to defend their chatelaine, but he would feel happier knowing that Fitz Renier and Malchat were in residence.

Isabel agreed without demur. She had been with him at Loches for almost half a year, and was quite happy to return home in time for the birth of her fourth child.

And it worried Prince John, who thought seriously of defecting to the French. He had already suffered one severe shock this year – the sudden reappearance of Robert Pernel. The Crusader had greeted him civilly, then explained to Richard that he could well understand how John had mistaken him for a traitor. Perhaps he *had* been foolish to leave Rouen at such a crucial time. And perhaps he *had* been over-ambitious to think he could capture Philip. John had every right to doubt his loyalty, and to air his beliefs.

The Crusader scratched at his throat and gazed directly at John, not smiling, not scowling. It brought John to the verge of panic.

What was Pernel up to? What did he mean by these generous admissions? Why didn't he yell liar and go for his sword? Hell's dripping fangs, what *was* his game?

Since then, John had worried day and night, and his bed-chamber resembled an armoury. Pernel was re-established as Constable of Rouen, and he invited the prince to every conference, however trivial the agenda. Then he gazed at him, until John began to sweat.

In the leafless October of 1187, John was leading a patrol through one of the shallow valleys, east of Rouen. The patrol was surprised by a large French force, and the riders scattered. John managed to reach a nearby village, where he bribed a group of local children, who grudgingly directed him to one of their hay-store hideouts. He stayed there until nightfall, then fled back along the valley, leaving the children to divide a Byzantine bracelet into five equal segments, hacking at the silverwork with a borrowed hoe.

When he had regained the city, John barricaded himself in his chamber and surrendered to a spasm of tears. He could take no more of it; not Richard's bellowed encouragement, nor Pernel's penetrating gaze, nor the tension, nor the dangers, nor the miserable quarters he had been allotted, look, the place was alive with insects!

He would do what he should have done years ago. He would write to Philip.

When he had fled from the Louvre Palace and surrendered to his brother at Lisieux, John had claimed that he'd supported Philip for fear that the French king would have had Richard assassinated in Durrenstein, or Berengaria murdered in Aquitaine.

Now he told Philip an opposite tale. Justifying his flight from Paris, he said he had returned to Richard for fear that the Lionheart would punish the guiltless Hadwisa.

'You know I don't love my wife,' he wrote. 'It is your own sister, Alais, who stirs me. But, in all conscience, I could not leave Hadwisa to Richard's vulgar mercies. That was the only reason I left you, and I will rejoin you whenever you wish.

'Now that I have been with my brother again, after his absence in the Holy Land and in Durrenstein, I know he offers no future for me. He is a gross, rancid creature, more like a tusky boar. And, as you may know, he is unnaturally attracted toward you. He disgusts me, my dear Philip, and I would rather be with you, whom I admire and respect.

'Your recent victories have caused consternation in our camps, and it's time my brother made some reasonable settlement with you. When I join you, I will help you arrange the terms.'

As soon as he had dispatched the letter, John worried again, sure that he had overdone the sentiments. But, within a few days, he received a secret and compassionate reply. The King of France did not yet invite him to defect, but asked a number of searching questions, all of which required long and thoughtful answers. John replied as best he could, in the privacy of his insect-infested chambers.

And in that way he fell headlong into Philip's trap.

Chapter Nine

THE TRAP

November 1197 – April 1198

This was not the first castle he had designed, but it was to be the finest. Château Gaillard, on the outer bank of the Seine where the river looped eastward between Vernon and the recaptured city of Rouen. Château Gaillard, built to defend that city and command the eastern border of Normandy. Château Gaillard, named by its designer and meaning vigorous, hearty, insolent. Château Gaillard, as the monarch-turned-architect might have been called Richard Gaillard.

The chosen site could not have been more suitable. A long, limestone rock reared three hundred feet above the river and was surrounded on all sides by near-vertical cliffs. As though this was not already a perfect foundation for the castle, nature had levelled the top of the rock, providing a plateau almost six hundred feet in length. The rock was shaped like a galley, its prow to the south, and from the plateau one could look over the entire loop of the Seine.

Beyond the valley that entrenched the northern, or stern end of the rock, was the village of Les Andelys. A small island was situated in the middle of the river, due east of the village, and this added still further to the natural advantages of the site. A watchtower would be erected on the island. The land between the inner banks of the loop would be walled in. The village would be fortified with walls and turrets. And the river itself would be barred in two places, directly opposite the rock and downstream, on either side of the island.

When that was done, and the island, village and foundation rock had all been incorporated in the outer fortifications, work could begin on the castle itself.

Richard had visited the site many times before, but he never ceased to be amused by the ignorance of his predecessors. It was true that he looked at it with a militarist's eye, and that he'd had first-hand experience of the great fortresses of Palestine. But even so, he was astonished that no one had ever thought to build on the rock. It *invited* a castle, and its size and shape demanded something more than a simple keep and curtain wall. God's legs, he thought, the walls are already there. One need only add another thirty feet to the existing three hundred.

The man-made structure would, of course, follow the edge of the plateau, so that not even a goat could make its way around the cliff-top. Towers would be constructed here and there, five of them in the prow section, seven on the larger body of the rock. A deep ditch would be chipped out between the two sections, then linked by a narrow causeway. The lie of the land was such that the castle could only be approached from the south-east, and that, if it was to be taken, it must be taken piecemeal.

First the prow, or outer bailey, must be stormed. Then the causeway captured. Then, confronted by the main section, with its seven massive towers, the attackers would have to break through into the central bailey, the midship area. That done – and how could it be done under a constant rain of arrows, crossbow quarrels, boiling oil, spears, rocks and lime? – the enemy would find themselves faced by a third walled enclosure. If they could get through that they would be super-human. And at the foot of the towering keep . . .

Since his first visit to the rock above Les Andelys, the king had drawn scores of plans, which he had then amended and embellished. He was assisted in his task by three architects, Sawale, Matthew and Henri, but it was Richard Lionheart who positioned the towers, decided on the thickness of the walls, the depth of the dividing ditch. His assistants corrected his geometry and assessed the strains and stresses, but they bowed to the king's superior knowledge and experience. He was, without doubt, the most perfect soldier of the times. A skilled tactician, an expert horseman, adept with the crossbow and sword, lance and battle-axe, blessed with tremendous physical stamina, and with the ability to rouse a flagging army and lead it to victory. He also understood the need to control what he had conquered, to keep open lines of supply and communication, to be merciless with cowards and to embrace the brave.

And with all that, he was unequalled as a military architect.

He told Sawale and the others, 'This place will combine the old with the new. We'll take advantage of all we know of our castles here and in England, and of what I've learned of those gigantic strongholds in the East. Krak des Chevaliers, Kerak of Moab, the harbour fortress at Acre . . . You should see them, messires, they're worth the trip.

'All castles are built to last, that's implicit, but this one will outlast them all. In five hundred years from now, people will still visit Gaillard and wonder how it might be attacked.' He nodded, and the trio nodded with him. They had no reason to disagree. They felt honoured to be involved in such an ambitious undertaking, and were content to measure and check. They had decided that, when the castle was finished, they would ask the king if they might chisel their names somewhere on the walls. Nothing too boastful; just to show that they had contributed toward it.

By the end of 1197, the island tower had been erected, Les Andelys fortified, the land between the loop of the Seine enclosed by a nine-hundred-foot-long semicircular wall. Two moveable barriers spanned the river, and work was in progress on the plateau.

With Marshal and des Roches holding the line in Touraine, and Robert Pernel in command at Rouen, the king spent less time with his army, and more with his architects. But he had left John as his deputy in Normandy, and the prince had neither the will nor the aptitude for the job. The Norman leaders appealed to Richard to entrust the construction to Sawale and the others, and prevent further French incursions along the border.

'Our spies report that King Philip is preparing a three-fold assault. In the north, between Aumale and the sea; south of Freteval, and once more into Aquitaine. Des Roches and Marshal might hold him down there, but Prince John –'

'What of him? He was willing enough the last time I saw him.'

Patiently, the barons told him that the last time was three months ago. 'Since then, he has scarcely left his rooms. We don't know what he's waiting for, but it's not a battle with the French. And, if we may say this, king, he has gathered around him many of his old cronies, Belcourt and the like.'

'Watch your words,' Richard warned them. 'You sound as if you suspect him of something. Now, let me tell you, I know my brother, and I've seen how he's changed these past three years. He's found the courage that hitherto eluded him, the Plantagenet streak I always knew was there. God knows, you cannot expect from him the leadership you get from me. But we are stuck in the depths of another winter, and Philip

will not move against us in the snow. At the first thaw, we'll
launch our own attacks. What do you think of it?'

'Of what, king?'

'The castle, man, the castle! Château Gaillard, that's what
I've called it.' He laughed steam into the cold air. 'I tell you,
confrères, if Philip does overrun us, we can all move into
Gaillard!'

But the humour was lost on them, and they would not leave
until Richard had agreed to return to the army within a week.
He was loath to do so, for like anyone who is having a house
built, he took a proprietorial interest in every brick and beam.

He was on site, three days later, when a small French craft
came downstream and moored against the eastern bank. Ice
fringed the river, but it was still possible to make way in mid-
stream.

King Richard's bodyguard, composed almost exclusively of
the men he had recruited at Nottingham, scrambled down to
the bank, swords at the ready. But the craft only contained
seven men, six of whom were sailors faced with the unen-
viable task of rowing the vessel back upstream to Paris. The
seventh was a messenger from King Philip, with letters for
the Lionheart.

Richard was perfunctory in his greeting, and made the man
accompany him about the snow-swept site. Workmen toiled
around them, their hands and faces whipped raw by the wind.

'Memorize what you can,' he told the messenger, 'though
it's too soon for you to gauge the details. But you're free to
look. Tell King Philip it's called Château Gaillard, and that
he must come and see it for himself. I'll personally conduct
him around, and we'll end the tour in the dungeons. They're
going to be over there, if you're interested. Deep pits, dug
from the rock. There'll be no doors or windows, just a hole
in the roof, to let down the prisoners and their food. And the
rain, I suppose, to refresh them. Philip's will be, let's see . . .
Oh, when the time comes, he can choose. What's the matter?
Why are your eyes streaming? Are you mourning him in
advance?'

'It's the cold,' the man stammered. 'We will not need to
attack you here. You will all perish from the cold.'

Richard clapped his own shoulders with his hands. 'Must
I give away other secrets? Behind you, down there, you see

that hole? Sunken fires, Frenchman. And the trenches that criss-cross the yard? They're to take the pipes. The fires will be kept burning throughout the winter, and the pipes will conduct the heat into the buildings. I've made a study of Roman fortifications, you see. One of them wrote a book, *De Re Militari.* And I've seen how the Arabs heat their palaces. Cold, you say? Surrender to me next year, and you'll be warm enough, I promise you.' He broke off to discuss something with Sawale and Henri, then returned to ask the shivering messenger the nature of his visit.

The man was too cold to reply, but merely produced a bundle of letters and thrust them at the king. Then he bowed and hurried away, his hands cupped over his mouth. Richard glared after him, surprised by his abrupt departure. The man was either ill-disciplined, or the letters did not require an answer.

. He walked to the river wall, clambered on the five-foot-high parapet and stood there in the driving snow, peering down at the river. Beside him, workmen were lashing together bamboo poles to make scaffolding, while common labourers trudged across the plateau, dragging ashlar blocks and barrels of flint rubble that would be poured into the core of the walls. When it was finished, the surrounding wall would be thirty feet high, and between eight and twelve feet thick. It was as well that the labourers could neither read, nor write, nor count, for they might despair if they knew how many barrel-loads would be required, or how far they would have dragged the brick carts in the next twelve months.

The messenger stumbled aboard the vessel, and it was pushed out into the river. The current carried it several yards downstream before the six oarsmen managed to turn it and start the long pull back to Paris. Snow plastered Richard's face, but he would not leave his vantage point until the craft had started along the southern arm of the loop. Then he jumped down from the wall, shouted encouragement at the workmen and strode toward the one completed building, the gate-tower that led to the causeway. Below the bridge, more labourers chipped at the rock, deepening the ditch that separated the prow section from the main body of the castle. Looking down from the gateway, Richard could see the men, stooped over, fifteen feet below. But he had stipulated that the ditch should be at least twenty feet deep and twice as wide, so they'd be busy all winter, picking at the rock.

He retired into one of the gate-tower chambers, purposely choosing one in which the fireplace was empty. He would drive his men hard, and expect them to work in any weather, but he would not be caught crouched before a blazing fire, a warm king in a frozen kingdom.

Although he was physically strong, and could deny the need for sleep and food or water, the wind-borne snow had turned his hands blue, and it took him a while to fumble his dagger from its scabbard and tear open the letters. As he did so, he noticed they were marked, precisely, *Première, Deuxième, Troisième,* and so he read them in that order.

The first was from King Philip.

After the initial, courteous greeting, Philip had written:

'We have been enemies now for some time, Richard of England. It is not a happy state for us to be in. But, as you fear I shall advance into your lands, so I anticipate your desire to encompass mine. We have made our treaties, and they have been broken, I shall not say by whom.

'But, once again we find ourselves at war. Would to God that it were otherwise, for I have always admired you, and wanted you as my friend.'

Richard wiped away the tears of winter from his eyes and re-read the passage. *Not a happy state? I have always admired you? Wanted you as my friend?* This was incredible!

'They are my own words,' he growled. 'This is what I told John. And where's the gross and noisome beast, the belching monster who was told to mount a tusky boar? It's not possible . . . It's not possible . . .

He shook his head with anger, and went back to the letter.

'I knew, after you drove me from Freteval and made me wade the river, I knew you would find the box containing my personal papers. And I knew they would deepen your suspicion of me.'

But they didn't, Richard thought. They confused me, for I could find no trace of an insult. It was not as John had promised. And nor is it now.

'So,' (the letter continued) 'I have been careful to support the claim I am about to make. Regard it, too, with suspicion, King Richard, for it concerns your own brother.

'You will think I am merely planting the seeds of fraternal discord. But not so. Nothing is further from my mind. You will believe what you wish, and I know I cannot dissuade you.

'This then is my claim, as a king to a king.

'Your brother, Prince John, is working against you. During the last year he has addressed several letters to me, but it is only necessary for me to include the last. He would have rejoined me in Paris, long ago. Indeed, he might never have left, had he not been convinced that you would take vengeance on his innocent wife. For myself, I find it hard to believe, but Prince John seems to believe it. *Coeur-de-Lion,* maltreating his brother's wife.'

Richard leaned back against the wall. He needed time to think. John claimed this, and Philip swore that. John said Philip said. Philip said John said. And out of it all came a grotesque picture of Richard Lionheart, slavering after the King of France and abusing the Countess of Gloucester. It was a fantastic distortion, and if Philip thought he could turn the Plantagenets against each other –

But he had to read on.

'When John reached you at Lisieux, he told you some tale about how I would have had you killed in Durrenstein, or, failing that, have killed your queen. And you believed him, it seems, even as you now disbelieve me.

'But does it not occur to you, Lionheart, that your brother sees death in every step? You, yourself, in that German prison . . . Queen Berengaria, in some sunny house in Aquitaine . . . The Countess Hadwisa, abandoned in England . . . John, I would say, has murder on the mind.

'But, before you decide, read the *Deuxième,* in which he speaks of you as a gross and rancid creature, akin to a tusky boar. Read how he says he cannot leave his wife, whom he does not love, to your vulgar mercies.

'And then, as you surely will, condemn the letter as a

forgery, the work of the cunning King Philip.

'And when you've done that, read the *Troisième*.'

And that's where Philip ended, understanding Richard Lionheart far better than Richard understood himself.

Of course it would be a forgery! Did Philip think he could delude Richard of England? Philip, who would not even go near a horse, for fear it would kick, or buck, or fall on him? Philip, who hated all sports, and had probably tried to banish his own shadow! It was laughable. The rabbit confronting the lion.

It was not John who had coined the vile insults and passed them back to Philip. It was Philip all the time. Philip, who thought himself so clever. Philip Augustus? God, no. More like Philip Labyrinthus.

Nevertheless, Richard hunched in a corner of the unheated chamber and read the *Deuxième;* John's letter from Rouen that began, 'You know I don't love my wife . . .'

A forgery, Richard agreed, no doubt of it. A perfect forgery, to be sure, an exact copy of John's spidery hand, but as false as the stone skittles at a fair. Throw the ball . . . Knock down the skittles . . . And what does the sportsman find? That the wooden ball bounces off painted stone, and that his penny's in the alley-owner's purse . . .

Of course it was a forgery!

Nevertheless, Richard hunched further into the corner and read the *Troisième*.

This was John's answer to Philip's carefully worded questions. A series of answers that only John could have given. They told of John's reunion with Richard at Lisieux, of the subsequent campaigns in Normandy and Touraine, of Richard's cruelty towards the speechless Aimer of Chaluz and of a dozen other intimate occurrences *that only Richard's brother could have known*. A spy could have known some of them. An Angevin could have known some of them. But only John could have known them all.

The spidery handwriting was identical in both letters.

They were not forgeries, for the *Troisième* could not be a forgery, so neither could the *Deuxième*.

What Philip had claimed was true. John *had* lied. Over this, and everything else. He *had* created the fiction of the sweaty, lovelorn boar. And he *had* maligned Hadwisa, and made an empty promise to marry Alais, and invented his fears about Durrenstein and Berengaria. And Robert Pernel? Yes, why not?

Stumbling blindly around the gate-tower chamber, the giant crumpled the letters in his hands. 'Oh, God,' he moaned, 'has he *never* spoken the truth . . . Have I really been duped all these years by a – a boy in silly heels?'

He came down from the rock and rode along the river path to Rouen. His bodyguard chased after him, and the workmen hurried across the plateau, using whatever wood they could find to make fires. Nobody could say why the king had left in such a hurry, but his face had been frozen into a mask of murder. Somebody was in trouble, that much was clear.

Within a month, Prince John had been dispossessed of all his lands, titles, incomes and authorities. He had become hysterical in the face of Richard's fury, retreated before the crumpled evidence, then fled when he saw the king's hand slide toward his sword. Had Richard not been consumed by private rage, he would have locked the gates of Rouen, then dragged John to a gibbet in the square. As it was, he burst in upon his brother, confronted him with the letters, then went after him, as though to cut him down.

But John made good his escape, as perhaps Richard had intended, and again the people of Rouen said they had not seen Softsword going anywhere, step-by-step. He had vanished, as from Le Mans, from Tours, from Mortain, from England, from Paris and, once before, from Rouen. If it was true that the dowager Queen Eleanor could turn into a bat, and Richard into a lion, it was doubly true that John could reverse his cloak and become invisible.

'I want him found,' Richard said, and, breaking the habit of a lifetime, offered money for his capture.

He was quite the best sailor in the family, and stepped ashore at Dover as though alighting from a dray-cart. But his state of mind did not match his stomach. Throughout the voyage he had kept his travelling hood closed around his face, and pretended he was ignorant of the language. For all the sailors knew, he was a traveller from some distant country, huddled against a typical western winter. They had already been warned to keep watch for the arrogant, high-heeled Plantagenet, but there was nothing arrogant about the monkish foreigner in his water-logged slippers.

However, John was John, and not even the fear of death could suppress his vanity. He went ashore, shuffled up into the town and spent half the money in his purse on a saddled horse, a pair of riding boots and a bird's bill cap. Half of what was left went on a night's lodging in a second-rate tavern and on a meal for himself and the young woman he'd found loitering in the porch. By morning, his purse was a sack of leather, the last few coins divided between the industrious whore and the tavern-keeper, who had kept them supplied with wine.

Then, without a penny in his purse, the most wanted man in Europe set out for Gloucester and a reunion with his wife. Things had not gone as well as he'd have liked in France or Normandy, but he was sure Hadwisa would be pleased to see him again. After all, he was her husband, home from the wars.

He announced himself to the guards, and they made him wait whilst they went in search of someone who would recognize him. He had been away so long that most of the garrison and household servants had never set eyes on him. They knew the king's brother was Countess Hadwisa's husband, and that his name hardly ever arose in conversation, but whatever else they'd learned about him had come from hearsay and rumour.

And now this thin, haunted-looking man, dressed incongruously in an old tunic and cloak, yet new cap and boots, turned up on the doorstep without an escort and without warning and claimed to be Prince John, lord of the manor. It bore checking.

Eventually, a cook and guard sergeant came forward, peered at him for a moment, then knelt in the snow. They had last seen him four years ago, but, by his appearance, it might have been fourteen. There was no trace of the strutting peacock, except in the narrow, bird's bill cap, and even that was made ridiculous by the frightened face beneath. Yes, that was the thing about him now. He seemed dressed in fear.

Nevertheless, he was still Prince John, and men hurried to take his horse, to inform Hadwisa, to lead him into the building. He moved unsteadily in his unworn boots, and his hand went to his cap, his fingers curled around the peak. As he approached the great, fortified manor, he practised his most winning smile, that of the prodigal returned, chastened by his own foolishness. Richard had never been able to resist it, so why should Hadwisa?

He would tell her – well, first he would find out what she had heard – and then he would tell her he was home to stay. If she knew that Richard had disinherited him, she would also know that her own lands were unaffected. She was still Countess of Gloucester, and mistress of several smaller estates throughout the country. They would administer them together, John and Hadwisa, and he would prove to her, and to Richard and England, that he had learned his lesson. His irresponsibility was at an end. He was older and wiser now, and content to stay within bounds.

He would not tell her that he had no choice in the matter and had come to Gloucester as a last resort.

He was somewhat irritated to be kept waiting in a non-descript downstairs room, and after a while he went in search of his wife. He had almost forgotten the layout of Gloucester, but he was too proud to seek directions from passing servants. Eventually, he found one of the men-at-arms who had been on duty at the gate, and asked the guard if Countess Hadwisa was in the solar, or her bed-chamber, or –

'Why are you out here?' the man interrupted. 'Weren't you put in the room by the main door?' He did not afford John the courtesy of a title, and barred his progress along the corridor.

John frowned at him. 'I'm out here because I felt forgotten, that's why. Now tell me where the countess – '

'You'd best wait in the room,' the guard said. 'I'll take you back.' He stepped closer, forcing John to retreat, then jerked his head toward the small, bleak chamber. 'Lady Hadwisa will be along in due course. You wait in there.' His attitude was cold and relentless. He might have been addressing a beggar or a backward child. He ignored John's mounting indignation, waited for him to move clear of the door, then leaned and pulled it shut. John blinked at the studded planks and felt the first tremors of doubt.

The guard would not have taken it upon himself to behave like that. He would not have dared. But there was one person who could have told him to restrain the visitor, only one, and that was Hadwisa.

He lunged forward and pulled open the door and the guard was there in the corridor, telling him it was best to do as he was asked, close the door again, you'll keep warmer.

Without realizing it, John obeyed, then moved absently to the window, to stare out at the snow. His doubts had become fears, and he plucked nervously at the green woollen peak.

When she entered, she did not come alone. The Abbot of Gloucester was with her, and various clerks and armed knights and, at the end of the line, the bald and portly Roger Malchat, steward of the kingdom.

John realized now why he had been kept waiting and out of sight. It was a coincidence that Roger Malchat was present, but the others, the abbot and clerks and feudatories had all been sent for. It would be difficult to stage a marital reunion in front of these unsmiling witnesses.

Hadwisa looked at him, then inclined her head in the slightest gesture of recognition. He bowed in reply, but she did not wait for him to straighten up before she asked, 'Won't you doff your cap for me, husband?'

'What? Oh, I bought it so recently, I –'

'Well, that's a relief.'

'My lady?'

'We know you have been disinherited, and that King Philip has furnished irrefutable proof of your treason. I expected you to come here, but in need of money. It's a relief to know you're not destitute, not while you can still buy such jaunty caps.'

He opened his mouth to explain, but she did not give him the chance. 'Is it my memory, or the French diet you've been used to? I do believe you've shrunk. I remembered you as, ah, I see. New boots, and not so high in the heel. They go well with the cap, really they do.' She looked at him, then, very slowly, expressed growing bewilderment. 'Allow me to ask – Why *are* you here? I won't embarrass you by suggesting you were drawn to me by some late-flowering love. No, don't look so awkward. We all know that Princess Alais – How did it go, Malchat? What did my lord John write to King Philip?'

'That Alais stirs him,' Malchat said flatly. 'That Prince John does not love you, but that Alais stirs him.'

'Yes, that's right, so we need not be mired down by talk of love.' It was a cruel performance, but she would not be diverted. John had married her for her inheritance, and there was nothing extraordinary in that. But he had belittled her, flaunted his infidelities, derided her to his friends, squandered her money and sneered at her talk of fabrics and flowers. He had abandoned her for all the world to see, then announced that she bored him, that she did not stir him like Alais of France.

And that, too, was typical of John, for he was no more likely to marry Philip's sister than to ride in single combat against the leader of Islam, Sultan Saladin.

It was cruel, perhaps, but it was just repayment for nine wasted years and a thousand wounding cuts.

'What then?' she asked. 'Since you're not here for reconciliation, is it for refuge?'

'Why have you brought along these people, my lady? I would rather speak with you in private.'

'I know you would. It's the only thing about you that frightens me. You look worn down, husband, but I doubt you've lost your magic. You *are* a magician, you know. You can work the most amazing tricks. So these, *people*, they are your audience. I'm too credulous, but I don't think your sleight of tongue will fool Malchat, or these hard-headed knights. They'll judge why you're here, and they'll write it down and seal it and hold you to it, for once in your life!' Her measured cruelty had turned to anger, and she knew it was time to stop.

But John could take it no further, for she had successfully destroyed his reasons. His mind was already racing ahead, away from Gloucester, westward across the Black Mountains to the boot-tip of Wales.

If his own wife would not help him, he would appeal to another man's wife, a much prettier creature altogether.

Two weeks later he was faced with the same problem; no one recognized him at the gate.

Before he had left Gloucester, Hadwisa had learned of his indigence and given him two hundred marks, a second horse and a magnificent, bearskin cloak. She had told him there was no need for him to go. But, if he stayed, he must expect Richard to find him and, in all possibility, banish him from the kingdom. So which was it to be? Would he wait – in his own rooms, of course – and face the king's retribution, or ride on into the world?

He took the money and the palfrey and the cloak and headed westward through the snow.

It had been a hard two weeks, for he had chosen to travel through some of the most inhospitable countryside in England. But it was not England now, it was Wales, and his solitary journey was chorused by the wind, and his progress marked by the drumroll of avalanches. There were wolves in the mountains, and the light seemed to fade before it ever filled the sky. Villagers gave him food and let him sleep with the horses, and asked nothing in return. Lunatics were thought to be touched by God, and he was clearly a lunatic, crossing their country in mid-winter.

And then he reached his destination, and once again there was doubt as to his identity. It was only when the grizzled Fitz Renier, far from his shrievalty of London, came down the steps that the guards stabled the horses. Things must be in a poor state in Normandy, they thought, if the king's own brother looks this ragged.

It was only by chance that Fitz Renier and the chatelaine of Pembroke had heard of John's disgrace. They had received no overland visitors for several weeks, but a fishing boat from Brittany had been blown far off-course, past the western tip of Cornwall and up the Welsh coast. Luck and good seamanship had guided the battered vessel into the estuary below Pembroke, and Isabel had insisted that the fishermen be entertained in the castle, whilst their ship was being repaired. It was not the first time she had done this, nor was it entirely selfless. She welcomed visitors, particularly if they were from Brittany or Normandy, for there was always the chance that they would have heard of a certain William Marshal, very dark-skinned, a friend of King Richard and the mighty des Roches . . .

They hadn't, but they had heard of John's treason and disappearance. *Couteau-du-Beurre*, isn't that what he was called? Buttersword, or something?

Now Fitz Renier crossed the yard and, with grave formality, welcomed John to Pembroke.

'Where have you come from, prince? Was your ship driven ashore –'

'Gloucester,' John said bitterly. 'I've ridden from Gloucester, after a blissful reunion with my wife.'

'You came on horseback – '

'It's the usual mode of travel. In fact, two horses; one a Christmas gift from Hadwisa. Now, for God's sake don't tell me you doubt it. Nothing I say is believed these days.'

Nothing ever was, Fitz Renier thought. But he could not entirely conceal his admiration for a man who could traverse the Black Mountains in the depths of winter. It was probably the most courageous thing Softsword had ever done.

They went into the keep, to find Isabel engaged in a noisy game with her children. The youngest, a girl, was in a crib by the fire, but the three boys were scattered about the large, square room, shouting directions at their mother. Isabel's eyes were covered with a strip of cloth, and one glance was enough to dishearten the prince.

A guard had reported that there was a rider at the gate who claimed to be Prince John. But both Isabel and Fitz Renier had been so sure it was a lie that the lady of Pembroke had not even interrupted her game. It seemed to be a recurring pattern at the castles he visited. John here? Nonsense. It must be an impostor.

He sighed and edged toward the fire, and Fitz Renier moved unobtrusively between him and the crib.

John's eyes widened in horror. 'My God!' he howled. 'I have not come to this! I am not – *harmful*!'

The boys stopped in mid-yell, suddenly aware that they had a visitor. Isabel pulled the blindfold from her eyes, glanced at Fitz Renier, then at John, and sensed intuitively what had happened.

The sheriff stood, unrepentant, in front of the crib. John had halted a few feet away, and now the room blurred before his gaze. Disgrace and rejection and the rigours of the long winter journey combined to rob him of his remaining strength, and he stood in that strange, distant place, his hands loose at his sides, tears dripping from his jaw.

Still unseeing, he whispered, 'I am not harmful, you know . . .'

His wild shout had brought other men into the room, but Fitz Renier waved them away. The children sidled toward their mother, and they, too, were sent off to play elsewhere. They were annoyed, because the stranger had ruined their game. Who was he, anyway, howling his harmlessness, then bursting into tears. And how comical he looked, a weeping bear with a skinny neck and a bird's beak.

When they had gone, Isabel and Fitz Renier exchanged a glance, and the sheriff handed John a large mug of mead. It was a potent brew, warm and heady, and John shivered his thanks. His vision had cleared by now, and he made his way cautiously toward Isabel. Fitz Renier kept pace with him, but did not interfere. Perhaps he'd been wrong to shield the baby. If so, God would punish him for it. But, before he submitted to divine judgement, he'd tell God that Prince John was a strange creature, then cite his extraordinary pilgrimage across Wales. Surely even God was surprised by that.

Holding the mug down at his side, John bowed to the chatelaine. He was in no mood to judge feminine beauty, but she looked remarkably well for a woman who had borne four children.

He said, 'My Lady de Clare . . . I apologize for startling you . . . You see . . . I have ridden here from Gloucester, and it is not the easiest journey, not for . . . for several reasons.' He looked across at Fitz Renier, who had somehow moved into a position that protected the chatelaine without further insulting the prince.

'I am an uninvited guest –'

'No,' she said, addressing him for the first time. 'If we only saw people by invitation, we would be very far from the world. As you say, it is not the easiest journey and, whatever your reasons for making it, you are welcome to rest.' To prevent any misunderstanding, she added, 'Sheriff Fitz Renier is the constable here, in my husband's absence. He has the same authority as Earl Marshal, and shares with me the administration of my husband's lands. Also, we are both aware that you have been dispossessed, and that you chose not to remain at Rouen. But we are the only ones. So far as I know, Pembroke is otherwise in ignorance, and will remain so as long as you wish.'

Very slowly, John bowed again, spilling mead from his mug. He could not remember having heard such a delicate phrase as that; chose not to remain at Rouen. Not fled, or returned to England, or made your escape. But simply, and without accusation, chose not to remain.

John thought, when I next see Marshal – if he ever lets me within earshot – I'll tell him he was brilliant in his choice.

The mug embarrassed him, and he set it on the table, 'I will not over-tax your hospitality, Lady de Clare . . . But I have travelled this far to speak with you and, yes, I would be grateful for some food and a bed. Tomorrow, when I have put my question, or rather, when you have given your answer, I'll be on my way again.'

'That's understood,' Fitz Renier told him. 'While there's a reason for your visit, you're welcome to stay. But don't imagine you'll turn the lady's generosity to your advantage. And, so far as I am concerned, you are a traitor, a deserter and a coward.

'I don't know what force controls your actions, prince, but you are unique in this. You deserted your father, King Henry, in his hour of need, then signed the list of those who had turned against him. Later, you sided with the French against your brother, the lawful King of England, when he was fighting for God's cause in Palestine. A few months more, and he was in that German prison, giving you the opportunity to foment insurrection in England and Normandy. A year more, and you heard he'd been released, so you deserted Philip and ran to grovel at King Richard's feet. And now you have tried once more to defect to the enemy, and would probably have done so, had you not been crossed by the Frenchman.

'Everything you have done has been to further your own aims, regardless of the price that others would have to pay. You have brought this present disgrace upon yourself, and, in my opinion, you have out-lived your time.'

John raised his hands to ward off the blows. 'Christ, Fitz Renier, you're salt on wounds! I know what I've done! There's no call to engrave it. I'll say my piece in the morning and leave. Be satisfied with that!'

Fitz Renier rewarded his outburst with a shrug. 'You are not here for my satisfaction. You're after some favour from Lady de Clare. But she is a gentlewoman, and I don't want her pity aroused by any abject emotions. I may be salt in your wounds, but you inflicted them on yourself, remember that.'

John ate with them in the evening, and was given a bed for the night. In the morning he would be allowed to speak with Isabel, in private. It did not meet with Fitz Renier's approval, but Isabel insisted.

'I am in no danger from him. You are merciless with him, though what you said is true. He's spent half his life working for the downfall of somebody or other, though his greatest successes have been to trap himself. Don't worry, I shall not be swayed by his tears. But, to be honest with you, Fitz Renier, my pity *is* aroused. The more so, because I think I know what he wants of me, and I cannot give it.'

'What does he want?'

'A letter of commendation, at a guess. He'll ask me to use my influence with Marshal, and encourage Marshal to sweet-talk the king. He will tell me how foolish he's been, and how he was always led astray by stronger men, but that his only ambition now is to earn Richard's forgiveness and be given a final chance to prove his worth. I may be wrong, but I cannot see why else he has come here.'

'And why won't you commend him to Marshal? I know I wouldn't, but I don't feel a twitch of pity for him.'

Isabel thought for a while before answering. John had not yet been given the opportunity to say his piece, and she did not wish to pre-judge him. But, the more she thought of it, the more certain she was that he had made the arduous journey in order to gain the king's ear through the Lord and Lady of Pembroke.

'There are two reasons,' she said. 'Firstly, because if I do ask Marshal to plead with Richard, he will do so. Not, perhaps, for John's sake, but for mine. And I will not put him in such an invidious position. I'd have him plead for you, or Malchat, or a dozen others we know, but not for Prince John.

'The second reason denies the existence of the first. If I do allow myself to be persuaded, and my husband does make the necessary overtures to the king, and Richard does show that magnanimous side of his nature, John will desert him again, sneering at his weakness, and all Marshal has worked for will be at risk.'

Fitz Renier nodded. He made no comment, but thought Lady Isabel had taken a long route to the truth. She was saying, in her own way, that John was not to be trusted, in sight or out. The sheriff could have told her that with half a breath.

Next morning, he made work for himself in the yard, whilst John petitioned the chatelaine. Then, as the light began to brighten over the estuary, the prince came clattering down the steps and started toward the stables. He was dressed in his bearskin cloak and peaked cap, and carried a flask of wine.

Fitz Renier glanced back, saw Isabel in the doorway of the keep, and went to join her.

'As I said. I've never been so right in my life.'

'Where's he going now?'

'Down to the harbour. I gave him one of our boats. Send a man down to alert the crew.' She glanced up at the sky. 'The sea won't be too high today. Tell them they are to take their passenger wherever he wants to go. But don't say who he is.'

'You gave him his letter?'

Isabel shook her head. 'When I refused him, he said, well, he was understandably upset, but in the end he said it was of no importance, there was another woman who would hear his appeal, much more influential.' She saw Fitz Renier's scowl and added, 'His mother. He's going to find Eleanor.'

But Eleanor of Aquitaine was no longer involved in the ways of the world. John did not reach her until early spring, where he found her in the gardens of the abbey at Fontevrault. She was stooped over, a stick in one hand, two seed bags in the other. Slowly, she edged along the flagstone path, digging a hole with the stick, tossing in a few seeds, then scraping the earth back in place.

He had lost his bird's bill cap *en route,* but Hadwisa's two hundred marks had enabled him to buy a wide-brimmed pilgrim's hat, an ideal disguise now that he was back in the same duchy as the Lionheart.

He came along the path and called quietly to his mother, and they stared at each other without recognition. Eleanor was seventy-six years of age, thin and brittle, her eyes large in their sockets. And John, who was just thirty-one, seemed to have lost weight in sympathy. He had heard that King Richard had called off the hunt and was now worried by John's disappearance. Richard's fury had once again been replaced by fraternal concern, but John was too terrified to rely on rumour.

His mother would know if it was safe to surrender to the Lionheart. He should have come to her first of all, he realized that now. She would have pacified Richard and calmed John's fears and brought them together, the last of her sons. He should never have bothered with Hadwisa, nor let her enjoy such a vindictive triumph. And the visit to Pembroke – Well, he'd been given the means to return to Normandy, but it was an odd place from which to cross the Channel. If it had not been for the stony Fitz Renier, he felt sure he could have secured a letter from Isabel. But no matter. He should have come straight to Fontevrault and Eleanor.

He let his hat spiral to the path and they embraced gently, each concealing the distress they felt for the other's starved appearance. 'Thyme and hissop,' Eleanor said. 'Now's the season to plant them. It's good soil here; one can grow almost anything. We use the hyssop to give an aroma to the holy-water. And in cooking. Nothing's wasted within these walls. You'd be surprised what we can do with things the world throws away.'

John was not sure if there was a double meaning to her words, but they seemed to apply to his own predicament. He took the stick, followed Eleanor's directions and preceded her along the path, digging the holes, waiting for her to drop in the seeds, now from this bag, now from that, then refilling the holes.

'I have been in England,' he said. 'You must have heard about the letters, how Philip betrayed me to Richard. I went to see Hadwisa, but she'd have no more of me.'

'Did that surprise you? She has been waiting for years to hear that her marriage is annulled. You *are* cousins, remember. Or would you have divorced her on some other grounds?'

'For Alais?'

'It's what you said.'

He shook his head. 'I don't know. Events ran away with me. I have not been in control of my own destiny.' He flinched as Eleanor clamped a bony hand on his wrist.

'Events never outstripped you, John, and you know it. Richard is one for the sudden, aimless gesture, but not you. You have always known what you were doing, and why. You created the events, but you made a poor job of it. As you're doing now, the holes aren't evenly spaced.' She relaxed her grip, and they went on along the path, warmed by the sun as it vaulted the high stone wall.

He spent most of the morning with her, planting and talking, gradually allowing her to peel away the layers of excuse and justification. At one point, he accused her of loving him less than Richard, and she immediately agreed. 'I'm a bitch with two grown puppies. Richard has become the hunting hound, but you still prefer to gnaw bones in front of the fire. And savage your brother, when his back is turned. Do I owe you love for that?'

'Perhaps not, but you never gave me the guidance –'

'To go where, in God's name, to go where? Richard was always the leader, as your bastard brother Geoffrey was always the most intelligent. But you, with wit and cunning and the ability to disarm, where did you wish to go? Into bed with whores and serving girls; into the shop that sold fine clothes, for which, hopefully, someone else would pay.'

'You make it sound so simple.'

'Space the holes. No, it was never simple, but it was never as difficult as you like to think.' She took the stick from him, then leaned on it, and let the seed bags hang by draw-strings from her waist. 'I *knew* how it had been for you, always in Richard's shadow. I know how much you wanted some sunlight of your own, and why not? But you were given the sun when Richard bestowed on you those seven counties in England, and the fief of Mortain, and Heaven knows what else. He made you independent, and did so against the general advice, but did you thank him for it? No. You thought that, if so much was so easily come by, there might be more, and you confused his generosity with weakness.'

She paused, then decided to say what was on her mind. 'I don't know which came first, John, your jealousy of Richard, or your hatred of yourself. But I do know that things were made too easy for you when you were young. Oh, you can look affronted, but it's true. You were not *given* anything, I'm not saying you were, but no demands were made of you.'

'Agreed,' John said. 'I was not given anything. Not even guidance. But I was always served second at the table, and brought out to admire Richard's prowess on a horse, or his unerring accuracy with a crossbow. You quote his gift of lands to me, but what use is a ship to someone who has never seen the sea? I may have wit and cunning, but when was I ever encouraged to use them? And when did you ever admonish Richard for calling me boy? You never thought to, did you, my lady? It seemed the obvious title. What else was I, but boy John?'

'I heard from the king recently,' Eleanor said. 'He wants you with him again.'

'Did he say why? Is he going to banish me, or is he embarrassed that the world knows I live in fear of him?'

'It's enough that he forgives you,' Eleanor said tartly. 'In his place, I might not.'

'In his place? But you *are* in his place! You were never anywhere else.' He kicked a scattering of earth from the path, then asked, 'Are my lands to be restored to me?'

'He made no mention of it. He wants you with him, and offers you the guidance you say I never gave. The Earl of Pembroke has agreed to take charge of you.' Her tone changed, and she implored him to accept. 'It will be a fresh start for you. Find your brother and make your peace with him, then be advised by Marshal. Please, my son, please, before we – those of us who are left – before we destroy our own house.'

'Under Marshal,' John mused. 'That'll be a cat-and-dog affair. I remember trading insults with him during Richard's coronation. And I suppose des Roches will be there, to push me about.'

'Des Roches is dead,' Eleanor told him. 'He went blind quite quickly, but he kept it secret. Anyway, long enough to fool his friends and ride with them into a skirmish. They say that the Frenchman who killed him was so horrified to discover he had slain a blind man, that he exchanged his armour for a scrip and staff, and has gone on a pilgrimage to Jerusalem. I imagine he has a hat like yours.'

There was too much sincerity in the story for John to put up further resistance. He nodded wearily and asked where Richard was to be found.

'He's at Château Gaillard,' Eleanor said. 'He seems to have made his home there, as mine is here.' She touched John's sleeve with the tips of her fingers, and managed a semblance of the smile that had so many times won her her way. 'If you want to regain his favour, compliment his castle.'

Chapter Ten

THE ARROW THAT FLIETH BY DAY

April 1198 – April 1199

The prow section was complete; a small fortress in itself, with its five towers and triangular bailey. Work had progressed apace on the main section and, by the end of April, a well had been sunk through three hundred feet of solid rock, and the first water was hauled up in a leather bucket.

King Richard was invited to taste it. He lifted the bucket to his lips, twisted his face in an expression of disgust and told the workmen the water was tainted. They'd have to start again, twenty yards to the north. For an instant they blanched at his decision, then, as he swung the bucket high in the air, spraying water across the inner face of the wall, they roared with relief and thanked God he'd been joking.

John arrived, to be clasped in his brother's suffocating embrace. 'All is forgotten,' Richard boomed. 'You're back and safe, and you've been punished enough. Here, arm-in-arm, that's it, come and see Gaillard. Marshal's due in soon from patrol. He's promised to take care of you. You look wasted away, boy. We'll get some roast lamb into you. They breed good meat around here. You see those pigs? They mark the perimeter of the keep. Nearly fifty feet across. And we're having another wall built around it, and a moat between. The gates will be, wait, let's get down there and you can see for yourself . . .'

Still boy, John thought, still boy.

He accompanied his brother on a tour of the massive, triple-walled stronghold. They climbed steps and stairs, balanced precariously on the unfinished ramparts, scaled ladders that had been roped to the inside of the towers. John was shown the island, with its watchtower, and the fortified town of Les Andelys, and the long, castellated wall that linked the inner banks of the river. He remembered what Eleanor had told him, rehearsed his compliments, then said, 'It has your mark on it. It's the most confident fortress I've ever seen.'

The word pleased the king, though he could not resist

commenting, 'That's because you never came East with me. If you'd seen Krak des Chevaliers . . . Still, you're right, it's a manifestation of my own confidence in Normandy. Its name implies it.'

John nodded and suggested some architectural feature that he knew Richard would reject. It gave the king the opportunity to launch into another lecture, then add, 'I'm glad you're showing an interest. I thought it would be beyond you.'

'That I'd be too stupid to see why it's the way it is?'

'Don't be so hard on yourself. Not stupid, no. Ignorant.'

'Ah, yes,' John murmured, 'that's a better way to put it.'

Marshal arrived with a cavalcade of Norman barons, the leaders of the various patrols, and Richard presented them with due ceremony. He told John he was being placed in the hands of a proven champion, and should obey Marshal in everything. Then he told Marshal that he was being entrusted with the care of his beloved brother and that the past was forgotten; John would be a most receptive pupil.

A pupil, John thought. I once controlled the entire southwest of England, and was Lord of Ireland and Count of Mortain. And now he speaks of me as a pupil. A boy pupil, of course.

Nevertheless, he swore obedience to Marshal and they exchanged a formal kiss of fealty. As they moved apart, Marshal said, 'That was a long ride you made to Pembroke, prince. I trust you sent back the boat.'

'Why wouldn't I?' John retorted. 'You are going to make a soldier of me, aren't you, not a sailor?'

'Well,' Marshal said, 'that's an ideal. But I'm going to try.'

They gazed at each other until Richard intervened to lead Marshal away and hear his account of the patrols. The barons went with them, leaving John on the plateau, looking around at the half-grown walls.

King Philip's spies reported that, when Château Gaillard was finished, it might well prove impregnable.

'Nonsense,' he remarked. 'The Lionheart is too boastful. I could take it if it were made from hammered iron.'

The observation was relayed to Richard, and his reply recorded by his delighted clerks.

'Tell King Philip he is too optimistic. I could hold it if it were made from patted butter.'

In all honesty, Marshal did not believe he had been excessively harsh with the prince. For one thing, the warlord was nearly fifty-three years old, and had never made John do what he, himself, could not. For another, he was kept in constant check by King Richard, who demanded regular progress-reports.

How well could John tilt at the quintain? Did he catch the shield square on, or did the wooden arm swing round and clout him on the neck? Was he more respectful toward his peers and elders, or did he still love to let slip a sarcastic comment? Was he awake bright and early, or did it require a fanfare to get him going? And how adept was he with the sword, how patient with petitioners, how well-versed in the law? Was he growing in stature, or did Marshal's expression mirror his failure? *Their* failure, for, if the pupil had failed, so had the tutor. Perhaps that was it. Perhaps the tutor was at fault.

'Stop there,' Marshal rapped. 'Don't be carried away by your own delusions. If you suspect I cannot school him, give him to someone else. I could almost request it, if it did not offend my pride. But you have known me too long, king, to think me incapable of instruction. It is not that I cannot teach him. It is simply that he will not be taught. What is his latest complaint?'

That you made him ride in the full heat of summer, without a drop of water, then forced him at sword-point to find water for his horse. He was kept dry all day, he says, even when he was in sight of a river.'

Marshal was genuinely surprised. 'You find that worthy of complaint? How many times have you ridden beneath the searing sun of Palestine, only to find that the Moslems have filled the wells with rocks or filth? And then who comes first, Richard Lionheart? Who first gets the water in the flasks? You know the horse must be watered, so it can still carry its weakened rider. And this is Normandy, not the salt deserts of Palestine!'

'Very well. Your point's taken. You asked what he'd said, and I – '

'I asked for his latest complaint, not when he had last raised a thirst! By God, we must have some balance here, or he'll be telling you he wants a servant to fan away the flies.'

'Yes,' Richard said, angry in all directions. 'Yes, the point is made. Just do your best with him, that's all I'm asking.'

Marshal allowed him the last word, nodded curtly and went away. Richard pitted his right hand against his left, bruising them both. Marshal was right, of course, if uncompromising. It was a pity that John's last complaint had come to mind, for it was a weak one, and indefensible. But, somehow it had sounded worse, the way John had told it, driven on under the pitiless sun by a man who despised him. Richard had felt protective toward the gasping prince, and had imagined him with a swollen tongue, his skin blackened by the sun, lolling in his saddle. But Marshal was right again, for the image was of Palestine, not the summer fields of Normandy.

Perhaps it was not the tutor, after all, but the pupil . . .

When John reached breaking point, he snapped in silence. He had now undergone almost a year's instruction and, in that time, he had lodged countless complaints with the king, who had acted on none of them. Worse, John had twice appealed for the restitution of his lands. On the last occasion he had heard Richard laugh, then watched him shake his head and hold up a hand, fingers splayed.

'Five years, if you're the man I hope you are.'

'Five years to what?'

'To restitution, John, that's what. You convince me you're worthy to govern, and I'll give you all the lands you want. But you have fooled me too often in the past. There's no one so sanctimonious as a felon-turned-friar. Nor one so suspicious as a man whose beliefs have been shattered. I've told you often enough in the past, you're not evil, you're weak and wayward. But your lies about King Philip – they cut me deeply. And then your letters to him, in which you described me as gross and bestial – those cut across the cuts. I opened my heart to you, young John. I thought you and I, well, that you would understand. I felt some – ' He rocked his head from side to side in an attempt to recapture his dream ' – some affection for the Frenchman, you had no right to pervert it. Nor to turn my admissions against me, as you did. I made myself vulnerable, but I shall not do so again.' He looked at John for a while, then recovered his spirits enough to tap the outstretched fingers. 'Five years of hard work and loyalty, and after that we'll see.'

But they'd see far sooner than that, John decided. Five years of waiting at Richard's table? Five years as one of Marshal's liege-men, in command of nothing more important than a grain-store or a watchtower? Oh, no, not while there was a quicker way, quicker and more decisive.

He sent word to the only person who could help, then announced that he was going to spend a few days with his mother, at Fontevrault.

It was a gold table, according to the first reports. Then a gold table, surrounded by figures of Christ and the Twelve Apostles. Then a complete statue on a solid gold base, the piece fashioned in the German style. It had been dug up in a field near a small castle in the Limousin district of Aquitaine, and some coins had also been unearthed, Roman coins and bracelets, a cartload of jewellery, an unparalleled treasure-trove ...

The story continued to expand until Richard could no longer contain his curiosity, and strode to his horse. He left Château Gaillard in the care of the architect Sawale and a dozen barons, then rode south, accompanied by Marshal and a hundred knights.

'If it's in Limousin, it might be on my lands. I've heard it's five feet across, the table, and that the whole thing stands two or three feet high. God's legs, it must be worth a fortune!' He grinned at Marshal, who advised him to curb his enthusiasm.

'By the time we get there, wherever it is, your trophy will be too heavy to lift. Is it really worth a three-hundred-mile ride, chasing a country rumour?'

'I don't bother you with these things,' Richard said confidentially, 'but I'm being pressed to settle some of the accounts for Gaillard. Imagine, the King of England, pestered by quarry-owners. The trouble is, I've exhausted their goodwill for miles around. If I can sell the table and pay off my debts, we'll have the place finished before the winter. And you know how cold it was there last year. Even I felt it.'

They went on a way before Marshal asked if the king would visit Queen Berengaria whilst he was in the south. Richard said yes, quite possibly, if there was time and if she came some of the way to meet him.

Which means no, Marshal told himself.

They passed through Anjou and Touraine, and Richard

thought of detouring to visit Eleanor at Fontevrault. But he was anxious to see the treasure and claim it for the crown. He'd call on his mother on the way back. And tell John to rejoin Marshal and continue his education. But first the gold table, and the candelabra and the wealth of coins and plate.

On 26th March, they reached the district of Limousin and were escorted to the man on whose lands the treasure had been discovered. He would not say what the treasure comprised, but that it was still there, in the field where it had been found, and was being kept safe inside a well-guarded leather tent. He added that it was his property now, and under no circumstances would he surrender it to the king.

Everything he said had to be repeated, for the field was beneath the walls of Chaluz, on the domain of Aimer, Viscount of Limoges.

Richard was in no mood to be crossed, and reacted furiously to Aimer's challenge.

'Even if your impediment prevents you from speaking sense, you can still hear it from others, can't you?'

The melancholic viscount uttered his strange, unintelligible sounds, and his interpreter repeated them. 'Neither my lord's hearing, nor his good sense have deserted him . . . He is quite clear as to what he told you, king. The treasure belongs to him . . . If he shares it with anyone it will be with the man who unearthed it, not the one who ridiculed him at Loches.'

Richard glared at Aimer's misshapen mouth. 'A joke about your voice? You call that –'

'Don't dissemble,' the translator said. 'Don't take us for fools. We remember how you behaved, and so do you.'

'So you refuse me what is rightfully mine?'

'We do, and will dispute your claim in every court in the land.'

That'll take years, Richard fretted. As soon as the Germans learn that the statue is in their style, they'll lodge their own appeal. And, if the rumours about the Roman coins are true, the papacy will be quick to take an interest. God's legs, every nation in the West will lay claim to some part of it, and Château Gaillard will never be finished.

He adopted a less belligerent posture. 'There's no need for animosity, Limoges. Will you not extend the hand of friendship, and treat the incident at Loches for what it was?'

'We know what it was, king, a calculated insult.'

'Well, at least let me inspect the treasure. I've ridden this far –'

'Inspect it to what purpose? It's not yours, and eyeing it will only make you greedy.'

Richard abandoned his efforts to make peace. 'This is very wrong,' he warned, 'very dangerous. I shall have the contents of that tent, one way or another. Now, I'll ask you for the last time. Will you surrender the treasure to me, or shall I be forced to – Where are you going? Limoges? *Limoges*! You dare walk out on me? I shall have that table, do you hear me, the table and – And then I shall have your title, your lands, every castle and manor on your domains! Do you hear me, Limoges? Everything! Everything, do you hear?'

He did not give his hundred knights time to assemble, but hauled himself into the saddle and set off in the direction of Chaluz. Marshal and a man named Robert of Breteuil were among those who managed to keep pace with him, but it was a disorganized rabble of riders that cantered across the open ground below the castle. Marshal noticed that the king had removed his helmet, and he spurred forward to warn him. There was no trace of the tent below the north or east walls, so Richard swung his horse along a bare ridge of rock and followed it as it curved past the south-east corner of Chaluz. Marshal went after him, with Breteuil and twenty others in pursuit.

They emerged beneath the south face of the castle, and there was the leather canopy, surrounded by mounds of earth, wicker fences, and a strong protective force.

Richard was still some way off, but he was sure he could glimpse the soft glow of gold inside the tent.

If he doesn't rein-in soon, Marshal thought, the guards will believe they're under attack. And for God's sake, Lionheart, conceal your mane.

As if in response to the unspoken warnings, the king halted his horse and jammed his helmet on his head. Then he turned and shouted at Marshal and Breteuil, 'Did you see it, my lords? There's enough gold in there to pay for Gaillard, *and* a barrel of wine!'

A shadow flickered across his eyes, and he glanced down at the crossbow quarrel that had whirred past and buried itself in the ground. Marshal raised an arm, pointing at a window in the south-east tower. Breteuil called to the king to come back, then sent his palfrey galloping across the sun-baked field. The tent guards watched them, the butts of their spears rammed into the ground. They saw Breteuil unsling his shield, ready to pass it to the giant, and heard someone – Marshal – shout, 'Watch the window! There's another bolt – '

It flew down, passed a few feet in front of Breteuil's shield and caught Richard full in the shoulder. An arrow would have been accurate over a greater distance, but a crossbow bolt was a fearsome weapon at short range. Short and heavy, it was loosed at tremendous velocity, and its iron, mace-shaped head could penetrate a three-inch-thick oak door. When it hit a man, its effect was terrible.

Richard cartwheeled from the saddle, snapping the thick shaft of the quarrel as he crashed to the ground. Breteuil sprang clumsily from his horse and drove the point of his shield into the earth, to protect the king from further missiles. In fact, a crossbow bolt would have passed clean through the shield, though the curved metal might have deflected it.

Marshal came off his horse, caught Richard around the chest and started dragging him away from the tower. Breteuil shared the burden, and together the warlords carried him out of arrow-range. His face and neck were webbed with blood, and two things were immediately obvious. First, that he had not been wearing his link-mail hauberk which, again, might have deflected the bolt, and second, that the bolt had entered his left shoulder, turned inward, and was lodged under his collar-bone. It would require careful cutting to get it free.

The riderless horses had trotted back to rejoin Richard's horrified escort, and now there was only Breteuil's upright shield to mark where the incident had occurred. The tent guards watched, unmoved, as the wounded man was draped over his horse and led away. They did not know who he was, but Lord Aimer had warned everyone in the district to keep clear of Chaluz, and the intruder should have heeded the warning. The man was a fool, charging in like that. What else had he expected, a fanfare of trumpets?

It was after the physicians had operated that Richard Lionheart knew he would die. They had cut deep and wide in their efforts to remove the bolt, but they had done nothing to prevent the wound becoming infected. Their instruments were filthy and the weather was hot and, once they'd extracted the arrowhead, they regarded their work as finished. There was some indecent squabbling as to who should keep the grisly souvenir, but when that was settled they were content to wait and let nature seal the wound.

But neither Marshal nor Breteuil were so complacent, and they sent for Eleanor and Berengaria.

Richard's mother was the first to arrive, though without John. 'He left Fontevrault four days ago. I sent your messenger on to Château Gaillard; John said he was returning there to continue in your service. You must be having an extraordinary effect on him, Marshal. I never saw him so happy as during his last visit.'

'John happy? I don't see why. He loathes instruction. He lodged a complaint a day with the king.'

'Nevertheless, he spoke well of your methods, and seemed excited at the prospects of rejoining you.'

Marshal had too much else on his mind to spare more than a thought for Prince John. But happy? Excited? That was not how he'd left Gaillard.

He shrugged aside the contradiction and prepared Eleanor for her reunion with Richard. 'When you see him, you must not expect him to know you. Sometimes he is lucid, other times he relives the past. His tremendous strength is in his favour, and the physicians seem sure he will recover.'

'And you? Are you sure, Marshal?'

'I am not a physician –'

'You are a soldier, so you should know at a glance if an injury is fatal. *Will* the king recover, strong as he is?'

'If he does not completely lose his senses, and the wound does not become infected, then, yes, there is the chance he will survive.'

Eleanor looked at him, nodded at what he would not say, and asked, 'Will you wait for me here, Marshal? When I have seen the king, there is something I must discuss with you.' Then she bowed her head and moved into the dimness of Richard's pavilion. Marshal closed the flaps behind her.

The pavilion had been pitched on the edge of the field, so that, when the king grew strong enough to see, he could lie propped up in bed, looking directly at Aimer's treasure tent.

The viscount had expressed deep regret over Richard's injury, and had agreed to leave the treasure where it was until the king was well again. But he would not put the pieces on display, nor verify the size and description of the fabulous table. Richard's escort began to wonder if the table existed at all; or, indeed, if there was anything in the tent but a tent-pole. It would be a cruel joke if Richard Lionheart had ridden down to claim so much gold, then been rewarded with a bolt of iron.

She emerged from the pavilion and hurriedly drank the water Marshal offered. When she had finished, he took the mug from her, tossed it to one of the guards and escorted Eleanor to his own tent. She looked back once and said, 'He will never leave there, you know. I had no idea – ' She had already taken his arm, but now she caught at it with her other hand. 'I did not imagine an arrow could inflict such a wound.'

'Crossbow quarrels are worse than arrows. The king has been hit by arrows before.' He led her gently into his tent and lowered her into a large, leather-strapped chair. The chair could be taken apart and slipped into a sack for travelling. Isabel had given it to him during the first year of their marriage, and he had hired a wood-carver to engrave their names in the plain, flat chair-arms. In an excess of zeal the man had surrounded the names with a simple hunting scene, so that the chair was now admired by visitors, and uncomfortable to rest in.

But Eleanor leaned forward while she spoke. 'I could get no sense from him, Marshal. He seems immersed in some wild dream, in which he and Philip of France are somewhere in the East, and the sand is really powdered gold . . . And he talked of Gaillard, and said someone must cover it from the sun, before it melted . . . He is dying, isn't he? You know the signs better than I. You know by now if your king is dying . . .'

He waited, but she insisted on an answer. 'And the truth. I have always expected the truth from you, and I have always got it. You remember how I set you on the road, how surprised you were when I called you to my chambers in Lusignan and showed you those chests, full of clothes and armour?'

'I remember, my lady.'

'I saw you as a man of honour, even then. So you can tell me. Will Richard die from this wound?'

'No one can tell you that he will, or will not. But it is likely.'

She nodded, and the movement of her head became steady and rhythmical, as much an act of solace as understanding. 'I thought so, when you sent for me at Fontevrault, when you said it was a crossbow wound. What I told you earlier, that was not quite true. I do know the difference between a simple arrow wound and, one of these . . .' She made a vague gesture with her hands, then slammed them on the chair-arms, her palms taking the imprint of ISAB- and MARS-.

'So he's caught at last, and by his own greed! Brought down by some nameless archer in this backwater place! Brought here by the chink of rumour! The King of England, lured *here* to die!' She stopped, and they exchanged a sudden, sharp glance. *Was it so? Had he been lured to Chaluz? Had Aimer finally repaid him for his ridicule? Was the story of the treasure just bait, and Aimer's tent filled with nothing more substantial than his strange, gargled laughter?*

But Marshal could not shake from his mind another unanswered question. Why had John appeared happy and excited at Fontevrault? Was it because the prince was anxious to put his mother's mind at rest? Had he shown a rare maturity by pretending to be happy for her sake? Or had he – No, that was too much.

Or had he . . .

No.

Or had he known . . . Had he known what would happen?

Had he arranged things with Aimer of Chaluz, Viscount of Limoges, and had they both lured King Richard on to the whirring bolt?

No, Marshal rejected, it was too much. But the very thought etched lines in his forehead.

'What I want to discuss with you,' Eleanor said, 'is whether or not you will support my other son. We are agreed that King Richard will die and, Christ knows, there is nothing we can do to prevent it. But if that happens, will you give your support to John?'

'I saw King Henry die,' Marshal said, 'and I have spent ten years in support of King Richard. If I am to see him die, then I shall be loyal to the next King of England. I have little imagination in this matter, Lady Eleanor. I would support a rabbit, if it was lawfully elected.' He looked down at the dusty floor of the tent, arranged his thoughts, then added, 'I had no fondness for your husband, King Henry. Nor do I feel particularly warm toward King Richard. He shares his father's excessive brutality, and would rather lead an army into battle than a nation into peace. May I go on?'

'You must, Marshal. You're the only source of truth left to me.'

'Then I'll say this. If King Richard dies, Prince John will inherit the throne of England. Oh, there will be contenders, but John is the only one with the right to govern. So I shall support him. He cannot be compared with either Henry or Richard, but I shall support him and, hopefully, continue his instruction.

'My hardest task will not be to envisage John as king, but to erase everything else I know about him. You are the only member of your family, Lady Eleanor, whom I have ever liked. It's a pity we can't give crowns to our friends. But, rest assured. I shall see it goes to John.'

It was not easy for Eleanor to smile, with her son dying in the next tent, but, when the rhythmical nodding had ceased, she treated Marshal to an expression he had not seen for many years. He wanted to tell her that when she smiled in that way, she shed thirty years, but he was loth to remind her of her unsmiling age.

Richard of England died on 6th April, 1199, in the pavilion near Chaluz, his head cradled in his mother's arms. He had never fully regained his senses, though, in brief moments of lucidity, he made Marshal promise to finish Gaillard, and see young John on to the throne.

'. . . And don't let Aimer keep that table . . . *Ayay uh Ahuse* . . . I told him I'd never master his language . . . You get it from him, Marshal, and pay those damned quarry-owners . . . John is not so bad, you know, but when the wind blows his cheeks fill out . . . You take care of him, sire, I know you never kept him thirsty like he said, he always exaggerated . . . Have you seen the table, is it really that big, ten feet across and –'

'Yes,' Marshal lied, 'even finer than the descriptions. It'll settle all the accounts for Gaillard, and I'll see to it that the walls are topped by winter.'

'. . . On the main section . . . As you go across the bridge, I want the north-west tower strengthened . . . I'm not well

enough today, but tomorrow I'll show you on the plans . . .
Don't forget to remind me . . . The north-east, I mean the
north-west . . .'

'We'll deal with it tomorrow, king. At first light.'

'. . . I saw my mother in a dream . . . She came right into
the pavilion . . . I wish God had not let her die . . .'

'But she is not. She's with us –'

'. . . It was magnificent, though, her death . . . Leading our
men against the French . . . God's legs, I never saw Philip run
so fast, he's so ugly, Philip, have you noticed how hideous he
is, with his twisted mouth?'

'Too ugly for you,' Marshal murmured. 'He would never
have done for you.'

'. . . The west tower, remember . . . I'm a little tired at
present, but we'll deal with it tomorrow . . .' He closed his
eyes, mumbled something through parted lips, then succumbed
to the gangrenous infection of his wound.

Marshal and Eleanor stayed there, while priests and bishops
crowded in around the bed. It did not seem possible that the
giant had been brought down. If one believed that, one would
doubt the future of the great Angevin empire, for, if the
Lionheart was gone, what would happen to his hunting-
grounds?

The gentle and passive Queen Berengaria arrived on 8th April,
two days after her husband had died. She had travelled all
the way from her principality of Navarre, determined to be
with him and aid his recovery. She was placed in Eleanor's
care, and the two women wept together, the mother who had
been forced to play the extra roles of confidante and lover,
and the wife who had been excluded from them all.

Robert of Breteuil took charge of the funeral arrangements,
leaving Marshal free to ride north to Château Gaillard. On
the way he realized that he had not seen inside the treasure
tent, so he still did not know if the table existed, or if the
melancholic Aimer had laid and sprung a trap. Aimer, or
Aimer and John?

At Gaillard he was welcomed by the prince, who told him
that Sawale had worked wonders with the remaining stocks
of stone, and that Richard would be delighted when he
returned.

'Did he find the treasure? Is he bringing it back here, or

is he sending it to Rome to sell it? That's where he'd get the best price, from one of the Italian guilds.'

Marshal gazed at him and saw that he had once again adopted high-heeled boots and slipped new rings on his fingers. He did not answer the questions, but said, 'Your mother told me she never found you so happy as during your last visit to Fontevrault. She said you spoke well of my teaching, and were elated at the chance to return to me. Is that true? It's what you told her, but is it what you felt? *Is it?*'

'Don't snarl,' John objected. 'Don't pester me, Marshal. I told her that to pacify her, why else? Now, I've answered your question; you answer mine. Did Richard find the treasure? We've all heard of its existence, and Sawale is desperate to know if Gaillard can be completed.'

'Don't you know? Haven't your spies told you that the lure was successful?'

'Listen,' John said. 'Southern air does not agree with you. What did happen, hmm? What lure?'

'Then you do not know that your brother is dead?'

'You come storming back, accuse me – What did you say? What did you say, Marshal? Richard is *dead*?' His astonishment was faultless, the way he slumped against the half-built wall, the way his mouth sagged open and his arms hung limp, fingers fluttering. One could not accuse John Softsword of regicide, however likely it seemed.

'Yes,' Marshal told him, 'King Richard is dead. He took a crossbow bolt at Chaluz, and died of the infection. Didn't the message reach you? Your mother sent the rider on from Fontevrault. What happened to him, I wonder, between there and here?' Then he drew his sword and, for no apparent reason, hurled it across the outer bailey of Gaillard. The long blade bent as it hit the ground, sprang straight and sent the weapon wheeling against the wall. Fifty men watched it bounce from the ashlar blocks and fall back into the yard. John stared as Marshal unsheathed his dagger and sent it spinning after the sword.

'What is the matter with you? Is this your expression of grief, or have you resigned your office, or what?'

'Neither. I just do not trust myself to be armed, at this time. It's better for both of us. It makes it easier for me to tell you – you-are-to-be-crowned.'

His height and confidence restored by the leather wedges

on his boots, John said, 'Must you abandon your weapons and clench your teeth before you can call me king? That'll be a handicap, won't it?'

'I haven't called you king. I said you're to be crowned. Only God knows if the two things will relate.

'King John of England?' And he pressed his tongue against the roof of his mouth, sucking in the future.

The story of King John and the House of Pembroke, of Château Gaillard and of the events that led to the meadow known as Runnymede, is continued and concluded in *The Wolf at the Door.*   G.S.

Maureen Peters

Maureen Peters brings the great women of history, and their times, to life. Each of her books is a vivid tapestry of the kings and courts, the passions and the tragedies that surrounded her heroines.

The Cloistered Flame

Joan of the Lilies

Anne, the Rose of Hever

Elizabeth the Beloved

Henry VIII and His Six Wives

Princess of Desire

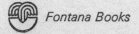 *Fontana Books*

Victoria Holt

The supreme writer of the 'gothic' romance, a compulsive storyteller whose gripping novels of the darker face of love have thrilled millions all over the world.

On the Night of the Seventh Moon

Bride of Pendorric

King of the Castle

Kirkland Revels

The Legend of the Seventh Virgin

Menfreya

Mistress of Mellyn

The Queen's Confession

The Secret Woman

The Shadow of the Lynx

The Shivering Sands

 *Fontana Books*

Victoria Holt *also writes as*

Philippa Carr

The Miracle at St. Bruno's
The Lion Triumphant
The first two novels in a series that will follow the fortunes
of one English family from Tudor times to the present day.

 Fontana Books

and as
Jean Plaidy

'One of England's foremost historical novelists.'

Birmingham Mail

All available in Pan Books

Fontana Books

Fontana is best known as one of the leading paperback publishers of popular fiction and non-fiction. It also includes an outstanding, and expanding, section of books on history, natural history, religion and social sciences.

Most of the fiction authors need no introduction. They include Agatha Christie, Hammond Innes, Alistair MacLean, Catherine Gaskin, Victoria Holt and Lucy Walker. Desmond Bagley and Maureen Peters are among the relative newcomers.

The non-fiction list features a superb collection of animal books by such favourites as Gerald Durrell and Joy Adamson.

All Fontana books are available at your bookshop or newsagent; or can be ordered direct. Just fill in the form below and list the titles you want.

FONTANA BOOKS, Cash Sales Department, G.P.O. Box 29, Douglas, Isle of Man, British Isles. Please send purchase price plus 6p per book. Customers outside the U.K. send purchase price plus 7p per book. Cheque, postal or money order. No currency.

NAME (Block letters)

ADDRESS